THE VICTIM

RUTH HARROW

COPYRIGHT

CONTENTS

Books By Ruth Harrow

In Her Footsteps
You're All Mine
In Her Wake
Dear Sister
Just One Lie
The Silent Wife
The Victim

PROLOGUE

It's been a normal day at work. It's the journey home where it really hits the fan. I'm over halfway back to my house when something terrible happens.

Just like every day, I unfold my headphones and slide them over my head. Immediately, the sound of traffic is muffled. Familiar melodies flow into my ears and the day I've spent handing out cups of coffee and cakes blows away in the cool breeze.

I push my chin down into the furry grey snood Mum bought me from Next. She got the same one for Claire too, but in blue. Mum still fusses over the two of us like we were still twelve. I smile. Neither of us would change her for the world.

My feet ache. My back does too from wiping up tables and clearing away used cups and muffin crumbs all day. I only have this evening to recover. At home, my best friend Claire is always happy to run me a hot bubble bath or ease the tension out of my shoulders with her skilful Shiatsu.

Then tomorrow I will have to do it all again. But I don't mind much. It's nice to see so many faces, regular and new. I don't know how I would manage my job if it wasn't for the friendly ones. But the customers keep me busy and I love hearing about their lives, especially if they are more interesting than my own. That's virtually a given.

Twilight falls as I reach the gravel path that leads beside the nature reserve lake. Seeing the swans and geese floating serenely atop the water calms me. The white of their shapely bodies glints out from the falling darkness. This is what I need after a noisy day of rushing around after others.

My feet carry me automatically home along the path I tread every day. Claire says it isn't good to follow the same route all the time. *You shouldn't make yourself predictable. You never know who is watching*, Uncle Tony said in agreement once too.

Then there is Mum who nags me about everything, from walking alone to disappearing into my music when I'm out and about. None of them understand I need this - the soothing music and the walk alone. If I couldn't wind down after a busy day, then I wouldn't be able to do it day in and day out.

It's funny though. The words of my loved ones are what I hear when someone suddenly grabs me. Even beneath my music.

Now I'm locked in a tight grip I can't break free from.

I'm quick to spring to action, jabbing frantically with a bent arm. Beneath the thick winter coat Mum got me for my birthday the sharp point of my elbow does nothing. My black plimsolls kick about wildly too, but I know the impact is tiny against the strong legs of my attacker.

Wild white stars dance in front of my eyes. My favourite song still plays in my ears and it occurs to me that this will be the last time I ever hear it.

CHAPTER ONE

Now

OK, so feminism has taken quite a hit in the last decade or so, but women should still expect to walk home alone after work without incident, shouldn't they? Even if it is dark and the winter nights drawing in mean daylight starts fading at 4 PM.

My best friend Leah was one of these women.

Now she is gone.

Leah was always going to do whatever she wanted and no one would stop her. She fell foul of this way of thinking because she had the unshakable belief that she was safe. Hard as nails.

This was in spite of the horror stories I had told her about the truth of human nature. And I certainly had gleaned a tale or two from my early childhood in care. Too much for a young child. That was before Leah's mum adopted me as a twelve-year-old.

'Any bloke who comes near me is in for a shock,' Leah had laughed once punching her fist in the air. It was one day after school when her mother, Helen, pointed to an advert for self-defence lessons in the newspaper.

Helen had later dropped us both off anyway at the Snowdome leisure centre in the centre of Tamworth for the classes. But our adventurous fourteen-year-old selves didn't take them seriously. We had instead used the unchaperoned opportunity to venture elsewhere in the building during every session.

We raided the vending machine for Sprite and Doritos and laughed through the glass at the newbie skiers as they scrambled around, limbs akimbo, on the indoor snow slope. On hotter days we would venture out to the lake at the edge of the car park, the water rippling the sun across our faces.

Leah thought bad things only happened to people in the news. Until one day she became a headline herself. She paid for her stubbornness with her life. Guilt racks me these days when I think of how I agreed to abscond our self-defence classes in our youth.

There hasn't been a day since when I haven't missed her. She had a wicked sense of humour and a killer dress sense that hovered somewhere between current fashion and hipster. Whatever she wore, she looked amazing. We had lived together for the best part of twenty years and she would forever dip into my wardrobe to borrow clothes. She was always guaranteed to look better in my stuff than I did with her svelte, yet shapely figure and long chestnut hair. But I didn't mind.

She had been such a big part of my life since I first met her on my terrifying first day of secondary school. I was alone and scared, but when she sidled over to make friends with me, all my fear evaporated. Her smile and unforgettable sense of humour graced my life that day and never left. Until two years ago, when Leah didn't come home after work one evening.

All she had to do was make the twenty-minute walk from the Costa she worked at in Ventura Park to our two-bedroom semi over in Fazeley. Most of the streets were well-lit and next to a main road, save for a few. Like the path beside the nature reserve where she went missing. We had never had any trouble in all the years we lived in this town, which was our whole lives.

To be fair, Leah had every right to think she was safe enough to make the trip. She had done so every day for the last two years since she got that job.

CCTV footage picked her up leaving work as

8

usual. Other security feeds tracked her out of the retail park. She was spotted on KFC's cameras, then Marks and Spencers', then finally on the Costcutters system when she stopped to buy a packet of Haribo. I've pictured her a thousand times diving into that packet of Starmix for her favourite strawberry foam hearts.

The police think it was around this point that she went missing. The part-eaten packet of sweets was found on the footpath that runs along the nature reserve. She was so frustratingly close to home. A chill comes over me every time I consider some faceless assailant hiding unseen in the bushes beside the water and waiting for my friend. If I had known there was a creep hanging around, I would have made sure she wasn't alone.

The police concluded that theft wasn't the intention. Leah's iPhone was recovered on the pathway, noise-cancelling headphones still plugged in. Tones and I stuck on repeat. Helen told her daughter off for being deaf to the world when out and about, but Leah always argued it helped her mentally clock off from work on the way home. As did the solo walk itself.

She wore the orchid Fitbit I bought her a few Christmases ago religiously to count her steps.

'Another bonus three-thousand in the bank!' she would say every time she got in from work, her long dark hair flouncing, cheeks rosy from the cold. 'I wouldn't get that if I let Tony give me that ride home he is always offering.'

Tony is Leah's uncle on Helen's side. He is also our landlord. Well, just mine now that Leah is gone. He was generous enough to let me keep the discounted rent he allowed for his niece when she was still my housemate. He also lets me off with her half. I wouldn't have been able to afford to stay in the place if he hadn't. I'm so grateful. He could easily get more, especially in the current housing climate. Guilty thoughts of a young couple moving in here to start a family eat at me often. These days the house seems so big and empty with just me here on my own.

I'm glad I haven't had to leave home on top of everything else. Leah's disappearance has cut me deep enough. Although we weren't biologically related, we wouldn't have been any closer than if we were actually sisters. Helen officially adopted me when I was twelve. Leah's father had left when she was a toddler, never to be seen again. Helen never remarried and I was the sister Leah had wished for.

Tony popped in regularly throughout our teenage years. He acted as a sort of father figure, coming over for Sunday dinner and taking us girls out on trips to the cinema or out for bowling and burgers.

Like other men of his baby-boomer generation, he never rushes to talk about feelings, but I know he has been as devastated about the loss of his niece as the rest of us. He has had a sort of extra-quietness about him since her disappearance. As though part of him has died. I can relate.

As much as it is my home, the house has never felt so still. And lifeless. I tried to explain this to Helen one day in the first few months, but it only upset her. Desperate to talk to someone who would understand, I was caught up in my own grief and didn't realise what I was saying until it was too late. I was mortified when I looked across the kitchen table to see fresh tears forming in Helen's eyes.

'I'm so sorry,' I told her.

'Don't be silly, dear.' She pulled me to her in a tight hug then. 'I'm just glad I've still got you, Claire.'

That comment had sat uncomfortably with me. Something akin to survivor's guilt, perhaps. Or something else.

I'd been put into care as a four-year-old, confiscated from my addict mother who had never made any attempt thereafter to retrieve me from the system. Helen was the closest thing to a real mother I've ever had, even though I never called her mum.

She had dedicated the best part of her life to raising two girls. They had made it to adulthood at least. Just over thirty. But then one had been snatched away. Deep down, I know that some part of her must feel the loss of her biological child more than if it had been me. Leah was her only real child, after all.

Yet, I think of Helen as my mother. She is all the family I have. She still knocks on the door with a traybake of chocolate brownies or lasagne just as she did when Leah was here. The portions haven't changed either, despite the fact that I'll be the only one eating the offerings.

I know without asking that Helen finds the thought of producing a smaller serving in light of Leah's absence as distressing as I do. The rims of her eyes were red every single time she dropped by with home-cooked food, packs of vitamins or even a warm jumper for the first winter.

It is Helen that I think of when I'm leaving my local one night. As I wrap my scarf around me, I know the evening has been a waste of time. Part of me even regrets turning down Tony's offer of drinks out with him this evening.

I don't really know why I turned him down. It's hard to tell what I want now that Leah isn't here. Usually, I'm torn between wanting my own company and staying out of the eerily quiet house. The prospect of a dinner for one seems too much to deal with all of a sudden tonight.

I'm feeling restless. A trip to the pub should have broken up the isolation of the evening. Plus, I don't know, maybe I could have picked up some company tonight too. But like every other time I have tried to find a partner, I find my thoughts always springing back to the only person I've ever loved.

When a lone guy looks hopefully over to my table from the bar, I decide it is time to leave. He's roughly my age and attractive enough. But like all the others my best friend used to try and set me up with, he just doesn't appeal. I try to ignore the look of disappointment on his face as I down the icy dregs of my vodka and coke and stand up.

As I step out with a cloud of huff into the dark November air, an odd feeling strikes me. The feeling creeps over my skin beneath my padded parka all the way down Lichfield Street. When I reach the well-lit main road, it lulls me into a false sense of security.

I quicken my pace and glance around me as I make the turn onto the road that will lead me to my house, but I appear alone. My ears strain, but I can't detect any sound other than my own. I'm just a few minutes away from home now. But then again, my brain reminds me, so was Leah.

Did the man from the bar follow me? It's a wild thought and I try to dismiss it.

To distract myself, I try to focus on the hot bath I've been thinking of all day. My mind reels through a list of issues I need to deal with when I get back into work tomorrow.

A sudden rustling noise touches my ears. Before I realise what is wrong, I feel strong hands on me. They snatch at my hair and pull me backwards in the dark.

My mouth is quickly covered to stifle my

shriek of alarm. For some reason, all I can think of is Helen. I claw and struggle frantically. My handbag drops to the asphalt. The pepper spray Helen gave me to carry is inside, uselessly too far to reach. Terror for my own safety gets mixed confusedly with thoughts of my would-be mum.

I know the mother hen will be devastated to lose another of her chicks.

My attacker snakes an arm around my neck. My chin is pressed so hard into the inside of their elbow that I think it might break the bone. But the worry starts to fade when my head quickly spins.

White spots appear before my eyes. The image of the dark shrubby street grows rapidly smaller and turns black.

CHAPTER TWO

Then

Nerves bubble in my stomach as I stir pasta into the rich sauce. Mushroom stroganoff. Leah's current favourite. When she made the switch to vegan last year, it was inevitable I would be going along with her.

Now it seems Leah and I have coconut in everything; the milk in our coffee and creamy sauces; we cook with the oil and scatter dried coconut on our cereal in the mornings. If I was to have an accident these days, I imagine I would spill out coconut milk instead of blood. But never mind. You get used to the taste after a while. More importantly, it makes Leah happy. That's all I want.

That is why I am so nervous now. Am I about to mess everything up? We have been best friends and lived together for almost twenty years. We love each other. Part of me is convinced Leah feels the way I do about her after all these years. At some point I can't quite identify, my platonic feelings have turned into something else.

Both of us are now in our thirties. We haven't been married, haven't been asked or even wanted to ask the big question. None of our relationships with other people has worked out for a significant length of time. When the inevitable break-up comes with a guy I'm seeing, I find I'm not upset.

At the end of the day, Leah and I always seem to have the best time with each other. We know each other best. That has to mean something, doesn't it?

Leah says a guy at our work, Gary, is interested in her. She works in another part of the local theme park than me, in one of the food kiosks near the zoo. I'm in maintenance. It's my job to help make sure everything is working for all the people that visit Drayton Manor. But we see each other plenty throughout the day and always have lunch together.

Leah says this Gary bloke is gorgeous and even asked her out a few days ago. But she hasn't said yes. So he can't be that wonderful. She pointed him out during our lunch break yesterday. But if he is so hot and funny and all the things she says he is, then what is stopping her from going out with him?

I think I know what. It's been bothering me for so many months. Longer, if I will admit it. And I am ready to now. It's been long enough. Tonight seems like a good time.

Now or never.

'This is gorgeous, Claire,' Leah says through a mouthful of creamy pasta. 'You're an amazing cook. You should work in one of the restaurants. Then you wouldn't be so exhausted at the end of the day running all over the park as you do now.' She adds cheerily, 'Plus, you would be closer to my kiosk!'

She shrugs casually as though this is an afterthought.

I smile. Another sign. Leah is suggesting we spend even more time together than we already do. What else could she possibly mean by that? Then there have been all those occasions over the years where I've thought we have had a moment. But I never acted on it at the time and it slipped away.

I won't let that happen again.

Nerves bubble inside me. This is it.

'Leah,' I say cautiously. 'There is something I've been meaning to talk to you about for a while now.'

I pause and look across the table.

My friend has stopped, fork-in-hand. She raises an eyebrow at me tentatively. 'What is it? Have you met someone?'

It heartens me to see her look worried at

this thought. Fine lines crinkle on her forehead. For a long time, I have noticed how Leah has behaved around my boyfriends, both prospective and otherwise. I've come to the conclusion that it is jealousy I've always seen. It has taken me a while to realise why, however.

'No, nothing like that.'

She relaxes a little, but her eyes remain watchful. She knows me well enough to know when something is serious. No one in this world knows me better than her. She is my soulmate.

I take a deep breath. 'I … Leah, the truth is that I'm in love with you. I have been for a while now and I just wanted you to know.'

Leah just stares at me blankly for a few moments, so I go on quickly, 'Don't worry, I'm not expecting anything from you. As I said, I just wanted you to know.'

I expected a more obvious reaction. But my friend just grins nervously. 'Claire, what are you talking about?'

My voice sounds loud in the quiet room. 'It's just … like I said. I love you. I have done for ages. I want us to be more than just friends … and housemates. I thought you felt the same way … '

As I start unnecessarily arranging my cutlery neatly on my plate, my face reddens. My words reverberate around my head.

This wasn't one of the many reactions I had pictured. In my head, Leah had been one of many shades of disgusted or horrified. Or on the other hand, pleased or even delighted; excited about the prospect of a new beginning.

One scenario was that she was even relieved that I had been the one to bring up the subject first.

But the real Leah in front of me can't process the revelation. Had I really judged this so wrong?

My voice is low now, matching my desire to crawl upstairs and under my duvet. 'It doesn't have to change anything between us. I probably shouldn't have said anything. Sorry. Just ignore what I said.'

My friend suddenly stops staring at me and shuffles about with things on her side of the table too for a few moments. She must realise now this wasn't a practical joke. 'No, I'm glad you told me. I think you're really brave.'

I smile awkwardly. 'Brave?'

'Yeah. It took a lot of guts to come out and say that. I thought you'd been acting funny today. You must have been really nervous.'

'I was.' I swallow down the lump that is forming in my throat.

'Oh, Hunny. Come here.' She stands up and moves around to my side of the table. She wraps her arms around my shoulders, resting her head against mine. Her warm vanilla shampoo fills my senses.

'Don't be upset,' she says softly. 'I love you. You are my best friend. The sister Mum never gave me. I just never really thought of you that way.'

'That's OK.' I dab my foolishly wet eyes on my sleeve. 'I understand you don't feel the same way. It should have been obvious.'

She drops onto the empty seat on my side of the table, still stroking my back soothingly. She reaches across for her glass of wine and takes a good glug.

'It's not your fault.' Her face forms her trademark grin and she gives a playful shrug. 'I'm just that irresistible. That's why Gary at work won't leave me alone.'

I swivel my own glass around on the table. 'So why aren't you into him? You said he's so funny and good-looking. I kind of took that to mean you were maybe into someone else.'

Leah looks puzzled for a second. 'Oh no, I never meant you to think that! He is hot and pretty hilarious when he wants to be. But he's also really into himself. He takes himself off to the toilets every chance he gets and does his hair. I mean, really! I can't be doing with that sort of bloke, you know that. Remember when I said goodbye to Mark from down the pub shortly after I realised he liked shopping more than I did?'

I shrug. 'At the time I thought you were just finding faults for the sake of it. Because … I don't know, I thought maybe your heart was elsewhere.'

Heat rises to my face again and I take a

generous sip of my drink.

Leah cocks her head to one side. 'Oh, Claire. I never meant any of that in the way you thought. I didn't realise. That was me just being picky. I thought you knew that. I won't just settle for anyone. You only get one life. It has to be the right person.' She looks at me and adds quickly, 'The right guy anyway.'

'I understand.' I shrug. 'You should probably ignore what I said then. Do you think you can forget this evening ever happened? I don't want things to be awkward. I love the way we are.'

Leah smiles and raises her glass to me. 'Sure. It's already forgotten, Hun.'

I raise mine too and the glasses touch with a hearty clink. My friend rests her head against my shoulder again as she has done so many times before.

Little do I know that, despite our promise, our lives are about to change forever.

CHAPTER THREE

Now

My body feels stiff. My muscles scream to be relieved. I try and turn over, but I'm restricted somehow. Then I realise my hands are bound together.

It's dark. Opening my eyes does nothing. I'm in the dark and I can't see a thing.

Vibrations course through my body and I slide sideways without warning. The wiry carpet beneath my tied hands prickles at me.

I'm in the boot of a car and it is moving. That's all I know.

My throat is dry and sore. All I can hear is the sound of the engine.

I know I should call out, but before I've managed to act on this thought, my eyelids become heavy again.

I jolt awake.

Stay awake, a voice says somewhere in my head. I open my mouth to call out but know it is futile. I will not be heard above the sound of the engine.

But I'm so tired. My body feels so heavy.

I want nothing more than to sleep.

I must have been given something to keep me subdued.

I try to focus on this last thought and fight, but my mind runs to nothing. Before I know it, all thoughts slip away from me again.

CHAPTER FOUR

Then

Despite my best friend's words and reassuring smile the night I told her of my true feelings, things did change between us after that dinner. It wasn't long before Leah found herself a new job at Costa coffee in the retail park in town. She said working with Gary was awkward after she rejected him.

She claimed he had taken it badly and made life at work tough for her. I never saw any evidence of that. She shrugged off my suggestion that we take it higher with HR, telling me she had already mentioned it.

Deep down, I knew why she switched jobs, but neither of us wanted to form it into words.

I was gutted the day she told me she had got another position. It wasn't just that I would miss my lunchtime companion, but I knew the switch signified a change in our friendship. I had messed up that night, after all. What had I expected? The biggest regret of my life was telling Leah the truth.

So now she works at a coffee shop. She talks with and meets loads of amazing new people every day, so she tells me anyway. I'm happy for her. Perhaps she will even meet *the one* this way.

Part of me is thrilled for her. Leah lights up when she speaks about her day and tells me all the gossip she has gleaned. Another part of me, the one I've tried to stuff deep down, misses her terribly.

But it is fine, I keep telling myself. Shortly after Leah's rejection, I worked myself up to ask James out. He is one of the zookeepers at the amusement park. He was nice enough. Probably too nice. For me, it was obviously a rebound fling and part of me felt guilty for keeping it going. Another part wondered if I would be able to keep it together.

Leah could tell I wasn't into him. She suggested I tell him it was over. But was I brave enough to go through with it? No. James took the initiative in the end and called time on our budding relationship. That was the closest I've ever been to upset after a breakup. Leah wasn't surprised when I gave her the news. She came at me armed with chocolates and sympathy and I felt better in no time.

When I see James around at work now, things are still awkward. We exchange a quick *hiya* and avert our eyes. I feel like I'm leaving a trail of destruction behind me where my love life is concerned. I just hope it is over.

Perhaps my next relationship will be the one, I think. *My thing for Leah was just a phase.* These are the lies I tell myself. I don't know why I bother when even I barely believe myself.

Anyway, now that my friend is working elsewhere she seems more comfortable with me again. It's been almost two years since my declaration and she seems to have mostly forgotten all about it. It is almost like old times.

When she gets in tonight we will order a takeaway and watch the film she has been banging on about for ages on Netflix. Leah missed it at the cinema because of Adam. He was the joker she was dating a few months back that didn't fancy it.

It wasn't long after that disagreement that she ditched him, which I'm pleased about. As she said, she won't settle for someone that isn't right for her. And she shouldn't. She is too amazing.

I set the box of Thorntons I picked up on the way home from work out on the coffee table. Then I get out the blanket we use for watching TV on colder evenings and leave it on the sofa for later.

As I do so, I feel a twinge of sadness for the friendship Leah and I used to have. Things are pretty much the same on the surface, but underneath regret eats at me. I feel like Leah second-guesses my actions sometimes, even when they are entirely as platonic as they used to be.

I should have kept my mouth shut.

At 8 PM, I open my JustEat app and order mine and Leah's favourite items for dinner. My best friend gets in from work every night at twenty past. You can set your watch by her. She always arrives ravenous too, that's another given. I also know how long the food order takes to arrive so everything is timed to perfection.

One thing about getting a theme park to run smoothly is making sure everything happens at the right times. Most of the visitors only come once a year or less and don't appreciate what goes on behind the scenes. It takes work for all the attractions to be fully working during their visit. It's a well-orchestrated effort by me and the team at work.

Time ticks on. I'm so used to Leah coming in at the same time every day that my brain conjures the sound of her arrival a few times. When I'm making some cups of fruit tea for us both, I'm sure I even hear her keys in the door. But when she doesn't emerge after a few moments, I go into the hall to find it empty. I must have been hearing things.

At quarter-to, I assume someone has held her up at the coffee shop end. Perhaps she is having to fend off another admirer. Or maybe she is flirting and exchanging numbers. I like to think it is the former unless it is someone totally flawless who really deserves her of course.

Another fifteen minutes later, I pull out my phone and send a tentative *'Is everything all right?'* text.

I don't get an answer, so I assume that Leah is closer than I thought and hasn't felt her phone vibrate in her pocket. She certainly won't hear it over her music. Perhaps she will walk in any moment now.

By twenty-past nine, I'm starting to worry. I make a few calls to her phone, but there is no answer. I can picture her strolling along with her headphones on oblivious to my attempts to contact her. But it's just a twenty-minute walk from work. She should be here by now.

Am I being unreasonable? I have more of an interest in Leah than most. It might be me reading too much into the situation. Maybe my friend being an hour later than any other day can be explained away simply. Perhaps she will sweep in with an exciting tale of a new friend she has met.

Or maybe she came across a stray or injured dog on the way home and had to take it home to its owners or to the vet. It is out of character for her not to text to mention it, but maybe she hasn't had the chance. She might not have a hand free if she has to carry the animal. Or if she is perhaps holding the hand of a pedestrian who has been hit by a car and is awaiting an ambulance.

All evening my mind comes up with all sorts of reasons why my friend hasn't called or texted me. But I know deep down, that is not what has happened.

Deep down I know something is really wrong.

CHAPTER FIVE

Now

There is only one thing worse than knowing that the person most important to me in all the world is gone. And that is knowing that what happened to her was all down to me and the fact I couldn't keep my stupid mouth shut.

I knew the reason Leah walked home from work alone that night was my fault. If I hadn't said anything about my feelings back then, she wouldn't have found herself another workplace.

Instead, we would have been strolling back from work that night laughing and talking about the day together.

But that isn't how it went. And I can never ignore that whatever happened to her was ultimately due to me. If there was any justice in the world, then it would have been me that was taken that night instead. After all, I travelled home alone that day too on a similar route to the same destination.

But then again, I may be getting my comeuppance today.

The warmth of the car boot has gone now. Freezing cold air sinks over me, but it is still dark. I struggle to understand why.

I'm shivering beneath my open coat. My scarf is pulled tight around my throat by my own body weight, but I can't move my hands to adjust it.

My bleary eyes struggle to focus. When they finally do, I see hessian texture close to my face. It obscures the light. A sack has been pulled over my head.

My body repeatedly bumps uncomfortably against whatever I'm lying on. I slide and my knees hit the hard surface of something to my left.

On my right, I fear an unseen abyss. I desperately try to keep my body as still as possible, wondering if I'm about to slip off and into oblivion. A nearby cliff perhaps?

There is a rumbling sound, like a tractor engine. Other banging and hissing sounds reach me too, but my brain is foggy from whatever I've been given to subdue me.

The engine sound rumbles through my entire body, as does each jolt. I could have been dropped into a trailer on the back of a tractor.

But is it high-sided? I can't tell. Will I fall off and onto nearby rocks if I move more than a single muscle?

For some reason, I can't get the craggy moorlands of Wuthering Heights out of my head. It's my favourite book. I've seen every film adaptation too.

Leah would laugh at the retro styling in the older movies. But none of the film interpretations neglected to feature the brutal landscape of the moors with its sharp rocks and unforgiving ravines.

Is that where I am now? I could have been driven hours away from the Midlands whilst I was slipping in and out of consciousness.

In my mind's eye, I see the vehicle I'm on following a rough path on an isolated farmland somewhere. Lethal rocks wait malevolently for me if I dare move out of line.

I have no idea how long I've been out, but it could have been hours. My kidnapper could have driven so far in that time.

The only bit of light I can see is through the gaps in the sack weave. And that light is a cool blue. The early hours perhaps?

How far have I been snatched from my hometown?

Where am I?

What is going to happen next?

CHAPTER SIX

Then

This is a disaster. Leah didn't come home at all last night. Helen is distraught. So am I. In fact, I've barely slept.

The police come over to the house in the afternoon. We give them Leah's life history, past and present. I help Helen answer the lengthy list of questions the police run through with us.

It turns out, I know more about Leah's personal life than Helen, especially where her daughter's love life was concerned. They asked us if Leah had any enemies. Helen became upset by this.

'Enemies?' She removes the tissue she has been holding to her face. 'Leah is so popular! She always has been. No one would wish her any harm.'

PC Taylor nods calmly. He is grey-haired and

obviously used to facing backlash from relatives. 'I understand, Mrs Bayliss.'

'Miss,' Helen corrects him.

He nods briefly again. 'But we need to get a clear picture of Leah's life. It is often someone not far from home that might know something. That is if Leah has gone missing at all. Most missing people return within 48 hours with a reasonable explanation.'

He turns to me again. 'Claire, I know you said Leah doesn't have a boyfriend at the moment but is there anyone who is interested in her? Maybe she has mentioned meeting someone recently, whether online or in-person?'

I wrack my brains. Leah has always been popular with men, but she hasn't mentioned any lately. 'Not for a while. Leah was dating a guy a few months ago and they went out for a few weeks before she called it off.'

PC Taylor makes a note of this. 'And what was his full name?'

'I only knew him as Adam, but I can't remember his last name. I'm not sure Leah even told me even though she spoke about him a lot.'

'And have you got any other contact details for him? His address, perhaps?'

'No, I don't.' I shake my head, frustrated for not knowing more. 'Leah only had his number on her phone, but I think she deleted it after they broke up. They met in the local down the road. She didn't go out with him for long.'

'Who ended the relationship?'

'Leah did.'

'And how did Adam take that? Was he upset?'

'I don't think so.' Doubt springs up inside me. I hadn't even thought of Adam. Was he angry my best friend said goodbye to him? 'He didn't get in touch again. Leah sent him a text to end things. But she didn't get a response back. A day or two later, he still hadn't messaged her, so we didn't think anything of it. I just thought that was the end of it and he wasn't that bothered. Leah said he didn't seem very into her towards the end. He obviously wasn't if he didn't even bother to reply to her text, was he?'

'People react to breakups in different ways. Are you sure he never tried to get in touch again?'

'Yes, positive. Leah didn't mention him at all after that.'

PC Taylor looks up at me with what I feel is scrutiny. 'Would your friend have definitely told you if he had?'

'Yes. We talk about everything. Especially relationships. If he had said or done anything bad, Leah would have definitely said something to me about it.'

The police officer poises his pen over his notepad. 'So Leah has had a negative response from any relationships in the past?'

'Well, no.' My mind springs back to what my best friend said about Gary from the theme park.

Was she telling the truth about him after all? Had he got nasty with her for rejecting him? But that was so long ago. Could it possibly be relevant now?

I bite my lip.

The police officer perched on my armchair notices this. He half raises an eyebrow at me. 'What is it? Have you remembered something?'

If there is a chance Gary is involved, I can't keep it to myself. 'Well, there was one guy she sort of had problems with. Maybe.'

Helen looks sideways at me. 'Who? Leah never said anything like that to me. Who is he? What did he do to my daughter?'

I shake my head quickly to reassure Helen. 'Nothing, exactly. Leah didn't really say. It was someone she used to work with when she was still at Drayton Manor.'

Doubt eats at me. Should I have kept my mouth shut, or did Leah really have a genuine reason to leave her job at the park? 'She just said that this guy was really interested in her, but she wasn't keen on him. So when he asked her out, she said no and … I don't know. Leah said he got a bit mean about it. But this was ages ago. She has worked at Costa for over two years now.'

PC Taylor jots this down quickly. 'This man was mean in what way, Claire? What did he do?'

'Nothing in particular that Leah mentioned. She just said it was really awkward being around him and he was making things tough for her. She said he stopped using her name and kept calling her *that employee* to other people and things like that. She said she caught him spreading nasty rumours about her too. But then other times, she said he kept finding reasons to be alone with her. She said it made her uncomfortable. That's why she left that job.'

Helen is quiet as she processes this new information.

PC Taylor scribbles down notes from what I have said and takes down all the details I know about Gary. 'Didn't she report this employee's behaviour to management?'

'She told me she reported him to HR. But she mainly just focused on getting out of there.'

I pause and think about the evening she told me she was going to get another job, insisting it had nothing to do with me. 'She seemed really keen for a fresh start.'

Now that I have said Gary's actions out loud, they sound more real. More serious and so much more toxic. This doesn't just sound like just another guy Leah rejected.

Had I really been so caught up in my own head and embarrassment at that time that I hadn't taken a real threat to her safety seriously?

But could Gary be involved? This was all so long ago. If it was him, why did he choose to act now?

And if so, what has he done with my best friend?

CHAPTER SEVEN

Now

I must have slipped out of consciousness again. As now my body slides painfully into the hard side of whatever containment I'm in. My forehead collides painfully with it and snaps me more awake this time.

The light is still a cool blue. It can't be much later than before so I must not have been out for as long this time.

I wonder if I am in any condition to run if I get the chance. But I can hardly see a thing. I could be anywhere. I can hear water sloshing somewhere nearby. A lake, perhaps? Noises still come at me confusingly. How long will it take for whatever substance I was given to wear off? What the hell was it anyway?

It's perishingly cold. I'm shaking furiously, even beneath my thick coat.

Without warning, strong hands grip me. The same ones that snatched me from my familiar walk home from the pub.

They drag me forward. My ankles twist and feel weak beneath me as they are forced to take my weight unexpectedly.

'What's going on?' I stammer. There is no response.

The sack is loose on my head. With every jagged movement, the rough hem swings and I catch a glimpse of the ground.

Dark rocks. Just as I suspected. But not quite as sharp as those I've seen a thousand times erupting from earthy moors.

I catch sight of my sensible shoes as they stumble over the stone and up a steep incline. My green suede loafers look so civilised against the roughly hewn backdrop of rock, and then grass. Long and springy at first, then firmer; cut by grazing teeth perhaps.

There is a familiar smell my confused brain can't quite place. Something from my childhood. A trip to the farm?

There are gaps in the weave of the hessian. Through them, I see the rough outline of various buildings up ahead of me. My suspicion feels astute now. I am being dragged towards the structures.

I'm quite certain it is a farmhouse that

looms ahead. I struggle against my abductor, determined I don't want to be taken inside.

I know I need to run. But it is important to pick my moment carefully. It needs to come as a surprise.

I need to make sure my abductor doesn't see my escape coming.

CHAPTER EIGHT

Then

I t is a bleak time when a few days later the police contact us to say they have found Leah's phone and headphones on the path beside the nature reserve. I'm over at Helen's house and she immediately bursts into repeating variations of, 'I told her so many times not to walk home that way! And with her music blasting in her ears too! You kept telling her too, didn't you Claire?! This can't be happening.'

But it is happening, I realise. This isn't just some female stranger who has gone missing on the news. This is Leah. She is my best friend. She has been my world for most of my life, or most of the parts that I care to remember. She can't be gone. Nothing could have prepared me for her sudden absence.

The police update us with what they have discovered so far. Leah left work alone as usual. But that we already know from speaking to her colleagues and employer ourselves.

Disappointingly, the police know as much as we do at the moment. TherThere is no hope of using her phone to track down Leah as it has been found abandoned on a path. The fact that she doesn't have it with her is a major blow to the investigation as much as it is devastating to us.

Leah is never without her phone. Nor has she ever before gone off somewhere and not told anyone. We tell the police this, but they seem to realise the seriousness of the situation now with the discovery of her device. No longer can they suggest that Leah has likely wandered off somewhere of her own accord.

The police inform us that they have questioned Gary, the man Leah claimed she had issues with. Apparently, he has only just come back from a seven-day trip to Dubai. The authorities are satisfied that he wasn't even in the country at the time of the abduction. It also turned out there was never any formal complaint made against him with HR at work.

Helen finds this most puzzling when she shares the news with me one evening over the phone. 'Why would there not be any evidence of Leah's complaint? Do you think this bloke has managed to cover it up somehow?'

'No, Helen, don't be paranoid. Maybe Leah didn't file the complaint in the end.'

'But why not? Do you think she was threatened?'

'I don't think so. She would have told me.'

The confirmation of Leah's lie doesn't surprise me. I wonder if she even made up the incidents with Gary completely. Or at least, stretched the truth a little. She didn't seem at all perturbed by the situation after she quit her job anyway.

A fizzling lead is naturally a disappointment. But had I really believed Gary had been involved in harming Leah all this time after she rejected him? I'd had the feeling my friend was fabricating the story at the time. Now I have even more reason to doubt her accusations with proof she didn't make the official complaint when she told me she had.

Maybe I was wrong to tell the police about Gary at all. But I couldn't keep quiet when they asked about enemies. Leah was so popular and liked by everyone. Rarely there were people who didn't always warm to her bright and bubbly personality, but she didn't have anyone actually hate her. Gary was the closest thing that fit that bill and he has an iron-clad alibi and a flimsy-at-best motive.

Soon, my friend's story is all over social media. I share the missing appeal everywhere I can think of. Local groups and those further afield. I get quite a few messages from our old school friends and customers who know Leah by sight. But no leads. No one has come forward with any sightings of her. It is almost like she has vanished into thin air. It is frustrating, to say the least.

Leah's beautiful face smiles at me from every appeal and the printed posters that a group of us have worked to put up around town. They appear to pop out at me on my way to work.

Helen and I chose three photographs for the poster. The most recent picture of the trio was one I took of Leah standing next to a statue of Robin Hood in Nottingham city. Autumnal sunshine highlights the warm tones in her chestnut hair that frames her face. It illuminates the vivid pattern in her blue irises.

My friend and I had gone up to the city a few Saturdays ago shopping and laughing off the breakup Leah had recently gone through with Adam.

It seems like so long ago now.

The 48 hours the police had initially suggested Leah might return in have now definitely passed. It feels like a crushing blow. Deep down, I know, like Helen, that Leah isn't coming back.

CHAPTER NINE

Now

The owner of the dirty walking boots I've that caught some glimpses of needs to have a shock. That is how I'm going to get away.

His grip is tight, but if I aim a kick in the right place, I can make a break for it. The fresh icy air has woken me now. As has the way I've had my legs forced to march towards the farm buildings.

But if this is a farm, then there must be a road nearby somewhere. Even though it might be far. Maybe that was why I was brought the last way of the journey by the tractor.

So which way do I run?

The silhouettes of the buildings become larger and more menacing. Yet, the familiar scent from my childhood that I assume must be a farm becomes more distant. I can't understand why. It's been ages since I have been to a farm. Can I even recall the scent now?

I know the closer I get to those buildings, the lower my chances of getting away are. I'm going to be locked inside somewhere, unable to escape.

I have made a mental picture of the parts of my abductor I can't see. Which is all of them, apart from their muddy old boots. They seem familiar because they are the same type Uncle Tony wears.

In my mind map, I have identified roughly where the groin is. I summon all my strength now and prepare to kick. As soon as he makes the turn towards the farmhouse, I will strike.

Any minute now.

I shift all my weight onto one side of my body and lift my leg, as I anticipate the turn of my abductor. But his shift in position is in the wrong direction than I expect. He turns away from the large farm building, not towards it. This causes me to tilt off balance and fall backwards.

I slide out of his grip.

But he grabs me roughly by the hood of my coat and my arms slide out of it, stopped only by my bound hands. I twist around onto my back, still blinded by the sack.

But his grip has loosened slightly though and I take the opportunity to kick out at him blindly. I take terrified gasps of air as I fight, the sack sucking into my mouth.

My foot collides satisfyingly with a part of him, and I'm suddenly released. Spurred on, I kick again.

And again. The heel of my loafer hits something softer this time, maybe his face.

With my hands still behind my back, I twist onto my front and up onto my knees. I almost make it blindly to my feet, before I feel hands dragging on my coat again.

I'm tackled to the ground and I come crashing down. Even through my thick parka, I feel the edge of a rock dig painfully into my spine.

There is an angry roar. He is enraged now.

Then, out of nowhere, a large hand delivers a punch to the side of my head.

I'm dazed. Like I was the time when I was four and my birth mother's companion gave me the smack of my life for *'looking at him the wrong way'*.

The sack weave spins before me.

Now my feet are forced forward again against my will. I'm still weakened and confused by the blow to the head and can do nothing.

The only thing I know is that I'm being forced through a doorway and everything goes completely dark like the boot of the car earlier, or last night, or whenever it was.

The only thing that registers with my senses is the smell.

That's what sets this building apart from the boot. It is the vile stench that tells me that aside from my abductor, I'm not the only body in here, just the only living one.

CHAPTER TEN

Then

One Saturday afternoon, a police detective pays me a surprise visit at home. It's a rare moment I'm either not at work or with Helen or Tony. The detective assigned to Leah's case introduces himself when I answer the door.

'I'm detective Halliwell. I've been handling your friend's disappearance.'

I am immediately put on alert at this surprise visit. 'Have you found anything?'

He shakes his greying head quickly. 'Can I come in?'

'Of course.' I offer the detective a spot on the sofa.

'Thank you.' He takes a seat and looks all around as he does so. His dark eyes scan the photos of Leah and I out on the coffee table.

I follow his gaze. 'That one on the top is from a trip to France we made a few years ago. It was December and freezing cold.'

He nods politely. 'Was it just the two of you?'

I shrug. 'Yes. We went for the Christmas markets to pick up presents.'

The detective leans forward and lifts a few of the other photos up uninvited. 'It seems to be just the two of you often. You said in your initial report that Leah had a stream of boyfriends over the last few years.'

'She did. Did you question Adam yet?'

'This is the Adam whose last name you don't know?'

'Yes, I'm sorry. I don't think Leah ever told me details like that. She just used to say what they had done together.'

He nods again, this time with a small grim smile. 'We looked into this Adam character. We can't find any record of Leah having a boyfriend during the timeframe you mentioned.'

'Well, there must be some trace of him. What about CCTV? I know Leah went down to the local with Adam. That's where she met him in the first place.'

'Did you two go on the pull together that night?'

'No. Leah was on her own when she met him.'

'Was that unusual?'

'I don't know. We aren't joined at the hip. She did things on her own sometimes.'

Detective Halliwell continues to watch me after I've finished talking.

I'm starting to feel like this is an interrogation. 'Why are you asking me these things?'

He purses his lips. 'Did you ever meet Adam?'

I have to think for a second. 'Actually, no. I didn't. Why? Do you think he is dodgy?'

'I'm not convinced he exists, to be honest.'

'What?'

'Every venue you told us Leah had supposedly been at with Adam said they hadn't seen them.'

'Well, they wouldn't have reason to remember one couple, would they? How can a cinema or restaurant remember every customer that walks in through the door?'

'Fair point. But we showed photographs to the staff. One or two remember Leah, but they claim she was there on her own. It made her stand out to them.'

'She can't have been. Maybe they just didn't notice Adam?'

'They noticed Leah, all right.'

'Well, anyone would. Look at her pictures.'

The detective eyes me closely again. 'What do you mean by that?'

I shrug. 'Nothing. Just that Leah is

attractive. She always attracted all the attention when we went out together.'

'I see. Did that upset you?'

'What? No, of course not. It didn't bother me. Leah is my best friend.'

He casts around the room. 'Do you have a boyfriend at the moment?'

'No.'

'You don't have a partner at all?'

'Not at the moment.'

'I suppose all this with your best friend and housemate has put a dampener on your love life?'

I swallow. 'I don't know. I'm busy with work too. I don't really have time.'

'OK.' He looks down at the photographs again for a few moments. I feel like he is drawing his own conclusions, but when he speaks again he seems to have moved his thoughts back to Leah's ex. 'At the end of the day, it looks like this Adam character doesn't exist. We can't find any evidence of him anywhere, and when we traced the texts Leah sent from her phone to his number, we found something surprising.'

'What?'

'The number Leah pretended was Adam's? It actually belonged to her.'

'I don't understand. What do you mean by pretended? Adam was real. I saw the texts back and forth between them.'

'Leah had a dual sim phone, yes?'

'Yes, I think so.'

'When she sent the texts you saw going out to *Adam*, she was actually just sending them to her other sim card. She had blocked her main number, so the messages wouldn't show up on her phone and give her away.'

My mouth opens at this. 'That's crazy. It can't be right. Are you sure?'

'Yes, positive. Our forensic team have been over it. It didn't take them long to figure out what Leah had done. So when she was texting Adam in front of you, she was actually texting herself knowing she wouldn't get a response. Then later, I assume she would have sent replies from her other sim when you weren't around.'

It takes a few moments for me to follow the thread of what the detective has said. 'Leah broke up with Adam via text. But he never answered. She didn't even seem bothered at the time.'

'That's because the whole thing was invented. There never was any Adam. That was why you never met the man. It probably explains her indifference over the supposed breakup too.'

I shake my head. 'That can't be right. I don't know why Leah would do that.'

'You don't? It sounds like she invented the allegations about her coworker, Gary Stewart too, apparently just for you.'

'They weren't exactly allegations. If she never made an official complaint and only ever told me about it, then what does it matter?'

'But your friendship is important by the looks of it. Why would your best friend lie to you about something like that?'

'I've no idea. Maybe you have got it wrong.'

'There's no mistake. Leah made up having a boyfriend seemingly for your benefit, Claire. That makes me ask myself one question - why?'

*

This morning, I'm joining a group to start the search from where Leah was last seen. I don't know what good it will do as the police have already been over the area, but it seems one of the only proactive things we can do. Mostly going through the motions of my usual routine of work and shopping as though nothing has happened has been driving me crazy these past two months.

Tony picks me up and drives us over to Helen's house. I'm taken by surprise when he rings my doorbell and leads me out to his car. I'd been expecting his usual Ford, but he leads me to a silver Vauxhall Insignia instead. Everything is unfamiliar lately. Why has the life I've known for so long slipped away so suddenly?

Tony has never been a man of many words, but this morning, he seems particularly quiet.

His fingers tremble as he reaches for the gearstick. I've never seen him so nervous. The image is at odds with his usually casual demeanour, shuffling around the place in his peeling hiking boots and casual shirts. It makes me feel worse about today. Is he expecting us to find something grim today?

Leah's disappearance has left me feeling out of sorts. I feel uncomfortable in my own skin, as though I'm almost missing a limb. Leah has been at my side for so long, it turns out I don't know how to function properly without her.

My attempts at small talk with my would-be uncle fail when I get nothing but one or two-word responses. So it is a relief when we finally stand on Helen's front doorstep. Although I dread to think what state she will be in.

At first, Helen's lined face looks tear-free and calm enough when she opens the door. But then she greets me by moving forward and grasping my hand tightly. She raises it and kisses my forearm absently.

The almond-shaped eyes Leah inherited are blank and sort of glazed. My worst fears are confirmed. She is beside herself with grief. In her mind, she seems to have decided today is the day we will find something none of us wants to see.

I was planning on bringing up the subject of Adam, Leah's alleged ex. I was hoping to get Helen's thoughts on the matter when I do sometimes when I'm baffled in life, but there is no way I'm going to do that today.

Tony shifts his weight from one foot to the other. I expect him to move forward and hug his sister but he doesn't. He looks pale and his dark eyes are distant too.

Helen moves back to the kitchen and we follow her down her narrow hallway. The beginnings of the morning coffee she always has been underway in here. The kettle has been boiled. A teaspoon and an empty mug rest lonely on the worktop. Helen returns the top to the jar of coffee, her mind obviously elsewhere.

I take it from her gently. 'Here, let me make your drink. Go and sit down.'

'No.' She shakes her head and puts her hand on mine. 'I can't, Claire. I'll be sick.'

'Have you had anything this morning at all?' I watch her empty the kettle into the sink with a cloud of steam. It condenses on the window.

'No. I'll be fine, honestly dear. I just need to get through today.'

'You don't have to go if you don't want to. I'll go and help with the search. I'll tell you straight away if we find … anything.'

'No. I have to do this. I can't just sit around in this house and wait for everyone else to search for my little girl. If Leah is out there, I want to know.'

I put my arm around Helen as we all head out to Tony's car. He opens the passenger door for his sister and I steer her inside.

Helen was pretty young when she had Leah. She has always seemed like a fun mum. She was more like a big sister sometimes when we were growing up, but now she seems to have become so fragile overnight.

We drive over to the nature reserve in Fazeley where Leah was last known to be.

The three of us get out of the car in silence and approach the spot on the path where Leah's phone was found. Police have marked the spot with white spray paint. But not only that, the exact area is now made obvious by a spread of flowers, teddy bears and notes with kind words from well-wishers.

Tony wanders over and crouches down to read a few of them.

Something unsettles me about the mini-shrine. All the people that laid these things are acting like they already know Leah is dead. But we don't know that. I refuse to consciously acknowledge the thought until I have proof, and it would be a sad day if I ever got it. I don't know if I would even be able to stand it.

Volunteers from the local search and rescue team hover around the area to, in their red high-viz jackets.

One of them is connected by a leash to a lively liver and white spaniel who looks alert and ready. Members of the public are here too. I recognise a few faces from secondary school. They have obviously seen the social media appeals. I return their sad smiles and thank them for their words of support as they saunter past Helen and me.

As the search kicks off, it turns out that

the effort is focussing on and around the many bodies of water in the area, whether the still lake, streams or river. There is a quarry not far from here too.

When I see the map the team leaders show us all, I realise this task borders on unimaginable. On it, areas of rough terrain and areas of water and wetland are marked. Anything or anyone could have easily become lost beneath the surface of any one of those bodies of water inset within the coarse landscape.

The search is on and the team spreads out. I stay close to Helen. Our feet sink deep into the marshy wetland that surrounds the main lake of the nature reserve.

Waders delve into the edge of the water nearby. Kayakers work the deeper middle section.

Those of us on foot scour the edges of the water and search along the path. I dread to think what we may find. The weather can't have been on our side lately. The rain that has kept the reserve damp and cold for the wildlife has meant it is hard for us humans to trudge through it.

Within twenty minutes, I'm soaking wet up to the knees. Dew darkens the bottom half of my bootcut jeans. The old trainers I always use for walking do nothing to keep the water out and my toes are numb already.

My hand had hovered this morning over the

Wellington boots that we have in the shoe rack at home. But then I realise that those boots actually belong to Leah. She used to wear them when she was stationed at a different position in Drayton Manor.

She used to be in charge of the outdoor displays in the dinosaur section. We have always shared our things and worn each other's clothes and thought nothing of it.

But to do so now just feels wrong. I realised last week that the handbag I've been using until recently originally belonged to my friend. She told me the one I had chosen from down the market was frumpy and insisted I use a spare one of hers instead. Nevertheless, I found that frumpy one out of the back of my wardrobe that day and recommissioned it. I'll keep the other one safe.

I don't like the idea that Leah will never come back. I like to think of it more that I'm keeping her things in good condition for *when* she reemerges. She would no doubt make a jest about what I've been up to in her boots to get so dirty if I had slipped them on earlier. Besides, I don't want to distract the sniffer dog with a false trail.

Helen trembles beside me and not just from the cold. She is having the same thoughts as I am. There is something utterly grim and sobering about the scene we are part of today. I can't imagine it from a mother's perspective.

I link my arm with hers securely. She grasps my hand in her cold one. She nods blankly, unable to speak as she continues to scrutinise the ground.

Tony accompanies the sniffer dog and his trainer up ahead. I see the pair talking, but they are too far away for Helen and me to hear what they are saying.

The dog appears eager, but doesn't pick up any particular scent or pull in any specific direction. That's good news, right? He isn't tugging his trainer over to a crop of bushes where we will make a gruesome discovery, at least.

Or does it just mean that it has been too long since Leah went missing? Maybe the dog won't find anything at all? Has all trace of my would-be sister been washed away in this past month by rain or the wind?

I can't say for sure what the weather has been doing lately. I've been so caught up in worry that I have hardly noticed what has been going on any further than mine and Helen's worlds.

By the afternoon, the waders have concluded their search of the lake and confirmed they have found nothing. They have now moved onto the marshy streams that lead into the River Tame.

I'm still torn by my expectations for the day. Part of me is desperate to know what happened to Leah, the other part hopes that we will find no trace of her. I cling to the hope that she has gone off somewhere and is completely fine. But in the despair I feel on this cold grey day it is hard to imagine that she is OK. Helen seems to have come to this conclusion too.

She turns to me as we take a quick break to gratefully sip the hot drinks the rescue team hand us. 'It's the not knowing that is the hardest thing, isn't it?'

'Yes. I know exactly what you mean. It's so hard just to get to sleep at night. My mind just keeps turning over all that we know and that isn't much.'

'I mean, even if it is bad news. I just need to know.' She looks distantly at the sky stretched above us. The dark grey clouds are reflected in those irises that hold a similar coloured pattern as her daughter's.

I've always been enamoured by Leah's eyes. Whoever said they were the window to the soul, wasn't lying. I could lose myself in her eyes sometimes when she would talk and everything and nothing; they are so different from my own dark green ones I've always felt are dull. Leah always felt so beautiful compared to me.

There is a sudden exhalation of breath behind me. I turn around and see Tony turn on his heel and head over to where he parked the car earlier.

Helen watches him go too. 'I've never seen our Tony so upset. The big daft sod.'

Helen's unusually composed face scrunches into tears. A lump forms in my throat too, but I swallow it down as I pull Helen close to me in a firm hug.

She sobs into my shoulder for a few minutes. I know I can't break down too. I have to be strong as the remaining daughter.

I'm virtually all she has left.

CHAPTER
ELEVEN

Now

I'm torn between gasping from the adrenaline of the last scuffle and holding my breath to keep the disgusting stench out.

It is dark in here. And cold. And the smell …

I blink and strain my eyes in all directions. I know from the taste of the air that I am not alone. I just can't tell the direction of the source.

My buttocks are numbing now from the cold stone floor. My abductor tethered me to something before he slammed the door behind him and left. I know it is definitely a *'he'* for sure now. I knew as soon as I landed that kick to his groin. It's not like it is a surprise though. The real shock would have been if it was a woman. But it very rarely is in these situations, is it?

I need this stupid bag off my head. I know I'm trapped, but not being able to see is causing me to panic more.

I rest my head against something cold and hard nearby that I assume is a brick wall. The rough texture catches obligingly on the hessian and a few manoeuvres later I'm sliding myself out. It feels like a small victory, but it doesn't help much.

It takes a good few minutes before I'm able to detect so much as a speck of light. After a few more, I realise that the tiny white dot has a sort of wooden texture directly around it. Other than that, I can't see anything as it is so dark.

I can only assume I'm inside some kind of ramshackle old building. The windows must be boarded up to block out all the light. The floor is gritty with rubble beneath my loafers. I can feel debris through my jeans too.

Now that I am alone in the quiet and the darkness, I realise how much my body aches.

My head throbs. Both from where it has been struck and probably from what I was given earlier. It feels like there might be a sore lump on my hip where I assume the needle went in. Unless that is another injury I have yet to identify.

I bet I'm dehydrated too. The glass of vodka and coke I downed last night has long worn off. The liquid has strained down to my bladder which begs for release now. But fully clothed with my hands bound behind me I have few options.

Is this what Leah faced? Was she ever here? I know in my heart the answer to that question. I squeeze my eyes shut as I think of her.

I just hope that the stench of this building is not the silent answer to the question I've been asking since my best friend's disappearance.

CHAPTER TWELVE

Then

It's now been three months since Leah went missing. The days have been long without her, but to find that so much time has passed without any trace is alarming.

In a way, the Adam thing gives me reassurance that this unseen ex I never met wasn't involved. On the other hand, it makes me wonder what the heck Leah was thinking of by inventing a boyfriend to talk to me about. At great length, sometimes,too. She told me what a great kisser he was. How Adam was all about the touching and the physical contact.

We even went on a breakup shopping spree afterwards to mend Leah's broken heart. Looking back, she hadn't even been upset the day the relationship came to an end. Was it really all a lie? Who did the untruth benefit?

Helen, Tony and I try to remain proactive, even in the face of the wall of silence we have been met with.

Adrian Jenkins, the admin of a relatively high profile Youtube channel sends me a private message on Facebook one day. He asks if I'd like to talk about Leah in his next true crime video. I decide any publicity is good and quickly accept.

Adrian records our interview for his show over Zoom. Once it is published, the video quickly racks up tens of thousands of views. It goes viral in various Tamworth and West Midlands groups, so a lot of locals see it.

If anyone witnessed anything in the local area where Leah went missing this will be a good chance at connecting with them in addition to the appeal the police put out themselves. It's a good feeling to think I've managed to do something useful.

Helen is grateful when I see her after the video gains traction. She is still disappointed that the national news hasn't picked up Leah's story as it has with the high-profile cases we see sometimes, but Adrian's video gives her the boost she seems to need.

As the weeks pass, however, no new leads come in. The comment section is alight with personal theories though, some are even quite spiteful.

One user has gone as far as to speculate that I'm responsible in a bid to be the sole occupant of the house I share with Leah.

It takes all my resolve not to comment back and put them right.

*

One Sunday, I'm doing my new usual routine of retracing Leah's walk home from work. This route is now as familiar to me as it must have been to Leah. I'm seeing it from her perspective now. It's obvious seeing this nature reserve through her eyes that she was drawn to the peace and tranquillity it offered in bountiful quantity. I've even taken food and fed the swans a couple of times and seen no one else other than the odd dog walker moving in the long grass and reeds nearby.

It has sort of been helpful for me too. The lettuce is going floppy in the fridge before I can get through it lately with just me eating it. I take the leftover stuff and feed it to the graceful white creatures since we're not allowed to give them bread anymore. They gobble the scraps of leaves down when I throw them into the lake.

They enjoy some of the excess roast potatoes Helen brought over from last week too. She will no doubt come over later with another roaster or insist I pop over for lunch and take a doggy bag with me.

My phone buzzes in my pocket and I pull it out. Coincidentally, it is Helen. My stomach sinks as it has done lately every time she calls, just in case she has something big she needs to break to me. It's just a reflex now.

I answer straight away, hoping it is not bad news. Then I wonder if she wants to take me up on my offer of a meal out after all. She has been bringing so much food over for me since Leah went missing that I feel like I should return the favour.

It is like she is still stuck in mum mode and can't ever stop. I'm so grateful, but I worry she is running herself ragged. Not to mention all her behaviour shows she is firmly in denial. I mean, aren't we all to some extent? But I know she can't keep it up for too long. It wouldn't be healthy.

'Hiya.' I hate the false brightness that I've tried to inject into my voice lately. It doesn't suit me.

'Claire. Oh my goodness.' Helen stops for a sob.

Another jolt stabs at my insides. *This is it*, I think. They've found Leah. *Please, no*. 'What is it? What's happened?'

Helen draws in a breath around her sobs. 'It's the police. They just … '

'Go on,' I say breathlessly. 'It's OK. Just tell me what they said.'

'I was here at home with Tony. Oh, God. I can't believe this is happening. This can't be right!'

'What is it? What happened, Helen?'

'They arrested Tony!' Helen dissolves into a fit of crying.

I suddenly have the image of my mother figure with her palm on her forehead the way she always does when distressed. Like the time she found an overlooked bill down the back of the cereal cupboard. It must have slipped from the drawer above. By the time she got to it the water company had added on a heap of interest. Helen had been on the phone for hours trying to sort it out, getting redder in the face by the minute.

But that pales into insignificance now. This time, Leah isn't there silently stroking her mother's back in support. Nor am I there to put a plate of biscuits in front of her for her free hand whilst the other presses the phone to her ear.

Nor is Tony able to offer any help it seems. Uncle Tony. He was always there for us if we asked for help. Always happy to take us girls out for the day to give his little sister some time to herself when we were younger.

My head spins. 'I don't understand.'

'That's exactly what I said!'

Helen gives a loud sniff and seems to pull herself together enough to go on. 'We had Detective Halliwell over last weekend. After Sunday lunch. He arrived shortly after you left. I think I said something in passing about Tony having a new car. I didn't even think about it when I opened my mouth! Then he sort of latched onto that.'

'Why did Tony change his car all of a sudden? I don't think he really said.'

'I don't know. He loved that Ford. I didn't really pay much attention with all this going on. But the detective wouldn't let it go. He asked Tony loads of questions about his activities. He got him to confirm again where he was at the time Leah went missing. Now some officers have just come and taken him down to the station. *For further questioning*, they said! I'm so confused, Claire. I don't know what to think. Could Tony have - no! I can't even say it out loud. It must be a mistake.'

'He can't have ...' I say slowly as I try to process the information. 'It's Tony. He wouldn't. Maybe the police are just struggling for leads. The detective asked me some questions too. They have come up empty so far, haven't they?'

'Yes. Yes, maybe. That will be it, I'm sure.'

But Helen doesn't sound certain of anything. The doubt in her voice is deafening. It creeps down the phone and starts buzzing in my brain too. Could Tony have done something to his niece?

It sounds like something you would read in the papers. Not something that could happen to us. Uncle Tony couldn't be involved. He's a good man. To think of him stalking Leah in the dark as she walked home is ridiculous. At the same time, the image makes my blood boil.

Something the first police officer said to us

in the immediate wake of Leah's disappearance comes back to haunt me all of a sudden. *It is often someone not far from home that might know something.*

Was he right or wrong?

Tony could be innocent despite all this. It could be a mistake. But why does an innocent man change his beloved car the same week his niece goes missing? It must be a coincidence. It can't mean what I think it does.

Or could it?

CHAPTER THIRTEEN

Now

The silence is broken by the sound of the wind outside, wherever outside is; I still have no idea where I am. The cool breeze whistles menacingly through unseen holes in the building.

In the dark, I have the feeling I'm being watched. Does my abductor have a view of this place somewhere? I imagine one of those low light cameras observing the movements even I can't see in this place. Are my pupils large and dark, stretching over my green irises as they are depicted on a screen somewhere nearby?

I shiver, chilled to the bone on this horrible stone floor. I try to remember the outdoor survival presentation we got one day in school once. Didn't that mention something about how to keep warm in emergency situations?

Some extracurricular team came in and did an activity morning for us all in Year Eight. Did any of us kids really pay that much attention? None of us would have considered the fact that we would ever need to use it. Not one of us imagined we would even be in a situation like this.

Leah didn't pay attention that day at school; that I know for a fact. I remember like it was yesterday, the two of us sitting on the second to last row. Hannah Turner just had a new flip phone for her birthday and she was showing off all the features.

We all glanced up when we were hissed at by Mrs Jenkins. Just in time to see a Powerpoint Slide about sharing body warmth when trapped out in the elements. A few of the boys sniggered at the stock image on display then.

But what good is any of that to me now? There is no one here to share body heat with.

The sense that eyes are upon me is strong again. It suddenly occurs to me that there could be all manner of unpleasant critters that in here too. Watching and waiting for their next meal, perhaps. Maybe they fancy something fresh.

Panic flutters in my stomach. I sit up straight. The bonds strain painfully against my hands.

I stare around in the dark, hoping that my

eyes will somehow suddenly adjust. But they don't. I stamp my foot and shuffle around with deliberate noise.

Then I stay still and listen intently for a reaction.

Nothing. Surely rats would move a little after that disturbance? What if there are bats? Maybe not. They might spring to life later. But that is the least of my worries right now.

My only thought now is to find a way out of here. At the very least, I need to be ready for when my captor returns.

I'm disappointed I didn't get to see his face. I still don't officially know who has done this to me. It would have been nice to have concrete confirmation. But I have a good idea. It will probably turn out that mine and Helen's suspicions were correct all this time. It's too bad the police didn't have enough evidence to arrest that slimebag.

Hatred boils up inside me when I picture his face; a face so familiar I could pick up a stone and sketch it into the filthy floor beneath me.

This place must be one of his properties, one Helen and I didn't know about. I know Helen sat down one day and tried to make a list of places he had access to once we were convinced who it was that took our precious Leah.

Neither of us could have saved Leah, but soon enough I hope to know what really happened to her, and the other women too.

There must be others. I'm convinced of that now.

This fellow probably has a list. Only he knows the full extent of what he has done and to whom. I've often wondered if he keeps trophies somewhere from his victims. That's what they like to do, isn't it?

One thing I know is that he doesn't keep anything incriminating in his house. That was a lead I checked off already. I don't like to think about what that nugget of information cost to obtain though. My insides still squirm uncomfortably at the thought.

I can't say that I'm just going to be just another name on this guy's list.

I refuse to be just one more victim. I owe it to the only woman I've ever really loved. When this guy comes back, he will know that he made a mistake by snatching me.

Part of me even feels sorry for him. Well, almost.

CHAPTER FOURTEEN

Then

The thought of Tony being responsible for Leah's disappearance eats at me. He has always been part of the family. He was the only male family figure when Helen adopted me and has been around whenever we needed him.

The hours Tony has been held for stretch out across the whole afternoon. I go over to Helen's and help her with the Sunday roast she had obviously been planning for today; it turns out, she was partway through peeling the potatoes. I pick up where she left off as we talk about the latest development.

The logical part of my brain tries to tell me that this is all a misunderstanding. Tony can't be involved. It's Uncle Tony. We all know him. He wouldn't dream of such a thing.

But then I should know what monsters can lurk behind closed doors from my early childhood. The way my own mother treated me can never be scrubbed from my memory.

To her, I was an inconvenience. Something to be shoved into the bedroom behind a closed door if it suited her. I guess, a child needing to be fed, clothed or potty trained was a hassle if it got in the way of her permanent bender.

I used to dream of having a father to run to when my mum's mood swings became too scary. I've never had any idea which of my mother's friends or cohorts I was the product of. I wonder even if my mother knew herself. I imagine she wouldn't and if she did, she never mentioned his identity to her only child. Besides, If he was with my mother, even for a half-an-hour encounter, then he surely wouldn't be the hero I desperately needed back then.

Was Uncle Tony hiding his true self behind a genial mask all these years? If so, why did he choose now to strike?

These are all questions Helen shoots at me at random moments over Countryfile, after we have picked at the roast dinner. Neither of us is really watching the program.

'And why Leah?' Helen mutes the television when the Antiques Roadshow theme tune pipes from the TV. 'Why choose to attack her? If

Tony was some kind of deviant, which we surely might have noticed by now if he was, then why not target some other woman? You don't have to go after your own family!'

'I don't know. They say it is usually someone the victim knows in these cases. But I'm struggling to believe Tony would do something bad. Let's just wait and see. I know it's not easy.'

'Huh! You can say that again. Waiting for news these past few months has taken it out of me.' Her voice breaks and she pulls a tissue from her pocket to dab at the corners of her eyes. She seems to keep a supply close by these days. 'I just need to know what happened.'

I stroke her back soothingly. After a few moments, she settles again. But we are both made to jump by the front doorbell which chimes ominously in the otherwise quiet house.

Helen scrambles to her feet and, despite her greater age, manages to get to the front door before me.

Tony stands on the doorstep. Raindrops run off his vintage leather jacket. He looks pale and exhausted, not at all ready for the onslaught of questions Helen fires angrily in his direction.

'Well?' Helen snaps, her lip wobbling. 'What have you got to say for yourself?'

He shakes his head. 'Come on, you daft cow. You know I had nothing to do with all this business with Leah.'

'It's not *business*! My little girl is gone!'

Tony takes the opportunity to step out of the rain and wrap a softer Helen in his arms as she breaks down. He strokes the back of his sister's blonde bob with one of his large hands as she sobs onto his shoulder.

I've never noticed how well-built Tony is before. I've noted how tall he is, but never paid much attention to the power in his shoulders.

A woman walking out alone would not stand a chance. Most men would have a hard job fighting him if they had to. Tony often takes on most of the hard labour of his property renovations and repairs himself and thinks nothing of it.

I remember how he gutted the kitchen of mine and Leah's house last year. He single-handedly moved the washing machine out into the back garden and tore and threw out the old units into a skip out the front like they were as light as polystyrene. The new units were carried in with just as much ease.

I step around the pair and close the front door before looking back at Tony. 'How did it go today at the police station?'

Tony releases Helen a little. He keeps his arm firmly around her shoulders as he faces me. The sight of it makes me want to snatch Helen away. She looks too vulnerable, being a good few inches shorter than me.

My "uncle" shrugs. 'The police just wanted to ask me some questions. They picked up on the fact that I had a new vehicle. It all boils down to bad timing that I changed cars the week our Leah went, didn't it? The police wanted the details of the old car so they can track it down.'

I fold my arms across my chest. 'And you gave them the information?'

'Course I did. What do you take me for? You know I've done nothing wrong, Claire. The police will confirm it when they track the car down. I'm glad I got ripped off in a big chain part exchange now. Should be easy enough to trace. Not like the back street dealer who tempted me with an extra hundred.'

'Why did you change your car anyway? You never said.'

'It all got overshadowed, didn't it?' Tony shakes his head. 'My old Ford was knackered. The flywheel was going again and I know from the last time that would be a big bill. On an old motor like that, it wasn't worth throwing good money after bad. The rust was starting to eat at it. You might have noticed?'

'Not really.'

'The police say they will run forensics over it when they get their hands on it, but they are wasting their time unfortunately. That is the thing that is bothering me about all this the most. They are obviously stuck for answers if they are trying to drag someone like me into all this. Come on, Claire. How many years have you known me?'

Helen gives Tony a playful slap and rests her head on his shoulder. 'I'm sorry, for being a daft old sod. Can you forgive me? I didn't know what to think when they carted you out of here this morning. Deep down I knew it wasn't you who was to blame, but what's happened lately has made me question everything. I'll put the kettle on, shall I? You look chilled to the bone.'

Helen steers Tony into the lounge where Antiques Roadshow now plays in silence before moving into the kitchen. 'We've run out of that Green and Blacks you got me,' she calls to her brother. 'You'll have to have the cheap Asda stuff.'

'I don't mind. Anything is better than what I got down the police station.'

I remain standing in the hall. Through the frosted glass of the living room door, I watch Tony's large form reach for the remote control.

So that's it. There is a perfectly good explanation for Tony's change of car after all. My feelings have been in turmoil today and I don't know how I feel about this sudden change of events. One minute Tony is being hauled off, under suspicion. The next he is back at home like nothing happened.

But simply accepting all this somehow feels like I'm letting my best friend down. But I'm not entirely sure why.

CHAPTER FIFTEEN

Now

It's been hours since my captor ditched me in here. Not that it's easy to judge time, but I think this is how long it has been. My bladder certainly seems to think so, anyway.

It's still completely in the dark aside from that little speck of light. I want to get to it and rip the board off that must cover the window. But I'm tethered to something near the wall and I can't move.

I twist my hands around. Something tugs on my wrists. It pinches and rips at the hairs. It must be tape that I'm bound with. It feels like the thick, chunky stuff. *That won't break, but it will cut*, I think to myself.

I shift my weight and feel around blindly for

something sharp. A jagged piece of rubble will do. A stone. Anything.

But my hands come across nothing more than gravel, dust and a small piece of stone. I lean as far as I will go, pain searing my wrists as they take the strain. Then a weight shifts in my pocket with a metallic jangle.

My heart leaps with excitement. My keys.

Did that idiot leave them in my coat pocket? My phone was in my handbag, so that's a goner, but that creep might have overlooked the contents of my pockets.

A key would cut through this tape if I rub it long enough.

My coat is still open, so I twist and shift awkwardly a few times. I'm glad no one can see me now as I roll around trying to gather enough slack on my parka. I press my knees together and manage to grab the hem of my coat between them.

It's my favourite winter coat, a dark green one. I knew I had to get it as soon as Leah picked it out in Peacocks and said it was my colour. 'It brings out your eyes,' she said as she tilted her head and judged me appraisingly.

There is another jangle and then I feel, my bunch of keys slide out onto the stone floor. I nudge the cluster of metallic objects with my foot towards my outstretched fingers.

My heart leaps excitedly in my chest. Another small victory. But it feels as good as getting a promotion at work, or walking down the street and finding a ten-pound note and no one else around.

My fingers are numb from the cold and they fumble to find the right tool for the job. They grope the key for Helen's back door, her front door, my shed, and then the ones for my house. After a moment, I determine that the sharpest of the lot is my own front door key.

Then I quickly get to work. I have no idea how long I've got before I'm paid another visit. I just have to be ready for when I am. The last thing I can afford is t still be trapped on the floor when that front door opens.

I'll be ready. And that creep won't know what has hit him. His biggest mistake was picking me up last night.

It is slow and frustrating work. Sawing with a limited range of movement and with a blunt tool is tough. My hands cramp and my muscles scream with the effort. I don't know how long I've worked the tape before I get somewhere. The first snap sets my pulse racing again.

'Yes,' I breathe.

Finally, more of the plastic gives. Now I pull my arms as far apart as they will go. Pain stabs at my wrists again, but I keep going. There is a final snap and my hands are free.

I move gingerly forward and realise the right sleeve of my coat has been taped to something also. That was what was keeping me near the wall. I shrug off my coat entirely and stand up quickly.

Too quickly. The darkness in front of me instantly fizzes and I see white stars briefly again. I lean quickly down and press my hands against my knees, willing myself not to pass out again. How long will it take for the mystery substance to leave my system?

After a few moments, I straighten up and look over at the door, as though it will suddenly be thrown open. But it doesn't.

Shivering more than ever in my thin jumper, I move over to the little speck of light. It looks much bigger over here. Almost like an eyehole. I lean down cautiously.

The cold air outside tastes so fresh compared to the vile stagnancy in here. I take mouthfuls of it, before tilting my eye and instead peering through the hole.

Outside I can see grass, rugged and yellowing. Clusters of dark heather poke out here and there. As I watch, a rabbit streaks out and disappears behind a crumbled old brick wall.

The scene looks like the rolling Yorkshire moors. I wonder if that is really where I am, like my favourite book characters. It's hard to say.

It didn't take long to become so disoriented. I don't even know what time of day it is. Was this what Leah faced in her final days?

My heart breaks at the thought of her being locked up in here, her warm locks being slowly dirtied and saturated with filth.

'Leah,' I say to no one but myself. 'I miss you, Hun.'

Just saying her name makes me feel momentarily connected to her, and stronger too. I allow my lip to wobble briefly at the thought of my lost friend. Then I pull myself together.

I'm guessing Leah didn't escape from her confines as I have. Because if she had, she would have given the guy that snatched her everything she could. I wouldn't have liked to have been him.

I feel my way along from the window. The wall is rough and my nails catch on it until I find the door. I take hold of the knob and push all my weight against it. I try again and again until I'm panting with exhaustion.

It's a long shot, but I had to check it wouldn't give easily.

A noise behind me makes me turn and blink into the darkness. But I can't make anything out.

I turn back to the window and peer out again. If I press my face hard against the wood, I can just about make out the edge of the main farm building to the side.

Another noise behind me makes me spin around. This time my heart thumps and doesn't stop, because I'm certain now that I'm not alone.

CHAPTER SIXTEEN

Then

Being at home is a different experience without Leah. I had no idea how much her energy influenced the space around us, even when she wasn't there.

Her perfume used to linger in a trail behind her as she left the house for work each morning. I hadn't noticed so much at the time, but now she is gone the absence seems impossible to ignore.

I'm also missing the folded corners of the magazines on the coffee table. My best friend would always fold over pages she thought I would like. And she was right every time. She knew me so well.

It is a relief these days to go to work. I find myself requesting overtime when I can.

And when I can't, it is always tempting to find somewhere else to be.

Spending time with Helen is a double-edged sword. I love her and want to support and be there for her as much as I can. But I will turn around at random intervals when in her company and see elements of my best friend looking back.

Then there is Tony. He will call by unannounced. No change there. But I'm not sure how I feel about him any more. Not when doubt has become lodged in the back of my mind.

What happens at lunchtime today only proves to add fuel to the flames where the subject of him is concerned.

After spending the morning arranging repairs on the ostrich enclosure, I head to the nearby tearooms for my lunch break. It's usually quieter at this end of the park, especially on an off-peak weekday. Since Leah's vegan influence went missing along with her, I order a chicken salad baguette and a bottle of orange juice and sit at one of the outdoor tables to eat.

Despite the cool weather, I find it less claustrophobic being out here. Just as well really, since my ex James decides to turn up today with a similar idea. He joins the end of the queue which, in contrast to when I ordered, now extends outside. There aren't many people waiting inside the tiny eatery, but it means that James now hovers awkwardly at the end of the line. Coincidentally it happens to be right near the table I chose. Now I regret not sitting inside.

I haven't seen James close up for a while. I can tell he is watching me out of the corner of his eye.

At first, he decides to pretend he hasn't seen me, then changes his mind. 'Hiya, Claire. You all right?'

My mouthful of baguette has a hard time going down all of a sudden. 'Yeah, fine thanks. How are you?'

'Fine, yeah. Good, good.' James takes his weight from one foot to the other.

There is an awkward moment that I decide to fill up with taking another bite of sandwich to avoid small talk.

James seems to feel compelled to make conversation though. 'I'm really sorry about Leah.'

I give up on the crusty bread and take a glug of orange juice, spluttering on it slightly. 'Yes, so am I.'

'I heard her uncle was arrested.'

'Yes. Well, no. Not arrested exactly. The police just wanted to ask him some questions. That was all.'

'Oh. My mistake. Some of the lads were talking about it a few weeks back. Bloody Chinese whispers, eh?'

He laughs nervously and taps his payment card against his thigh as he waits for the queue to move, which it doesn't.

Great, so Leah's fate has been reduced to nothing but work gossip. Something to pass the time until the end of the shift. But it piques my interest because I didn't think the news about Tony had left Helen's house. Tony wouldn't be likely to mention it either.

I look back to James. 'Who was talking about it?'

James looks surprised that I've said something more. 'Oh, I don't know. Just Liam and Joe, I think. Liam's brother rents one of Tony's properties. I guess that is how he heard about it. I suppose he was worried in case his landlord gets sent to prison. The rental market is tough right now.'

'Yes, it is. Tony is my landlord too.'

'Oh, yeah. He is, isn't he? But you don't think he was involved?'

I open my mouth to answer but I'm not sure what to say.

'Sorry,' James says quickly. 'I'm being nosy.'

'No, it's not that. I just ... I don't know. I thought I knew him. But lately, I don't know. Changing his car a few days after Leah went missing is a bit suspect. But he has a satisfactory explanation for it.'

'What, that he messed up the interior with building rubble? He has done that sort of work for years, hasn't he? Why did it bother him all of a sudden? And that very twenty-four too? He must have really made a mess of his car to rip out all the interior as he did.'

'What do you mean?'

'Liam's brother needed the cooker replaced in his flat around about the time Leah went missing. He said Tony had pulled out the boot carpet and had ditched the parcel shelf when he saw the car. He thought it strange at the time. I mean, Tony's car was always a mess inside. Comes with the territory when you manage properties as he does, doesn't it? On top of that, he went and switched cars the next day too. It's a bit fishy if you ask me.'

The line starts to move now. James is compelled by those behind him to finally step inside the building. As soon as he does, the family with a crying baby behind him take his place. 'Well, I guess I'll see you around, Claire.'

I turn and face my unfinished lunch but I am no longer hungry.

Tony never said he had messed up the inside of his car. He said there was a mechanical problem.

And James is right. Tony always had splodges of paint or strips of wood with rusty nails poking out in his car somewhere. The boot was forever full of tools or old disused appliances that leaked and tore the interior. It was always a mess. It would have made no sense to switch vehicles for that reason.

But it could be a case of Chinese whispers.

After all, Tony wasn't officially arrested. His tenant got that fact wrong, at least. But is he right about the car?

I pull out my phone and tap out a text to Helen. I'm invited for Sunday lunch, but I can't wait until then. I need to ask her this now.

> *Hi Helen. I hope you are doing well today. It's a nice sunny day here in the park.*

Cut to the chase Claire, I think to myself. No amount of padding is going to distract from what I'm going to ask.

> *I was wondering, did the police check out Tony's car yet? He said forensics were going to give it the once over. Did he get the all-clear yet? xx*

It is a while before I get my answer. Helen works in a sandwich shop. She must be handling the lunchtime rush at the moment.

Later on in the afternoon, my phone buzzes with a reply.

> *Don't worry, that's all sorted now. Tony has explained to the police how his car is a workhorse and taking trips to the dump all the time is a normal part of his work. We all knew they weren't going to find anything. We let our imaginations run wild for a few hours, didn't we? Actually, speaking of the devil! Tony is picking me up after work to treat me to a cream tea. I'll tell him you were thinking of him xx*

I have the immediate urge to text back and ask her not to. But I leave it.

Besides, something troubles me now. Tony never mentioned the police being bothered by a trip to the dump shortly after his niece's disappearance.

So that is three question marks above his head now.

One, it sounds like he ripped out the interior of his car in the twenty-four hours after Leah was gone.

Two, he apparently made a trip to the dump straight after that.

Three, he then changed his car abruptly another day or two later.

A visit to the dump isn't unusual for him. Still, the timing and considering the other things make me suspicious. As does the funny feeling in the pit of my stomach.

CHAPTER SEVENTEEN

Now

My instincts were right before. I'm not alone in this ramshackle old building. Another living body is nearby. Watching.

I can sense them now. My eyes won't tell me, but the way my hairs stand up on my arms and on the back of my neck does.

I take a tentative step forward away from the window and further into the building. I have the feeling my legs will let me down at any minute.

Did my captor turn and enter through the back of the house as soon as he exited the front door? Surely, even in my disoriented state, I would have noticed such a brazen move.

Or would I?

'Hello?' I take another step into what I assume is the middle of the room.

I can't judge the size of this place well. I just know from feeling around that there is a door and two windows on each side at the front. But I have no idea about the back.

Perhaps there is a way out through a weaker back door?

I reach out my hands in front of me. I'm frustrated that they waver beyond my control.

Fear is nothing, I tell myself. *Leah went through all this on her own too.*

As I move forward, I stare around blindly as I take another few cautious steps. Then I hear something shift again. There is definitely something moving in here.

My heart hammers faster. 'Hello? Is someone there?'

My thoughts spring back to a wild animal of some kind. I don't know where I am, but might there be a fox or a savage dog locked in here too? Haven't there been stories of escaped large cats roaming moors and sparsely populated areas?

What if one has got in here by mistake? My captor might not even know about it yet.

Or maybe this is part of a game. Maybe that's what he wants. For me to be attacked and killed by some kind of creature. I thought I knew his motives, but maybe I was wrong. Who knows what makes these creeps tick? Or what goes on inside their twisted minds.

All I know is why I was brought here. I pulled too many threads; did too much digging when everyone else had let go.

In hindsight, I made it too easy for him to think he could take another victim. I knew too much. So it killed two birds with one stone.

Yes, I know enough to realise why I was taken. But it would have come as a total shock to poor Leah as she strolled home past her sanctuary of the nature reserve with her favourite song blaring in her ears.

My outstretched fingers suddenly make contact with another wall on the other side of the room. This place must be quite big. But then again, it is hard to judge without actually seeing it.

Despite this less-claustrophobic idea, the stench is overpowering. It makes me cough and gag as though it is getting stronger at the back of the property.

I feel my way along and find a rotten wooden doorframe.

It is just as dark at this end of the building. My hands map out the features on one side of the room as I tread carefully forward.

There is something that feels like it could be a farmhouse dresser of some kind. My fingers move gingerly over what could be shards of broken porcelain; then over a crusted surface that in my mind I imagine being one of those old range cookers.

My hands continue to follow the contours and dips of the kitchen. One such hollow causes me to plunge my hands into freezing cold liquid.

I gasp and pull them back, wondering what the slimy residue that coats my hands could be.

Bending down, I rub my hands frantically on my trouser legs. The smell makes me wretch some more.

An exhalation of breath behind me makes me freeze in my tracks and straighten up. My heart still pounds from panic in my ears and I struggle to hear over it.

'Hello?' I call out. My voice sounds breathless now. Afraid.

After a few minutes, I hear another noise. But it coincides with the whistling of the wind outside and I shake my head to dismiss wild thoughts.

It could be the wind that I'm hearing. That will be it. My lack of vision is playing tricks on my mind. My captor must know that. Perhaps that is why this place is set up the way it is. Maybe I'm being taught a lesson in fear?

I should have kicked him more forcefully earlier. Could I have fought any harder than I did? Maybe I should have gone for biting? I had just a split second to react earlier. Yes, teeth might have been more effective than the impact through my silly little loafers. I'll have to try it when I get the chance.

I feel the wall above where I put my hands. It surely must have been the sink. Which suggests that the area above it is a window.

I feel upwards and feel damp wood. It is quite soft compared to the boards of the front. I give it a thump with my palm.

I lean all my weight over, careful not to risk touching the substance in the farmhouse sink again.

The board give a fraction under all the force I can summon.

A tiny amount of light tells me I was right. I am standing at an aged porcelain sink. It is filled with a dark liquid. But I think it is green, not red or any other really untoward colour. It was just putrid algae I plunged my hands into. That is something at least.

The light doesn't do much for the rest of the room. I still can't make out much.

I twist my neck and try to stare around behind me. The strain of pushing against the board is making my arm muscles shake.

It's my own fault. I've abandoned any attempt at fitness since Leah has been missing. Leah and I used to go out walking at the weekends sometimes, we even discussed getting a dog together.

Now I hardly stay active at all. After work these days, I just flop on the sofa drained and mentally exhausted.

Helen was adamant that I should walk

home alone from work as her daughter had done. She turned up one day with a little red Polo to call my own and insisted I accept it. She wouldn't have let me rest until I said yes, so there went the little exercise I had on my short daily commute.

It takes me a few moments in the gloom now, but I can just about make out a pattern of vertical wood poles at a diagonal angle. That must be the stairs.

Then something I catch out of the corner of my eye makes me shriek louder than I have in the last twenty-four hours. I jump and the wooden panel slips from my fingers and back into place with a snap. I am once again plunged back into total darkness.

There was a figure at the base of the stairs.

That's all I made out, but I don't need to see any more to know that I am indeed being watched. Even in the low light, I could see a gleam upon the whites of their eyes.

Human eyes. The person was wearing a hood or had bushy hair. I don't know. I didn't see it for long enough.

'Who are you?!' I half-scream. 'Who is there?'

'Claire?'

It's a woman's voice; deep and croaky. But definitely a woman. Certainly not my abductor.

I blink. 'What's going on? How do you know my name?'

'It's me, Claire. It's Leah.'

100

CHAPTER EIGHTEEN

Then

I t occurs to me how convenient it is that Tony has everything neatly explained. He has Helen fooled. He almost has me fooled too. But something doesn't sit right with me about it all.

The vehicle switch was too much of a coincidence for my liking. Then James voiced his suspicions too. Then there is Liam and Joe at work. Not exactly the sharpest pencils in the drawer. Still, four separate people are unlikely to detect smoke without fire.

My enquiries at the police station get me nowhere. The female officer behind the desk told me I couldn't get information about the case or its suspects as I wasn't the one who made the missing persons report. Officially that was Helen.

'But I was there when she filled in the form,' I say imploringly. 'I even answered some of the questions for her.'

She holds up her hands. 'I'm sorry. We can only share information with the person named on the form.'

So I'm going to have to take an alternative approach. On Sunday, I text Helen to decline her offer of Sunday lunch when she tells me Tony will be there.

Don't be silly, Claire. I'm making your favourite giant Yorkshire puddings. You need some meat on your bones, especially lately. Don't pay attention to all these websites and magazines. Men like something to hold onto, you know xx

I tap out my response.

I'm not bothered by what men like. You and Tony have a good time. We will catch up next week, I promise xx

I imagine I'll get a doggy bag tomorrow overflowing with food, but I don't think about that now.

Now all my focus is on Tony. He will be occupied for a good while at his sister's house. Lunch, dessert, numerous cups of tea, more dessert and the obligatory scroll through the channels with a cocoa later will give me at least six hours. But what I'm planning won't take anywhere near as long as that.

Tony leaves a spare key in the backyard.

'Not under the mat,' he told us two girls once. 'Because that is too easy for opportunists. But under the rosemary bush in the border of the garden. Under a black stone. In case either of your two ever needed it in an emergency,' he would tell us. 'You can get in and make yourselves at home until your mum or I get there.'

Well, now I do need it, Tony. And you could call this an emergency. I hope you haven't changed your habits.

Nerves bubble inside me as I pull up in my Polo outside Tony's two-bedroom semi. He lives in Wilnecote. His car is gone already, just as I knew it would be.

This is not the largest of all his properties. I remember being inside it so many times over the years. It shouldn't take long to search. He uses his spare room as an office with all his paperwork. Tony is a stickler for records and receipts. He has a fair few properties to manage and maintain. And he keeps it all in his house.

I get out of the car and let myself through the gate at the side of the house.

I've been through my plan all night. Like I could sleep once I had this idea of coming in here. It's not called breaking in if you've been told repeatedly where the key is kept, is it?

Once I step into the back garden, I immediately spot the rosemary bush. It is a lot bigger than the last time I was here. Tony has obviously let the maintenance of his own place slip in recent times.

There is a tense moment where I feel around in vain for the black stone. But my fingers close around its smooth surface after some fumbling and find the single key underneath.

Through the conservatory next door, a Yorkshire Terrier goes nuts as I let myself into Tony's place. Its fuzzy little head bobs around above the low fence, shrieking and eyeing me with its beady black eyes.

It knows I shouldn't be here, but quietens quite quickly once I step in through the back door.

It has been a while since I was up here, but everything is pretty much as I remember. There is a new three-piece suite in the living room which wasn't here last time. I remember Tony mentioning that purchase a long while ago though, so that doesn't mean anything. It isn't evidence that has been disposed of recently.

The dining room and kitchen seem pretty empty and spotless. I head upstairs.

Tony's bedroom door is open. I think I will just walk past, but since I'm here, I might as well take a look. I step inside gingerly and wonder what I am looking for exactly. A trophy of some kind?

The double wardrobe holds nothing much more than a sparse rail of clothes. Tony often goes about in the same handful of apparel; torn and faded jeans and the same rotation of shirts.

Other clothes hang from the rails too, still with tags on. One of them looks like the jumper Helen got him for Christmas just gone. Then there is a dated suit and formal white shirt which I've never seen Tony wear ever.

There is a box of photographs at the bottom. A few baseball caps sit lonely on the shelves and a few retro ties too which I suspect might be older than I am.

The rest of the wardrobe is uneventful and empty. There is a box of coat hangers in another section of the wardrobe and a vacuum cleaner and cleaning supplies.

There is only one bedside cabinet. In the top drawer, there is nothing but a tube of lubricant and condoms; I am quick to close it again. The next drawer down has a box of tissues, cold medicines and a tub of Vaseline.

The last drawer has a mix of underwear and socks. I close it again carefully. What had I expected? Tony has proven he is good at coming up with creative hiding places just by the way he concealed the spare back door key.

When I straighten up, I catch sight of the double-framed photographs on the cabinet.

One side has a picture of a teenage Tony and

Helen. Helen sits on a sofa, her head thrown back in laughter and Tony sits comically on her lap, his own legs in the air. The two had the same dark hair back then. Tony's looks a lot fuller in the photo than it does these days.

In the other photograph, Helen and Tony have a hand each on my and Leah's shoulders. This shot was taken at a barbecue we had in Tony's garden one summer. Leah and I must have been around thirteen at the time. It was a day during that crazy heatwave we had one year.

My friend and I were both dressed in shorts and t-shirts. Helen is red-cheeked behind us; she can't tolerate the heat at all. Even Tony has ditched his usual shirt and is down to a vest too.

It's a colourful and sunny shot. We all look like a happy family with our de facto parents smiling behind us. We are the family Tony never had for himself for whatever reason.

Doubt creeps in now. Have I made a mistake in coming in here?

There is no point in not finishing what I came here to do. Something in my gut tells me something is off. The police seem to have let Leah's abductor slip through their fingers. I owe it to my friend to exhaust my search for her.

When I move along the landing and open the door to Tony's home office, I find the door shut. I fear for a moment that it is locked, but the handle gives easily.

Inside, everything is in its place just as I

remembered.

There is a desk with various folders, some open and with sheets of paper hanging out.

What concerns me is the folder from the last three months. Where would that be?

Conveniently, Tony has labelled all the files with his neat capitalized handwriting. I don't think he even knows how to write in any other way.

It doesn't take me long to take down the folder from last year and find receipts for various things, including the new car. The purchase was made on October 29th.

That was three days after Leah went missing. The rest of us were frantic with worry about his niece then, and Tony was buying a new car. That had been at the top of his priority list whilst Helen and I were making up missing posters on her computer.

Anger bubbles inside me when I think back.

I flip through other pages. There is a receipt for the dump. James was right. It is dated the 27th of October. Less than twenty-four hours after Leah was gone.

What did Tony discard that day? Obviously, something quite big if he couldn't dispose of it in normal household waste as he often does. But he didn't want to use a skip either on that occasion as he has done many times before. Was it merely the interior of his car that had been forever dirty as far as I can remember?

I flip back through the papers. My vision blurs as tears well in my eyes. I happen across the previous receipt. It is one from a garage on the 25th for nine-hundred pounds.

That only compounds Tony's guilt in my opinion. Why would he spend so much repairing his old vehicle just days before he bought a new one? He specifically told me spending any more on that car was "throwing good money after bad".

The house is quiet. So quiet I can hear the neighbours dog through the wall when it starts yapping away again.

Then I hear sounds downstairs. Keys and talking.

That can't be Tony! He was supposed to be with Helen all afternoon and most of the evening too. I've never known Helen not to insist on hosting him all day if she invites him over for lunch.

This can't be happening!

I hastily close the folder and try to remember exactly where it was on the shelf.

I'm just wondering what the heck to do now when I hear heavy footsteps up the stairs.

'I'm just going for a slash!' Tony calls over his shoulder to someone.

I glance over my shoulder in time to realise I left the office door open behind me when I came in.

Will Tony notice?

Can I make it over there in time to close it before he sees?

CHAPTER NINETEEN

Now

'Leah?' I repeat.

My mind spins. It can't be. I'd clung onto hope for the longest of all of us and even I'd admitted my friend was a lost cause. 'Is that you?'

'Yes, Claire. It's me.'

I blink furiously, willing my eyes to focus. Leah's voice is so different. My brain doesn't trigger a spark of recognition. What has happened to her to distort her voice so much?

I step forward and reach out blindly again. 'I can't see you. I'm coming over. Reach out to me, OK?'

Leah doesn't answer.

'Say something, hun, so I can find you.'

She speaks again in her hoarse voice. 'I've missed you so much, Claire.'

My chin wobbles. But I manage to speak again after a moment. 'I've missed you too, hun.'

I reach out and manage to connect with Leah's shoulders. They are bony and hard protruding from beneath a blanket. But I pull myself into her and hug her tightly. My senses are filled with stale sweat and unwashed-hair. The rest of her body feels unrecognisable against mine.

She must have lost a lot of weight in this place. Leah always had the perfect body. I was sometimes jealous of how she could eat anything she wanted and get away with it. She was slender but never skinny.

'Oh my god. What has he done to you?'

Leah doesn't answer as I cup her face with my cold hands. Her skin is like ice too. She doesn't flinch. I stroke the contours of her face gently, but nothing feels familiar. I feel a stab of remorse for what my friend must have been through. I wish I could see her.

It is so bizarre to have a reunion with someone you can't see. I never imagined reuniting with her again like this.

Or at all.

But I don't tell her that. I take her cold thin hand in mine. It again feels unfamiliar. There are several splits in the fingertips. 'I can't believe you are here.'

'Neither can I,' she croaks back.

'What happened to your voice? You sound so different.'

'I don't know. I got ill with some kind of throat infection not long after he took me. It's disgusting in here. So is he. I've screamed a lot too. It's made my voice weird. Maybe I've torn something. I don't know if it will ever be the same again.'

'It's OK.' I squeeze her hand, fearful of what she has been through 'I'm sure you'll get better when we get out of here. Where are we? Are we still in the West Midlands?'

I feel her shrug.

'Well, it doesn't matter. It seems to be some kind of farm. Does that creep come in here often?'

'Sometimes. He mostly leaves me alone. He goes back to Tamworth a lot.'

'Right, of course, he does. He is always in town.'

'How do you know?'

'I see him all the time, don't I? He's so close to home. That's why you were taken. Me too. Plus now he wanted me out of the way because he must have realised I'd discovered his secret.'

For the first time, there is a note of urgency in my friend's new voice. 'Did you tell the police about him?'

'Yes, but they didn't listen to me. They didn't have any evidence to link him to you or what happened to Helen and ruled him out. It was just me and your mum doing our own thing and poking around in the end. You know me. I can't let things go, even you. I mean, you know … especially you. It's been awful without you, not knowing what even happened. You just vanished into thin air, it seemed. But I've been trying to piece it together, monitoring that monster for ages. And now here you are. I can't believe this is real. I never imagined he had been keeping you alive out here all this time. It just won't sink in, you know?'

There is a pause after I've spit all the thoughts that have chased each other through my head for so long.

'I've missed you, Claire.' Leah repeats. She doesn't give an obvious reaction, despite the fact I've mentioned her mother several times

She must be in shock, I realise. I put my arms around her shoulders and hold her tight, unwilling to let her go. Her hair feels coarse against my cheek. It must be gummed up with two years of filth, far from the soft chestnut sheet that always fell over her shoulders.

I've dreamed and dreamed of the moment I would find Leah again. I even stopped believing it would happen. Now I can't believe it at all. I never expected my friend to be beyond recognition.

'What are you going to do now?'

I take a deep breath and take her hand. 'I'm going to get us out of here.'

CHAPTER TWENTY

Then

It turns out I don't make it over to the door to shut it in time.

'Claire?'

I stare back at Tony's face as his figure remains frozen in the doorway. His dark eyebrows curve in surprise. The thin lips of his mouth open. He is obviously speechless to come home and find me in his study.

I am lost for words too. I'm reminded of the time he caught me and Leah smoking behind the local shop. He gave us a stern telling-off. He seemed so big and foreboding suddenly in that moment when normally he was so placid and genial. After his outburst of disappointment and anger, he decided not to grass us up to Helen as we girls had feared.

I know I won't get the same chance today.

'What are you doing in here, Claire?' Tony manages finally. He laughs slightly. 'Helen said she thought you were on a date.'

'No. I wasn't. I wanted … ' I'm trying to find a plausible explanation, but there isn't one, so I just decide on the truth. This thing needs airing anyway.

'I heard you ripped your car interior out the day after Leah went missing.'

Tony looks knocked for six. 'Eh?'

'Someone saw that you took the entire contents of the boot out from your old Ford. Then you took it to the dump.' I gesture to the desk and folders of records behind me. 'I saw the receipt. It has the date and time on it. You can't deny it.'

I'm not sure about my would-be uncle's reaction as I watch it closely. His mind is obviously whirring fast.

'I don't know, Claire. That was all months ago, last year. I think I was looking into fixing the old thing up a bit. I considered trying to salvage what I could from it. That was my favourite car. Did me proud, it did. I didn't want to throw it on the scrap heap.'

'But you threw most of the back half of your car out. Why?'

Tony shrugs. 'I was planning on cleaning it all up and getting a new boot carpet and interior

115

put in. If I was going to pay to get that flywheel fixed, I wanted the rest of the vehicle to be a bit shinier too. So I took out the old stuff and took it to the dump. Why wouldn't I? What's all this about, Claire?'

'You did all that and then got a new car anyway just days later. I've seen the receipt for that too.'

'A bloke I work with told me I was wasting my time with that old thing. He told me I shouldn't throw any more money at it. He sat me down in his Vauxhall and said I should get one like his. So I did.'

'And all this was at the top of your priority list when Leah was missing, was it?'

There is suddenly a flurry of activity at the top of the stairs.

'Tony?' comes Helen's voice. 'Who are you talking to, you daft old sod? Your phone is downstairs!'

Helen's head peers around the doorframe. The smile vanishes from her face to be replaced by a look of shock akin to her brother's.

'Claire? What on earth are you doing here, dear? I thought you had other plans?'

'No, not really. I thought you were both having lunch at yours.'

'No … we decided I'd have the day off cooking since you weren't coming over. Tony suggested we order a takeaway from his place, instead. Why are you in here then?'

'I … just wanted to check something out.'

Helen looks from me to Tony and back again. 'You wanted what? What's going on?'

Tears prick my eyes now. 'I want to know why Tony was so worried about replacing his car when you and I were both out every minute we could searching for Leah!'

'I wasn't!' Tony sounds indignant now. 'I picked up the new car and was driving around all over the place looking for our Leah. How could you say I was doing anything else?'

'I saw the receipt in the folder!' I point behind me at the desk again. 'You purchased it three days after Leah went missing. How could you even think of anything else other than Leah at that point!'

I cup my hands over my mouth as it trembles beyond my control.

Helen tuts and steps over, pulling me into a hug and stroking my back soothingly. 'Come on Claire. You know Tony didn't do anything. You are desperate to make connections. We all are. But you can't be doing with sneaking in here like this.'

I pull myself free from her grip and turn back to face Tony. 'I had to. The car thing doesn't add up.'

Tony softens his indignance now he sees my tears. I don't want him to. I want him to shout at me until the truth spills out.

He shakes his head. 'It wasn't like that. I'd

already put down the deposit on the new car the day before Leah went missing. When I heard she was gone, I was distraught. I forgot all about the vehicle I'd reserved. Then the garage calls me up and tells me they have another buyer interested in it. They were going to take my nine-hundred quid deposit if I didn't turn up and pay the rest. I had to go, Claire. That was all.'

Tony's hazel eyes shine now. He sniffs and steps out of the room. Helen and I hear him blowing his nose loudly into a tissue.

I'm left feeling worse than ever since Leah went. I had convinced myself Tony was the one responsible. It gave me something to cling to. Something to focus on other than my overwhelming grief and denial over my best friend.

Now I've seen the undeniable truth in Tony's eyes that he is innocent, every ounce of despair and desperation comes crashing back.

CHAPTER TWENTY-ONE

Now

L eah's hoarse voice comes out of the dark. 'How are you going to get us out of here?' 'I don't know yet.'

I've felt my way back to the front of the farmhouse and I'm tearing at the tape that is still binding my coat to the wall.

Leah has told me she was bound in the same way when she first arrived. She says the creep wound the tape through a hole in the wall and looped it around the skirting board to keep her tethered at first. Leah says she has had a long time to figure it all out, despite not being able to see.

She uses her hands in the pitch dark to show me how to undo the remnants of tape. There is a loud tear, but we manage to get my coat free. I can't feel where the damage is, but I'm shivering uncontrollably now and grateful to slip it back on at all.

Leah seems to be wrapped in a duvet that has lost its padding around the edges. I try to get her to take my coat, but she refuses, insisting she prefers the blanket. Her fingers draw it tighter around her shoulders when I try to overrule her. I suppose she has been in it for a long time. It must be her only source of comfort in this place.

I take the deepest breath I can without inhaling too much. Now that I know Leah is alive, I have my doubts about its origins. Unless this guy has brought other victims inside and he has ... well, they haven't made it.

'How often does he come in here?'

My friend replies with that haunting voice. 'A few times a week maybe.' Her faint West Midlands accent is distorted somehow. It makes me wonder if she has had a head injury at some point too. 'It's hard to keep track of time. Once he left me for more than two weeks without bringing anything. I thought he was going to let me starve to death.'

'You poor thing.' I reach out and feel around to grasp her cold hand. I find it still gripping the corner of her thin duvet. 'It's OK now. I won't let him do anything else to you. He would have to get through me first.'

'Thanks, Claire.'

'You're welcome, hun.' I give her hand another squeeze. 'So when was the last time he brought food?'

'I can't remember. I think it was two days ago.'

'OK. How does he do it? Does he shove it or throw it in, or does he step completely in here?'

'I don't know. I can't think.' There is a pause. 'He opens the door a tiny bit and sort of chucks a bag of stuff in.'

'Right. Have you got anything we can use as a weapon?'

'What?'

'Like a loose brick or something. This place is falling apart. There must be something we can use. A plank of wood maybe. Anything. If there is one thing I learned from Tony it is how heavy and sharp strips of wood can be. Remember when we had work experience at school and we both chose to work with him? We thought it was going to be a right skive, didn't we? But he had us helping him out with fitting that new kitchen before he took us paintballing. Do you remember?'

There is a pause. 'I've been in here a long time, Claire. My head is fucked.'

'Sorry.' Leah's use of a swear word takes me by surprise. She wouldn't normally talk like that in casual conversation. But she has been through a lot. I suspect I won't even know half of it until after we get home.

Leah guides me to the area in the corner of the room she has used as a toilet and I finally relieve my aching bladder.

'It's a shame he doesn't step inside the building,' I say as I feel around each room meticulously with my friend's guidance. She clings behind me as I go. Her hands are on my hips as if she doesn't want me to disappear into the darkness and leave her behind.

'I am here with you now. I won't leave without you,' I tell her a few times.

'Thanks, Claire,' is all she repeats.

I venture upstairs with Leah's directions. We avoid the missing steps and practically climb over where the wood has rotted away.

Upstairs, there are a few gaps in the roof where several of the old slate tiles have come off. It still doesn't allow me to see where I'm going much better, however. It just means it is colder. Breeze filters in and the air is slightly fresher.

Leah's voice comes from behind me. 'I spend most of my time up here.'

'It must have been lonely.'

'Yeah. I'm glad you're here.'

My groping of the rooms upstairs comes up with nothing truly useful. Leah seems to have been provided with a flimsy plastic fork with which to eat at some point, but the handle has been broken.

She tells me she only has the clothes she came in with and no shoes. I offer her mine.

But again she won't accept them. She tells me she is used to life without shoes and has built up hardened skin on her soles now.

Back down in the kitchen, I feel my way back to the shards of ceramic I found earlier. 'This will have to do as a weapon. It's the only thing I can find.'

'What is it?'

'I think it is a broken plate. It's only thin china, probably antique or something. But it's all we have. On the bright side, it might be sharper because it is thinner.'

'What are you going to do with it?'

'I don't have much of a plan. But I'm thinking when that door opens, we need to be ready. I suppose you can't hear him coming? It's all soft grass out there. Anyway, when he opens the door to bring food, we will both make a grab for the door.'

I walk to the front of the building. The layout is becoming familiar and I've quickly built up a mental map of the place I'm in. I grab Leah's hand and guide it to the door to familiarise her with the size and shape.

'I think we should make a grab for the main wooden panel, rather than the knob. It will be easier to grab quickly in a struggle.'

Leah says nothing.

'Don't worry,' I tell her. 'I know you won't be as strong as you were. I'll go for the guy with the ceramic. Just make sure you put everything you have got into pulling the door back. We will have one chance to get it right. There are two of us and only one of him, remember?'

'I don't want to.'

'I won't let anything happen to you, I promise. But we have to get out of here. And the front door is our best shot.'

'What about the back door?'

'It seems to be boarded up like the windows. Does he ever use it?'

'He does sometimes. Like a few weeks ago. He left it unlocked.'

'What? How long for?'

I sense Leah shrug.

'I don't know,' she says flatly. 'It's still unlocked.'

'What?' I turn on my heel and head for the back of the property. I forget about treading carefully now. It's surprising how quickly I can judge my way around in the dark.

Or so I think. My hip collides painfully with the remnants of the kitchen counter. But this time my hands avoid the putrid water left in the sink.

I feel hurriedly over to the back door and my hands close around the vintage knob.

I try it, but it doesn't budge.

'It's stiff,' comes Leah's voice not far behind me. 'Lift and turn.'

My friend is right. The door budges as I lean my weight into it. Light bores into my eyes like it is my first day ever opening them.

We are free to step outside. I can't believe it.

I want to ask Leah why she didn't think to mention the unlocked door sooner.

But then I turn in the light of day to see my friend for the first time in two years. And I feel my stomach plummet through the floor.

CHAPTER TWENTY-TWO

Then

The first year without Leah seems to pass by in a blur of false sightings, futile tips and a feeling of general despair. Our lives feel as though they are all on hold waiting for news.

Seeing Tony for a while after I broke into his house was awkward. At first, he still took issue with the fact that I suspected him of doing something horrible to Leah. But we got over it. We have known each other too long to let a blip like that really influence our relationship.

'We are all in this together, Claire,' he said to me one evening when my boiler needed its annual servicing and the serviceperson stepped out to his van for extra tools. 'There is no point in us all falling out. Leah wouldn't want that. We have to stay strong for when she comes home.'

In the second spring since Leah's disappearance, the weather looks a little less bleak, but we still know nothing new. The police still update us now and then. They were inundated at first with tips, but they slowly fizzled out once Leah's face wasn't splashed all over social media any more. None of the leads turned out to be credible, they tell us.

It is now the Easter holidays for the local schoolchildren. Helen is tasked with babysitting next-door's little girl, Mia, as she often is. The parents find their neighbour's childminding service convenient, and best of all cheap.

Helen hasn't mentioned it, but I think she would still do it for free. She adores the girl. Since Leah has gone missing, it strikes me that Mia is the grandchild Helen never had.

'The Easter holidays have been taking it out of Mia's mummy and daddy apparently,' Helen says one Saturday with a smile as we make ham sandwiches for us all.

Mia sits in the garden at a little plastic table Helen got just for her. The little girl's favourite character, Queen Elsa, smiles up at her from the surface.

Helen lovingly cuts the crusts off of Mia's just the way she likes them. In reality, it is the only way her charge will eat them. 'I don't know why her parents struggle. She is a little angel when she is here.'

I smile. 'I have the feeling Mia isn't so good when she is at home.'

'Hmm. You might be right. I have heard the odd outburst through the walls now and then!'

We take the little picnic out into the garden and all sit on the small chairs around the little blue table.

It's a pleasantly mild day outside. The sun is working hard to poke through the clouds. The air is sweet with blossom and the first tentative lawn cuts of the year, there is no breeze at all. We are all warm enough in tops, blouses and jeans.

Mia pours us all a cup of imaginary tea using the set of miniature china cups Helen surprised her with earlier. We sip it with obvious relish.

After we have all eaten and drunk. Mia entertains herself by looking for minibeasts in Helen's small pond at the far end of the garden.

Helen watches her closely while we talk. She glances at me. 'You are wonderful with her, you know.'

'Am I? I don't really know what I'm doing.'

'That is what I was like with Leah. It was a right shock when I found out I was pregnant. She wasn't planned you know. I hadn't been out with her father that many times. He wasn't happy about it. Got in a right strop when I told him the happy news, he did!'

She laughs sarcastically as she watches Mia

pull her small fishing net up to her little nose and inspect it carefully. 'Anyway, as you know, Leah's dad didn't stick around very long. It's hard work when they're babies, but it gets easier. He wasn't here long enough to find that out though. I didn't realise it at the time either. I just fumbled through and hoped for the best. That's the thing about being a parent. You don't have to go on a course or get qualified. You have the job anyway.'

'I suppose.' Now I'm lost in thought of my adolescent years with Leah and the times we spent out in this garden ourselves in our youth.

'You would make a wonderful mum, Claire. There is plenty of time.'

I laugh nervously. I know on this side of thirty, a ticking sound has begun somewhere. But I have no intention of worrying about it. 'I think children aren't for me. I had enough of the young ones from when I was in the children's home. That's enough to last me a lifetime. I can't stand the crying.'

'But you must adore Mia. She's wonderful. Wouldn't you like a little girl to dress up and watch grow?'

'Mia is lovely. But you know she isn't this well-behaved most of the time. I just can't see myself doing it. It's not me.'

Helen goes quiet for a few minutes. I can tell I haven't heard the last of this though. She has worked this angle on Leah a few times over the last five years or so. With her only daughter missing, I guess I have to bear the brunt of it alone now.

Helen is obviously revving up a counterpoint. 'Leah got broody when you and she used to help me look after Mia. Wouldn't she be surprised if she could see how much Mia has grown lately?'

The afternoon seems to have had the shine taken off it by the suggestion that Leah has been gone for so long. I guess we are approaching yet another milestone: eighteen months.

I take a sip of my raspberry cordial. The ice clinks loudly against the glass. 'I don't know if she was broody exactly.'

'No? Of course, she was. I could tell deep down she was thinking of a child of her own when she saw how adorable Mia was.'

'Maybe.' I remember how Leah would shrug off the times we left Helen's house after helping to take care of next-door's child. Perhaps we got the harder times Helen was speaking of earlier. Either way, Leah was perfectly happy to pass a younger Mia back without a tug of regret and go out and do something fun with me afterwards, something that was more us.

I don't tell Helen this. Maybe I shouldn't ever mention it. Do we need to start remembering Leah how she was in the past only and not expecting anything new from her in the future? I envisage a future where we speak of our mutual loss in the past tense only.

Is now also the time to start shaping the mental image of a flawless woman? I get the feeling we are supposed to speak of Leah as though we never saw her on a bad day or perhaps during a minor disagreement we might have had sometimes.

She wasn't perfect, I know that. But lately, we seem to be crafting an immaculate image, one not to be tainted in any way. We aren't supposed to mention any memories that are less than perfect. Like the time Leah drank way too much at a house party a few years ago. She ended up in a blazing row with her boyfriend at the time right in front of everyone.

I don't think Helen heard about that incident, nor would I ever tell her. It wasn't really Leah's fault, she never could handle her alcohol well in excess. I have so many memories that were less than perfect too. In her early twenties, my friend dated a man for two months who turned out to be a fake.

She had luckily got out before it was too late, but hearing extracts of his behaviour disturbed me. She had wanted the relationship to work because he had seemed so sensible on the surface. He had insisted on meeting Helen and charmed her with flowers and an expensive bottle of wine.

Helen told her daughter he was a keeper. It was the very next day when Leah told me how he was starting to become behind closed doors.

Behind the smiles and his designer cologne, he made quite a few disparaging remarks about Helen and me too. Leah broke up with him that weekend.

Choosing to remember only the good times sit uncomfortably with me for some reason. It feels as though stripping Leah of her flaws only does a disservice to her memory. She was a real person with emotions and experiences, sometimes so raw. These nuances only added to her charm and made her all the more worthy of our love and respect in my opinion.

Now, it seems Leah is a static image, something to be loved and adored from afar. The thought distresses me more than I want to admit.

Helen's voice drifts back to me as I sit on one of her patio chairs. 'And you don't even need a partner to have a baby these days.'

I try to focus on what she is saying to distract myself from my own dark thoughts.

'I mean, you haven't truly needed a bloke for a while with sperm banks and all. They've been around for ages now. But it is more acceptable these days, isn't it? No one really bats an eyelid. There are all sorts of families these days, aren't there? Especially in the cities. Birmingham must have quite a few alone and that isn't far from us, is it?'

Helen looks at me now and I feel more under scrutiny at once. 'What do you think,

Claire? Are you going to give me a grandchild before I go, eh?'

'I don't know.' Like many times over the years, I feel a rush of gratitude towards Helen for thinking of me as family. She never had to. That's just the kind of person she has always been.

'Look, I know your love life has been a little sparse for a while. But why don't you try and find someone for you? I know you are lonely. Maybe it is time to start thinking of the future now.'

Heat rises in my face. Helen is right. I am lonely. Do I make it so obvious? Leah's absence only amplifies it. It is harder to pretend I'm not alone without my best friend.

'The right person for you might be out there on their own too. You won't know unless you make a bit of an effort. Maybe pushing yourself to get out and about might be good for you. The person of your dreams could be ready to walk into your life.'

The way Helen keeps saying *person* and not 'bloke' or 'man' is telling. What has she assumed about me? And is she right?

Fortunately, the heat of Helen's scrutiny is lifted by the ringing of the landline phone inside the house.

She sighs and heaves herself from her chair. 'Won't be a sec.'

I take a deep breath once she is gone. My shoulders relax a little. Is Helen right? Should I look to the future more?

My whole life has been on hold since Leah didn't come home from work that night.

We have all been waiting for news, but none has come. I can't believe it has been so long since I heard her keys in the door or we both sat together laughing at our favourite tv show.

Mia comes dashing over with some stones she has clutched in her chubby mitts.

I grin at her and lift my shoulders cheerfully, hoping I don't look too troubled after my deep conversation with Helen. 'Hi, Sweetheart. What have you got there?'

'Some magic crystals. They're sparkly when you look up close.'

'Wow. They are gorgeous.' They are ordinary stones, but veins of quartz glisten in the weak spring sun. 'Did Elsa make those for you?'

Mia nods enthusiastically, her eyes lighting up. Her face falls when there is a shuffling behind me to announce Helen's return.

I glance over my shoulder when Leah's mum doesn't step out into the garden. She hovers in the doorway, staring distractedly at the cordless phone in her hand.

The sudden change in Helen's demeanour makes me sit bolt upright in my chair. She seems to be struggling to find words suitable to speak in front of our young charge.

I put my hand on the girl's small shoulder and whisper to her conspiratorially. 'Mia, why don't you go and hide those crystals somewhere safe for Elsa?'

The little girl's big brown eyes look uncertainly back to Helen who manages a nod and a forced smile.

'Quick, before Prince Hans finds them,' I add.

Mia turns and scampers off to hide her handful of treasure around the garden.

I immediately turn to Helen.

She finally manages to speak. 'That was the police on the phone. They say they have found a body. It's a woman. They think it might be Leah.'

CHAPTER TWENTY-THREE

Now

I didn't quite make it out of the back door of the crumbling old farmhouse. I've pushed the door open. The brass door knob is clutched beneath my icy fingers.

But I stare open-mouthed back at the woman behind me in the ramshackle old kitchen; the person I've been trapped inside with for hours.

The woman I thought was my best friend.

This person isn't Leah at all.

She stares back at me with round dark eyes. A far cry from Leah's blue almond-shaped ones. The matted and wiry hair is far too dark and the hairline is too low. No amount of trauma could change my friend like this. This isn't her.

'Who are you?' I demand.

'No one. I'm nothing.'

'What are you talking about? Where is Leah?'

She shrugs. In the light of day, the coverless duvet looks dark grey with filth. There are stains all over it.

'But where is she? You said you were her. You lied to me!'

'Sorry, Claire.'

'How do you know my name?'

'I heard him say it. He mentioned he was going to bring you here soon. He said you would be company for me. Another pet for him.'

'Pet?' I repeat blankly. 'Where is Leah? Was she ever here?'

'Wouldn't you like to know?'

'Yes! I would!' I take a step back towards the building and this filthy bedraggled woman who has several teeth missing. 'Why don't you tell me what you know? Why are you being so unhelpful? I just want to find my friend. Please!'

'Your girlfriend you mean?'

'No - Look, it doesn't matter. Please help me.'

'You should go. He will be bringing food here soon. You don't have much time if you want to get away.'

'No. Not until you tell me about Leah. Was she here in this building? You know the truth.

Just tell me!'

'Yes. She was here.'

I glance around the weedy overgrown backyard, as though a sign of my friend might just spring out of nowhere. 'Where is she now? What happened to her?'

The woman shrugs.

'Don't be difficult. Where is she? How long ago was she here?'

'She was here for ages. Then about a week before you arrived he came in and dragged her out.'

'No. Where did he take her?'

'I don't know.'

'Yes, you do!' I take another step towards the woman. I want to shake her. She is concealing information from me on purpose. I just can't figure out why.

'Where would he have taken her? Have there been others too? Where are they?'

'It's hard to say.'

I groan in frustration. This woman seems to be determined to lie to me. Is she lying about Leah being here at all? I suddenly remember saying Leah's name out loud earlier. This woman had been lurking in the shadows at the time. She must have heard me. I'd been certain it was my abductor that took Leah. But then again, I'd been certain about Uncle Tony once too. And it turned out I was wrong.

I want to test this woman now to be sure.

'How do I know you saw Leah? Tell me what she looks like. What colour hair does she have?'

'Black,' the woman answers simply.

My heart sinks. 'Wrong.'

'No. She has black hair and eyes and skin. Even the whites of her eyes are black. Her clothes and shoes too.'

'What are you talking about? You're crazy.'

'No, I'm not. The whole inside of the building is black. It's pitch black! I can't see a bloody thing, can I? How am I supposed to see what the fuck colour your girlfriend's hair is!'

A branch of a weedy tree suddenly blows against the ruined garden wall with a thwack. We both look at it, afraid the movement was something else. The woman continues to stare at it, troubled.

I turn back to her and raise my hands imploringly. 'Look, you don't have to be sarcastic. I need your help. I can get us both out of here. But I'm not leaving if my friend is here!'

She looks at me, her round toad-like eyes bulging with urgency. 'She isn't here. You should go and get help. Before he comes back. He will be here soon.'

'How do you know?'

'Because I know his routines. You need to hurry. He could be here at any second.'

She looks up at the cloudy sky. Her muddy irises reflect the dark hue of the day. 'He usually chooses midday to bring food. He hasn't been for a few days. But he is obviously around somewhere if he brought you. Hurry. Go now.'

CHAPTER TWENTY-FOUR

Then

Waiting is the toughest part. All we have been able to do for the most part since Leah went is to wait. It has driven me half-mad. Helen too, I know. And now we have to do it again.

Suddenly, having Mia around is a drain on us. But her parents are spending the weekend at a couples spa in Stratford. They booked it months ago. Helen doesn't have the heart to bring their getaway to an abrupt end.

'Besides,' she whispers to me as she loads the washing machine later. 'I need someone to pick up after to keep my mind from running wild. Not that it isn't already. But I need something to keep my hands full.'

Tony arrives when Helen is making dinner with Mia. Helen texted him with the news.

Helen's counting and singing for the little girl's sake comes from the kitchen where I've taken refuge in the living room. Her voice is deliberately cheery, even when I know her heart is breaking inside. It distresses me. Somehow it reminds me of the children's home I spent my earlier childhood in. Besides, it is cramped in the tiny kitchen. Three is a crowd.

'Have you heard anything more?' Tony asks when he takes a seat on the sofa opposite my armchair.

'No. Not yet. I don't get why they called Helen to tell her they found something. Why not just call when they have made the identification?'

Tony sighs deeply. 'I guess they needed to give her a bell, in case she hears the news from someone else first. They have to put her on alert, like. In case it does turn out to be … well, it might not be … but you never know … '

'But it is someone, isn't it?' I say after a while in silence, with only snippets of cheery conversation drifting from the kitchen. 'Whoever it is. It is someone's daughter. Or aunt or sister. Someone is missing them even if it isn't us … '

Tony doesn't add anything to this, he just lets the silence spiral as he is lost in his own thoughts. So I flick the television on. It's the BBC national news.

Mia is occupied in the kitchen. Luckily dinner is a slow-moving beast when tasking a six-year-old to help you make it, especially when it is lasagne. So I leave the channel on for now.

But I can't concentrate on any of the stories. I just stare blankly at the screen. As does Tony. Doom and gloom surrounding the economy, the energy crisis and the realities of war can't hold our attention at a time like this.

Unfortunately, the local news starts afterwards before we realise it. The preview of the headlines reveals a reporter stationed outside the grounds of Dostill Quarry. My heart pounds in my ears and I can't quite catch what he is saying.

Unfortunately, Helen chooses this moment to walk in with Mia and announce dinner is ready.

Tony makes a sudden move for the remote control and switches the set off. Mia is none the wiser, but Helen gets the gist. She stares at the screen even though it has turned black.

Then she seems to come to her senses and realises she is holding plates of steaming hot lasagne and chips.

She resumes her falsely cheery energy and puts the plates down on the coffee table. She helps Mia settle into her seat with a lap tray. 'Careful, it's hot, dear. Remember to start around the edges. And don't be afraid to blow on it first.'

The thought of food makes my stomach lurch at this moment. 'Sorry, Helen. Can I just nip to the loo before we eat?'

Upstairs in the bathroom, I shut the door and slip my phone out. It doesn't take me long to load the Tamworth Herald site. There is an article with live updates on the quarry story.

But there isn't any news.

We know more than they do, in fact. All the local newspaper knows is that a body has been found in the quarry. Nothing more. The police told Helen it is definitely a woman. A woman that fits Leah's profile.

CHAPTER TWENTY-FIVE

Now

'**G**o now,' the stranger urges me. She stands in the doorway of the farmhouse. For some reason, she seems reluctant to step outside herself. Anyone would think she would be desperate to get away from the dark and the various odours. I know I am and I've only spent hours here.

'Once you get onto the main road, you can follow it away from here.'

'What about you? Aren't you coming with me?'

She shakes her head. Her wiry hair blows in the breeze. 'I can't. My ankle is busted. That shit broke it last month. It's not like I was able to get any help for it locked in here, could I? It isn't healing right. The bone is still sliding around in there when I step on it.'

I cringe and then look down at her ankle. There is so much filth and dirt on her bare lower legs and feet that it is hard to tell there is even an injury, never mind how bad it could be.

'I'll help you.' I move to unwrap her duvet, but her grip is surprisingly strong. 'You need to put your arm around my shoulders.'

'No!' She shrinks away from me. 'You just go. I'll be too slow. Bring help back here. Make sure that filthy old pig doesn't catch you.'

'What if he comes back when I'm gone? What will he do to you?'

'Nothing he hasn't done before. Besides, he mostly lost interest in me ages ago. But you should make sure you aren't here when he arrives.' She nods encouragingly to hurry me along. 'Good luck, Claire. I hope you make it.'

I glance around me, but I can't see anything beyond the outbuildings and jagged rocks. The buildings must be built in a dip to protect them from the elements. 'Which way do I go?'

The woman thinks for a moment. Then she points through the building to the front of the house. 'The road is straight ahead that way.'

'That's right, it must be. That is the way he brought me in. I think he used a tractor.'

The woman blinks at me in confusion and says nothing.

'But that way I would have to go past the

other farmhouse. He will see me for sure. What is in the other direction?'

I turn and look behind me but see nothing beyond the leafless tree at the side of the garden or the slope of the hill.

'I don't know. I haven't been outside for ages.' She looks over the yellowing grassy knolls with fear.

I wonder if she has become a little agoraphobic during her imprisonment. 'Are you sure you can't run?'

She nods. 'I know I won't make it. But you can. You'd better hurry.'

She watches as I turn away from the farmhouse and trot along the remnants of the garden wall. At the end, I lean on the inconsistent brickwork and turn and peer cautiously over to the other building.

There is no sign of a tractor anywhere. Or any vehicle. Nor do there seem to be any lights on inside the building. The day is overcast. Surely it is dull enough for indoor lighting?

Does that mean that creep has gone off somewhere again?

Maybe I can make it past without incident, after all.

I crouch low and trot over until I am flush with the exterior wall of the other farmhouse. This building is in much better condition than the other one.

The outside looks like it might have been

painted once, although not for decades. I can imagine in fifty years or so this one might be falling apart like the other place.

I wonder what is going on inside. Is my abductor in there? What about Leah? Was she ever in this place?

I stare at the crumbling render.

What is my abductor doing right now? Will he notice if I attempt to make a run for it?

There is only one way to find out.

I creep forward, surprised by how stiff my legs have become even just from my short time in captivity in the cold.

The air is freezing out here. It makes me shiver even beneath my coat. But it is a relief after being in that horrible crumbling building in the dark.

I peer carefully around the front of the building. The coast seems clear and I have gleaned that the front door is shut and the curtains at all the windows are drawn.

Yes.

I can make it. I know I can.

I turn and don't need any further prompting. I run as fast as I can. It's been years since I've last actually run flat out. My membership to the Snowdome gym has been long forgotten. If I'd had more warning last night when I was abducted, I would have run like I never have before.

Kind of like now. I would have loved to have

had the chance to get away from him last night and raise the alarm to bring down a ton of bricks on his head. I didn't get the chance though. And that was because he was a sneak. How long was he watching me before he took me?

Running is tough now. Especially when your muscles are seized up with the unrelenting cold.

It doesn't take me long to get away from the farmhouse. I glance over my shoulder so many times. It slows me down a little, but I am paranoid. This is all too easy.

And I have the unshakable sense that my captor will pop up out of nowhere at some moment. What if he has driven somewhere local? He might have gone to buy food and supplies from wherever the local store is.

But as I make it, gasping and panting, up the nearest slope towards where the woman was adamant there was a road, I realise that possibility is unlikely.

Especially when I turn around. I spin and do a 360. Like a Google Maps camera out of control.

'No!' I say out loud in shock.

No. No. No. NO!

This can't be right. Every direction I turn in gives me a view of the sea.

Dark grey waves crash aggressively inwards from all angles.

My heart sinks as the reality of the situation sinks in.

I'm on an island.

CHAPTER TWENTY-SIX

Then

It seems to take forever to identify the body that was pulled from the lake. I flit between terror and placating myself with all sorts of lies for weeks.

It probably isn't Leah. It could be anyone. So many other people go missing too. I've noticed their stories since Leah has been gone. Any one of these missing women could be the person that was found.

It is all I can do to keep myself sane. I repeat the same comforting words to Helen also, either over the phone or in person, but she doesn't believe them either. Nor does Tony.

All we were told is that the body is that of a woman. She was wearing a dark red top. From the description, it sounds like the one that made up part of Leah's uniform. Tony tried to reel off a list of other reasons the colour of the shirt would be the same. I forget what he suggested as my mind went whirring off with a list of possibilities of my own, each worse than the last.

Eventually, we get the call from the police we have been simultaneously dreading and desperate for.

It's not Leah.

The body was that of someone else, some other discarded human being. It definitely was a woman though. The red clothing they found on her turned out to be the remnants of a nurse's uniform.

They have also managed to ascertain that the dental records don't match Leah's so we are all off the hook. For now, at least. The jaw of the woman they found had several fillings whereas Leah didn't have any, despite her love of sweets.

The police don't elaborate further, leaving the rest to our respective imaginations. It isn't long before a piece in the Tamworth Herald appears on the discovery which answers the remainder of our questions.

Janet Wiseman, beloved daughter and aunt, the article starts. *A well-respected senior nurse at the local community hospital …*

The article goes on to state that Janet had been missing for twelve years.

As I said weeks ago without realising the

full actuality at the time, this woman was someone else's daughter. And sister and aunt too it transpires. At least now they have closure on their own mystery.

I wonder if the relief is so great of finally getting some closure numbs the pain of the loss a little. Probably not. Do we still have that to come? Or will Leah take us all by surprise and walk in through the door one day?

I can only hope it is the latter, but it is looking unlikely now.

After a busy May day at work, I drive over to Dosthill. I park my car on Slade Lane and walk through the remaining residential streets to the quarry on foot. The cellophane from the bunch of flowers I picked up from Morrisons on the way crinkles beneath my fingers.

It's been ages since I've been here. Tony used to bring us as teenagers to this place and to the nearby lakes on hot summer days sometimes. Our search for Leah didn't extend this way as it was so far from where she went missing.

I wanted to scour every inch of town and not rest until it was done. But it wasn't practical, I know that. Even if every Tamworth resident came out in force, we still might never find Leah with all the green areas, rough ground and bodies of water. The truth is there are just too many places to hide a body.

I approach the blue railings around the water. It's obvious I have the right place. There is already a floral shrine spilling from the fence. The heads of soft toys bob up here and there in the sea of tributes. The scene is so much like the spot where Leah went missing it chills me.

I lay the vibrant supermarket bouquet down with the rest. It is immediately overshadowed by a bountiful array of lilies and red roses nearby.

But it was important to me somehow that I pay my respects in some way. Perhaps it is my offering of gratitude that it wasn't my best friend's body that was pulled from the water here recently.

I feel better now that I have visited the scene for myself. The quarry is different than I remembered it. The day is warm, but the sky is grey. The dark cluster of trees today doesn't seem to benefit from the perpetual sunshine of my and Leah's youth. This evening the leaves rustle ominously, as though trying to speak to me.

Just for old time's sake, I venture down to the nearby Middleton lakes. I pass an elderly dog walker with a Bichon Frisé who gives me a cursory hello as we pass each other on the country track.

The place is almost as beautiful as I remember. But I feel the rose-tinted haze before my eyes is missing. Perhaps it is because it now occurs to me that the River Tame that runs beside the nature reserve in Fazeley where Leah went missing widens out a little here. The search team had briefly mentioned that if Leah had gone into the water up there then articles may have been brought down here. But it would be like finding a needle in a haystack they had said.

Still, this place feels a world away from my hectic day at work. With summer approaching head-on, the park is nearing its busiest time.

I watch a heron for a little while wading slowly through the water. Eventually, he flies off after a fruitless fishing session. I hope it wasn't me who put him off his stroke.

I tug up the zip on the outdoor fleece I've been wearing in the evenings recently. Leah wore this one too quite a bit, but I've relaxed my policy on using our shared things a little. Now, it seems like a way to bring her closer, when every day without news she feels like she has been slipping away from me.

The sun is becoming low in the sky now. I consider staying for sunset, but my stomach protests, reminding me of the measly packet of crisps I called lunch.

Besides, it will be getting dark soon. The various promises Helen has elicited from me about being out alone after dark weigh heavy on my conscience. So I head back the way I came.

As the wide track turns into a narrow muddy path, I spot a dog walker up ahead.

Or rather, his dog spots me. A big dark German shepherd turns and lifts his large head to stare in my direction.

Luckily it is on a lead. The dog seems to have gone still and watchful as I approach. The grey-haired man at the end of the leash gives it a rough tug to prompt his canine companion along.

The dog doesn't move and remains fixed upon me. The man mutters something to his pet and drags him over to the side of the path. The pair wait in the overgrown bushes and brambles for me to pass.

'Thanks,' I say hurriedly as I quicken my pace and overtake. The dog continues to stare at me intently and lurches forward. Without warning, it breaks into a booming bark which makes me jump out of my skin.

I slip my hands into my pockets and shrink into the fleece. There is still a Tesco receipt Leah scrunched up and forgot about in there.

My fingers close around it now. I've looked at it so many times I know exactly what she bought that day. Carrots and lentils for the soup she experimented with for dinner. It was a bit of a culinary disaster when she burned the onions, but I didn't tell her that. I don't have the heart to throw the little scrap of paper away now, even though it disintegrates slowly beneath my fingers.

The man gives an audible tug on the lead from behind me. 'Shut up.'

I'm thankful for the small head start he affords me, but it doesn't seem enough. The two figures manage to stay just at the edge of my vision for the whole walk back, right until the exit for the quarry. It is a relief to be walking on overlooked residential streets again.

But the dog walker still tags along behind me. It is only when I get inside my car that I feel truly safe as he passes by.

In my rearview mirror, I see the fifty-something man now gesture his dog into the back of a muddy four-wheel drive up the street.

The animal seems perfectly under control, so why would it go for me like that? Was it just nervous around people?

The man glances back towards my little red Polo before climbing into his own car. I expect his front headlights to spring to life, but they don't.

He sits in his vehicle for a while. I can't see through the windscreen much in this light, but it looks like he is just sitting, facing straight ahead.

I leave first, as it happens. Instead of turning around in the street as I had planned, I go straight on and turn onto the next road, intending now to take a different way home.

CHAPTER TWENTY-SEVEN

Now

I'm on an island.

For fuck's sake. How could I not notice that before? How could the other woman not have known either? She has been here much longer than I have. Years, by the look of her.

Then it occurs to me; the bumping of the tractor when I was drugged and confused. It can't have been a tractor at all. It must have been a boat. And the bumps were the vessel hitting the waves as it brought me here.

How long had the journey taken? My mind wasn't together enough to accurately guess.

Salty sea air bites at me. I can taste it on my

lips. That was the smell that reminded me of my childhood when I arrived. Days out at the seaside from the children's home, not the farm.

This place doesn't look like a working farm at all. There are no animals out grazing. The buildings are in a state of disrepair. The main farmhouse with the shut curtains looks the most civilised. And I'll bet that is where my captor is right now.

Fortunately, there is some cover nearby in the form of rocks protruding from the grass. I crouch down behind them whilst I try and figure out what to do.

Turning my back to the rocks provides me with some shelter from the relentless wind. Now I can see land. It might as well be on another planet, though, for all the good it is doing me. A stretch of sea separates the two pieces of terra firma.

I can't see a boat. It is surely moored on the side of the island facing the land, and that section is wide and craggy.

Which part should I try first? Will the keys be left inside the vessel? And if they were, will I be able to figure out the controls? As far as I know, the journey yesterday was the only ever time I've been on a boat. I have no idea how to operate one.

As I try and decide on a plan, a noise breaks through the wind. A noise that makes my stomach twist in terror.

Barking. Deep and booming.

I turn and peer cautiously above my rock. A large figure of a dark dog takes leaps and bounds from the open farmhouse door. His master follows him, running to keep pace.

I shrink back down behind my rock. I scramble over and slide down the slight incline before I get hurriedly to my feet.

I don't care where the boat is - I'm going to have to guess. Fast.

My heart hammers furiously in my chest. I recognise that dog. I've seen its wild eyes up close, heard its bark rumble through me at close range.

I can't let it get close to me.

I run down the slope faster than I should. My legs feel weak and wobbly beneath me. But I will myself not to stumble. A fall now would be disastrous.

My mind races with possibilities as my feet pound the ground. They carry me to the most plausible place a boat would be docked - the land at the furthest tip on this side of the island.

My shoe gets caught on a bramble hidden in the long grass and I hit the ground with such force that I'm momentarily dazed. The taste of blood fills my mouth, but I force myself to my feet. Just in time to see two figures emerge at the brow of the hill.

The barking is no longer muffled now. It cuts through the air as the pair move closer.

They don't seem to be moving at much of a pace. Not that I stick around to watch them. It just makes me think I can make it to the boat I know must exist.

It is a complete leap of blind faith as I set off again, trying to ignore the feverish barking behind me.

They are getting closer.

As I near the water's edge, the sound of the violent waves drowns out the approach of my pursuers.

Panic bites me - there is no boat.

I have no choice but to change course on a whim and head in the other direction.

There is no way I can stop running. Not with the animal so close behind me.

My breathing is ragged now. A stitch forms in my side. My thighs scream for oxygen.

If I wasn't literally running for my life, I would stop and collapse into the soft grass and gasp for air. The wind has forced the long blades so flat over the years it is like running on a spongy carpet. I don't have time to stop. I wheeze and pant my way over to the next tip of the island.

Then my heart leaps with excitement. There is a boat. It is tethered to a flimsy little dock that was obscured by rocks a few moments ago.

I can see it now. It is a small fishing boat. Old and battered like the rest of the things around here. It can be the only thing that brought me to this place though, so it can get me out of here.

The figure of the black and brown dog looms in the corner of my eye. I can't believe it hasn't reached me yet. Or the man. He can't be older than fifty-five and I know he keeps active. How have I made it this far without either of them catching up?

Maybe I can get away and find help after all.

As I approach, my hope intensifies. I'm sure I spot keys hanging in plain sight through the scratched old window. Luck must be on my side.

I can do this.

The small jetty is green and slimy looking. I only register this at the last second. My shoes don't gain the traction I need and I fall again. This time, my shoulder collides painfully with the rotten old wood and I shriek with pain.

Then I hear a snarling nearby.

My free arm automatically bends and comes up to protect my face, but I know it is not enough. My senses are ambushed by the sudden feeling of thick fur and hot breath. Angry snarling fills my ears.

It is then that I know I am going to die on this slimy old dock. Just when I thought I was about to escape.

CHAPTER TWENTY-EIGHT

Then

I'm unsettled by my evening out at the lakes and quarry. For the rest of the night, I can't focus on anything. I try scrolling through news coverage of Janet Wiseman on my phone.

Later, I switch on the television to try and stop the place from feeling so quiet and lonely. But Netflix doesn't have anything to fit my mood, which is most unusual. I end up scrolling through the screens aimlessly. Eventually, I switch it off.

A few times, I see car headlights driving down our quiet street. I get up and move the kitchen curtain aside each time. But it is just a neighbour or visitor who cruises by; cars I recognise, anyway.

There is rarely anyone else down the street. It has always been a good thing about living here, I guess. Our street isn't a through road to anywhere. Getting in and out of this part of Fazeley isn't easy. Tony said that was part of the reason he got the house for a good price as commuters would likely want somewhere else.

Helen texts me later in the evening. She says she has Mia for the half-term coming up and suggests the three of us go to the West Midlands Safari Park one of the days.

Sounds great, I text back. *I'd love to xx.*

Helen sends a reply back quickly. *Is everything all right, Claire? xx*

I look back at my message. Upon reflection, I would usually write a longer answer. Helen knows me so well.

Sorry, I tap now. *Just had a busy day at work. I'm very tired xx*

I hover over the keys wondering how I can put my uneasiness into words. I know I will feel a weight lift off me if I talk about my experience earlier.

I also know that Helen would fret and probably organise Tony as a chaperone-slash-bodyguard to get me to and from work. I can't have that. So I leave my message as it is and hit send.

Are you eating enough greens? Living on

nothing but carbs can make you sleepy xx

I smile for the first time since greeting the friendly Bichon Frisé owner much earlier. *Yes, I promise xx.*

If I admit to what my lunch was, I know Helen would be straight over here with a pot of home-cooked something. My ready-meal curry this evening wasn't too bad. Onions, garlic and tomato count as a serving of fruit and vegetables, right?

Helen texts back with other suggestions for the school holiday with Mia. I end up agreeing to a lot of it around my working hours.

Planning outings for the future feels positive. I guess that is why Helen is so determined to get me involved. At least I have some things to look forward to.

It is almost twelve, but I'm still wired. I should probably put my screen down or read a book or something, but I know I'm too restless to get into a story right now.

I end up scrolling through the various social media posts about Leah's disappearance. The interview I gave on Adrian's true crime YouTube channel has greatly slowed in momentum but is still slowly racking up extra views here and there.

I can't stand watching myself on the screen, so I mute the video and scroll through the comments again. Various users are still debating my involvement in the case in addition to speculating whether Leah had a secret boyfriend none of us knew about.

I know that can't be true, Leah would have told me if she had one. We told each other everything like that. I still can't figure out why she would lie about dating a man named Adam.

Now that I look back, however, it was odd that I never saw or met him as I had with every other of Leah's partners. After the detective pointed out the conclusion of the forensics team, I realise that I never did see Leah when she received a text back from Adam. She just showed me her side of the conversation when she sent messages out. Later, she would show me the response she supposedly received when I wasn't around.

Unlike her other relationships, she consulted me in deliberating over what she should say in her messages out to Adam, showing me her screen more than normal and asking for tips on how to word her thoughts and feelings.

At the time I thought it strange since she never obsessed over such things before. All of a sudden that was different. What did she hope to achieve by inventing a boyfriend and making such a big deal of it in front of me?

Was it an attempt to push me away? Was it Leah's way of gently telling me her interest was elsewhere, anywhere but with me?

I know by now that the detective was right

about Adam not existing. I found a cinema ticket for the film Leah said Adam caused her to miss. It was stuffed in a drawer in her bedside cabinet. It was the very film I had set up for us to watch the night she went missing. She had told me she was so excited to get to see it at last. In reality, she had watched it apparently alone weeks before that night. It is all so baffling.

Helen is just as confused as me on the matter. She is usually so wise and able to put the proverbial last word on any moral dilemma, but this one has her as stumped as me.

1:30 AM quickly rolls around now. I end up back on Facebook. This time, I realise I have unread private messages. Perhaps other influencers are reaching out to me? More exposure would do Leah's case some good.

The messages turn out to be spam or adult junk, apart from one. One message suddenly has me blinking at the screen in my hand when I realise who it is from. My head is so full, I don't clock the name at first, Carole Evans. But then the realisation has worms squirming uncomfortably in the pit of my stomach.

The message is from my mother.

This is the woman who allowed the care system to swallow me up for years starting at the age of four. If it wasn't for Helen, I would have spent my entire childhood surrounded by other unwanted or unfortunate (or both) children.

What on earth does she want now?

I tap the message to load it onto my screen.

Hiya, Claire. Long time no see. You're all grown up now! You look so much like your grandmother. Thankfully not like me with my horrible bulgy eyes! I saw your video on Youtube. Sorry about your friend. If you ever want to talk, I want you to know I am here for you. I'm so sorry I haven't reached out before now, but well, things haven't been easy for me. Love, Mum.

The words blur on my screen as I stare at them. I blink away tears I'm sorry to say form in my eyes. This is so unexpected, a bolt from out of nowhere. I don't need this right now with everything else that is happening.

How dare my real mother do this to me now?

I drop my phone onto the coffee table and press my face in my hands. A wave of hurt I hadn't realised I'd been carrying around leaks from me.

I'm so confused; I wish Leah was here. She would know exactly how to comfort me. My friend would understand what I'm feeling better than I do. She is the only person in the world who knows my whole story, even the bits I haven't told Helen.

Eventually, I switch the television back on. I have no idea what I'm watching. It all seems like inane nonsense when you can't take anything in.

My swollen eyes move frequently from the

screen to my phone lying on the coffee table. It is past four in the morning before I finally snap and tap out the words that have been forming in my mind for hours.

I don't know what message I've concocted for Carole in the end. I'm too tired and weary to go over it again. All I know is I've poured my heart into the message and sent it out to goodness knows where. I have no idea where Mum lives now. She didn't say in her message. Her profile is photoless and the details are private so there isn't anything to glean. There is no way to judge if the profile is even really hers.

If I wasn't already on edge over Leah, then I know I would have handled this unexpected interaction better. I would have had an extra layer of defence up. But I've uncharacteristically let my guard down. I've never felt so vulnerable.

I suppose I should go upstairs to bed. I'm exhausted enough to perhaps get in a couple of hours of sleep before I have to get up for work later.

When I finally do go upstairs, I realise I haven't even drawn the curtains up here. As I move over to the window, I catch sight of a vehicle I know I shouldn't be seeing. Not in my quiet little street. This isn't a through road after all. There is an open stretch of patchwork fields straight ahead of me. Pink scars appear in the sky above the horizon ahead of sunrise.

Usually, I am familiar with the vehicles on

this street. The spark of recognition now does nothing but stoke my nerves further.

It is the dog walker's vehicle parked outside, the one from near the quarry yesterday. The old black Land Rover.

I pull the net curtain back and stare down at it. As I do, the engine roars to life. I can just about make out arms manoeuvring the steering wheel in the growing light.

I know this vehicle doesn't belong to a neighbour or their extended family or their friends.

I blink in disbelief as it cruises to the end of the street and around the corner. Later, I will be furious with myself for not clocking the registration plate.

For now, I find myself dissolving into a pit of worry.

Two questions burn in my brain. Why did the vehicle from yesterday drive down my street? And what did the driver think he was doing?

CHAPTER
TWENTY-NINE

Now

T he dog tears into my arm. The sleeve of my coat is thick, but I feel sharp teeth sink into my arm in a tight and unyielding grip.

The jaws grip and the beast shakes its head back and forth, snarling in a frenzy.

Then his master appears in the corner of my vision. I hear a whistle and then the dog releases me. My savaged limb is somehow more movable than the other one which is still trapped painfully beneath me.

The dog does a small circle around his owner and sits down calmly beside him, licking his lips contentedly. He awaits further instruction.

I have just enough time to glance up at the face of my captor and get a spark of recognition. This is the first time I've clocked his face so close up. He is as old as his grey hair implies, mid-fifties. He is dressed in the same outdoorsy dark green coat I've seen him wearing around town. On this island, it makes a lot more sense. For the first time, I see his dark green eyes trained on mine.

Then I see what he is holding - the pepper spray from my handbag. The one Helen had pressed into my hand not that long ago.

'Who is this for?' he asks.

Despite the pain in my arms, I have a question of my own. 'Where is Leah?'

He ignores me and looks back at the tiny bottle. 'Did you buy this for me?'

'Where is Leah? The woman in the farmhouse says you took her away. What did you do with her?'

I don't have time to react.

The image of my captor swooping down, bottle in hand is the last thing I see before intense stinging pain erupts in my eyes. My shocked intake of breath backfires on me. I cough and gag as the burning starts in my nose and the roof of my mouth, too.

The dog's wet nose sniffs at my ear.

Then the man shouts to the animal, 'Get out of it you!'

I can't see a thing. But I feel myself being

dragged up from the ground. I feel once again myself being pulled up the slope and away from the dock. Just like when I got here in the early hours of the morning.

Tears stream from my eyes, even as they are screwed shut. But I am determined. I've never been so close to the truth.

'Where is Leah?' I shout blindly in between whimpers. 'I want to know where she is!'

He actually laughs. It's one of those horrible irritating laughs that grates on you. 'She is the least of your worries.'

I fight against the iron grip on my arm. But this creep has learned from earlier. He won't give me an opportunity to slip out of his hands again.

Neither will his pet. I feel a wet nose now and then on my ankle as we climb. I try to force my eyes open, but can't as the stinging is so intense. So it is a surprise to once again smell the foul air of the dark farmhouse.

But I hear further noises that I didn't the first time I was imprisoned. The ground feels unfamiliar. Are we going in through a different door?

An unexpected descent causes me to twist my ankle as I'm dragged down steps.

'Where am I?' I shout, unable to open my eyes.

I lose my balance and hit the floor. Once again hear a low growl close by.

'Leave it!' The man's voice calls. Then I hear

the dog's claws on the stone floor as he trots away from me. I hear something bang shut followed by a metallic click.

'Where am I?' I shout, trying desperately to open my eyes. I fail. They sting too much. One thing I register is how much worse the smell is down here than it was in the farmhouse.

In fact, I fear I have found the source.

CHAPTER THIRTY

Then

Helen tasks me with picking up Mia from school on the last day before half-term. She says it is because Mia's school in Mile Oak is closer to my house and she can stay with me until Helen gets home from work. I don't believe this reason for a second; I'm sure she has an ulterior motive.

I suspect Helen wants me to go through the motions of a school pickup; as though suddenly looking after Mia as if she was my daughter might make me inexplicably broody or something. Helen is usually so astute on some things, I wonder if she might even be right. But that doesn't happen when I drive over to Mia's school this afternoon. In fact, something else completely unexpected happens.

It takes me a few minutes to locate the right area to queue for pickup. I remember being at Mia's school once before when Leah and I collected her from her nursery class once. She was so much smaller then, but I remember the afternoon vividly.

So much so I feel if I was to glance around me, I would see my friend grinning and waving as she spots our little charge walking flat-footed across the playground with a backpack that is far too big for her.

Only when Mia finally emerges, she seems so much more grown up. Her bag isn't too big and her pigtails have been replaced by a French braid. At the end of the day, the effect of the plait isn't so neat, there are strands of hair coming free. She still looks smart though in a grey pinafore dress and white shirt. Leah would gush over her shiny black shoes and the cute pink bow holding her braid together too.

The little girl's face lights up when she sees me. She joins the bustling queue of other children filtering out of the gates.

Mia waves enthusiastically and I wave back with even more gusto. Helen is right, my interaction with children feels so natural. But is it what I really want?

I'm still waiting for Mia to file out of the school gates, so I don't have time to ponder this thought much. Something tugs at my senses and

I look over my shoulder.

I instantly spot the dog walker from last week amongst the crowd of parents. My insides turn cold. I felt he might have been staring before I looked around. Now he has his eyes trained on the children filing out of the gate.

What is he doing here?

Before I come up with a logical explanation, I see the man reach out his hand and link it with the girl who steps out just before Mia.

'Hi, Daddy,' the girl says. Now that I look at the pair together, I see the girl has the same dark eyebrows and a broad face not dissimilar to my own.

I open my mouth in surprise, but Mia throws herself at me now. 'Aunty, Claire!'

'Oh, hi Mia. Have you had a nice day?'

She nods enthusiastically as she pulls back from her hug. 'Mrs Davies took us out to the conservation area. The school tadpoles are starting to grow legs!'

'Wow! I bet that was cool.'

'It was! We got to draw pictures afterwards. Do you want to see mine?'

'When we get home.' I glance up at the father and daughter striding down the road ahead of us.

Mia follows my gaze. 'That's Holly Thompson. She's in my class.'

'Is she your friend?'

Mia shrugs. 'Everyone is friends in class. But

Holly doesn't talk much.'

'Oh. Is she shy?'

'I don't know. She says her dad is a bad man.'

'Why does she say that?'

'I don't know. Mummy says I should be friends with Zoe instead.'

'Why Zoe?'

'Mummy says her dad owns a restaurant chain and she would make a nice friend.'

'Oh. I'm sure Zoe is nice, but that's perhaps not a reason to be friends with her.'

Mia screws up her small nose. 'Zoe isn't *that* nice. She didn't invite everyone to her birthday party last week.'

'Oh dear. Maybe you should just choose someone you like the best. Someone who is similar to you and you get along with. That's how you will find your best friend.'

'Like you and Aunty Leah?'

'Yes, I suppose.'

I see the dog walker and his daughter have disappeared around a corner, no doubt to that vehicle that is now familiar to me. I kick myself again for not seeing the registration plate of the similar one that was parked on my street last week. I was sure it was the same when I was feeling vulnerable in the middle of the night. But then, I'd believed I had been digitally ambushed by my real mother out of the blue. Who knows what I was thinking?

I didn't get a response back from that

message I sent out. That was the big giveaway, wasn't it? The account it was sent from gave nothing away either. There wasn't even a photo attached to the profile.

Now that I have had time to think about the bizarre interaction, I feel like the whole thing was just a hoax set up just to get at me. No doubt the product of one of the online trolls who still believe that I was responsible for Leah's disappearance.

I've no idea how they would know my mother's name, but I haven't exactly worked hard to conceal my past. At least one person in town must remember me from the children's home. Any one of those kids knew my background and could be anywhere now. I often wonder what happened to them all.

'When is Aunty Leah coming home?' Mia whines suddenly. 'I haven't seen her for ages.'

'I don't know, sweetheart. Soon, I hope.'

I lead Mia over to my Polo and open the door for her. 'What else do you know about Holly and her daddy? Do they live nearby?'

Mia shrugs as she clips her seatbelt together. 'Somewhere in town, I think. I don't think Holly likes it.'

I check the belt is secure. 'Why do you say that?'

'We had to write a story in class. Holly wrote one about a knight coming to stab the evil king and rescue the queen and the princess from the dark castle. Mrs Davies says she shouldn't have put killing in the story.'

'No. That's not kind, is it?'

'No.' Mia watches houses go by as I start the car and pull out of this busy side road. 'Holly cries in class sometimes. Mrs Davies says we shouldn't stare at her when she is crying. Daniel Taylor got sent out of the classroom for making fun of her once.'

'So he should too. It isn't very nice to laugh when someone is upset.'

'*I* know that,' Mia says indignantly. '*I* just want to be Holly's friend. But it is hard to get her to talk.'

After a few minutes of driving, Mia forgets about the troubling subject of Holly. Instead, she chatters about her day excitedly, telling me about tadpoles and the completed pile of work she has brought home from school.

When we get to my house, she heads straight for the living room and unpacks her schoolbag, pulling out a wad of paintings, maths worksheets and various craft items. She hands them to me excitedly.

I drop myself onto the couch next to her to take a closer look at the pile of schoolwork. 'Wow, Mia, you have been busy.'

The one she said she did this morning is at the top. It has a variety of pond life and tadpoles with tails and legs that feature prominently in Mia's artistic vision.

Mia certainly seems to be overflowing with creativity. Her paintings are bursting with colour and detail. She beams happily as I tell her this.

Then I move on to another painting in the pile. This one is darker. There is a knight in dark grey armour in the foreground. He is holding hands with a woman with long blond hair and a girl with dark features.

I hold it up to look at it more carefully. 'What is this one about, Mia? Did you do a picture of a knight too?'

'No. That's Holly's. She sits at my table. It must have got mixed up with my pile at hometime.'

'Never mind. You can take it back after the holidays.' I look at the painting again. 'Is this the picture you mentioned earlier? It doesn't look as bad as you said.'

'That's the second one Holly did. Mrs Davies took the other one away.'

As I look at the picture, I realise at first glance it seems OK. But then again, the tip of the shining knight's sword is tinged with red.

CHAPTER THIRTY-ONE

Now

I t is a long time before I can open my eyes again. Tears stream down my face for what feels like hours as I lie on my back on a cold stone floor. As that other woman had said, it is hard to know how much time passes in this captivity.

I'm still kicking myself for not realising the true nature of my plight; I'm on an island.

I'm not the only one that made that mistake. The other captive woman saw me off fully expecting me to bring back help. There is no disputing she has been here for ages by the look of her. If she could be fooled into thinking this was simply a remote farm somewhere, then I can't really blame myself for thinking so, mere hours after I arrived.

I did learn something from my escape attempt though. That stupid creep keeps the keys inside his boat. They were clearly visible through the windscreen for a second; I have logged that fact. For next time.

Eventually, the stinging subsides and I open my eyes again. At first, everything is as black as it had been before in the farmhouse. But as the minutes pass by in this new place, some details come into focus.

There is a metallic grill in a corner high above me. Cold air from outside flows down onto my hot and swollen face. Without this, the bad smell of this place would be unbearable.

I heave myself to my feet. The teeth that sank into my arm left behind a painful throbbing. I can't see how bad the damage is in the dark.

I sniff. My sinuses feel stuffy. At least the cool air takes a slight edge off the stale atmosphere.

This must be some kind of cellar, I think as I get to my feet.

One of my shoes is missing. The floor is cold and rough beneath my feet. I tread carefully around, wondering if my shoe came off down here. In the rush of adrenaline of my attempted escape, it could have been lost anywhere without me noticing.

It is unlikely it survived the chase down the

hill. But it doesn't stop me from shuffling around in the dark trying to locate it. One-half of the pair is little use to me.

Besides, I move around to keep myself busy. Just as Helen and I have done since Leah went missing. We keep ourselves occupied to avoid dwelling on the various possibilities.

Away from the grill, it is virtually as black as the farmhouse. I tread carefully, taking small steps. But even this technique doesn't help when my foot hooks into something long and thin.

I struggle to maintain my balance. Then I tip forward, landing hard on my knees. When I swear and try to extricate myself from what I have fallen on, I'm not at all prepared.

My fingers connect with an unfamiliar texture. It takes me a moment before I recoil in horror.

It wasn't a simple pipe or strip of wood I have tripped over. It's a bone. And by the feel of it, it is still connected to the rest of the skeleton.

As I try to clamber out of my entanglement, a flicker of light draws my attention. Somewhere near the other arm.

I take a few moments to feel brave enough to reach out for the source of light. When I do, another wave of horror washes over me as I recognise the source as a watch display. Not just any watch either, but a Fitbit.

Just like the one I bought Leah. The one she was wearing when she went missing.

CHAPTER THIRTY-TWO

Then

Mia's words about the man's daughter haunt me. She is not one to make things up. She has no motive and wouldn't even know how to lie anyway. Then there was the painting. It can't be denied that this Holly girl is disturbed. Besides, it was she who had chosen to say those words about her own father. What six-year-old does that? Unable to contain myself further, I take my thoughts to the police station.

Unfortunately, Detective Halliwell doesn't share my enthusiasm for this new lead.

'How old are the girls in question again?'

'Six.'

The detective sighs. He couldn't make it

more obvious how disinterested he is about my tip. 'Just remind me what this man has done?'

I lean forward, across the desk. 'He was walking his dog near the quarry where Janet Wiseman's … well, near where she was found. And I saw his car later that day driving past my house. I've never seen it on my street before. It is quite a coincidence after seeing it earlier that day, don't you think?'

'It is probably just that you haven't noticed it before. Perhaps it is a new neighbour.'

'It isn't. I know my neighbours.'

The detective raises a greying eyebrow. 'All of them?'

'Yes, or I know them by sight. I always see them around anyway. I know this guy doesn't belong there.'

'He could be a friend or visitor of one of your neighbours.'

'It isn't.' I sigh with frustration. 'I've told you. The owner of the car is nothing to do with anyone who lives down my street. This is something to do with Leah's disappearance, I know it.'

'You have a strong feeling?'

I nod emphatically. 'Yes.'

The detective closes the folder in front of him. 'Many friends and family members of missing persons have these feelings and theories about people, but they usually always turn out to be false. You had this same feeling about Tony

Bayliss. Didn't you?'

'No,' I lie.

The same eyebrow is raised again.

'OK, so I did suspect Tony. But only briefly and only when you took him away for questioning. I was desperate for answers then and jumped to conclusions.'

'Has your desire for answers about Leah worn off since then?'

I fold my arms. 'No. But I know there is something in it this time. I just have this feeling I can't explain. Please.'

I know I'm losing the detective. He thinks I'm having one of those moments he spoke of that all relatives and friends of missing persons supposedly get.

But after a few moments, he sighs deeply and looks stressed. 'All right. We will look into this chap.'

He passes me a piece of paper and a pen. 'Write down all the details you have on him.'

'That's great. Thank you so much.'

'Claire,' he says solemnly. 'Don't get your hopes up. Please don't mention anything to Leah's mum either. She doesn't need her hopes dashing yet again.'

I nod. The last thing I want is to upset Helen more. If I am right, then she will find out soon enough anyway. I'm just terrified of where the investigation might lead.

And what it will unearth.

*

At the weekend, Helen, Tony and I lead a vigil for Leah. We've done several events like this before, but this one feels like a big deal. It is now the twenty-month anniversary of Leah's disappearance. Not exactly a significant milestone, but one we had the opportunity to draw attention to in the local area thanks to a connection of Helen's.

We all stand on the grass at the community centre in the castle grounds.

A group of other people have shown up as well including Helen's boss, June, and her coworkers from the sandwich shop she works at. There is also a smattering of people from mine and Leah's secondary school years.

A few people even introduce themselves as friends or family of Janet Wiseman too. This takes me by surprise. I guess Leah's story has had more coverage than I realised. They must have noted Leah's story as much as we have noted theirs after their recent news coverage.

Only now does it occur to me that they would have been told when a body was found in the quarry. They too must have endured the agonising wait whilst it was identified. Only their prayers weren't answered like ours were when it came down to the identification process.

Despite Leah's case getting a decent amount of attention, it just doesn't seem like we've achieved anything by spreading the word around. All it seems to have done is started the online rumour mill about me and my involvement in the disappearance of my best friend.

That was never what I wanted. If anything, this has detracted from the real perpetrator, whoever that may be. I have the strongest suspicion I know who it is now.

Everyone is huddled outside on the grass as twilight falls. I move around and light the candles clutched in many pairs of hands. It's a warm June evening.

I'm dressed in blue skinny jeans with one of the custom t-shirts we have printed with the image of Leah's missing poster. Helen and Tony have one on each too.

Tony is trying to talk a middle-aged couple into taking some shirts from the pile he has on the table. They are trying to remain polite, but I can tell they don't really want them.

The enthusiasm for Leah's case has dwindled somewhat in comparison to the initial breaking of her story. Now, this evening suddenly feels more like a memorial, rather than the boost of exposure I had been planning in my mind.

I don't like it. The group's acapella version of Amazing Grace seems oddly eery in the growing darkness. Faces are illuminated by candles, most of them I don't recognise. I suspect some are passers-by that seem to have attached themselves to us. Is this their idea of a summer evening out?

Then I spot someone that is familiar right next to the couple who wouldn't accept Tony's shirts. Something about the roughly hewn features of the woman's face triggers something long buried in my mind.

Then a rush of recognition leaves my insides feeling crushed. The mismatched warbling ends and the gathering sort of scatters. But I don't move, I remain rooted to the grass in my canvas pumps.

Helen is busy accepting hugs and the same old supportive messages from the group. She doesn't notice the woman first tasked with the job of looking after me is here and heading straight for me now.

Suddenly I feel like a small child all at once as my mother draws level. I feel if I look down, I would be wearing the same badly fitting hand-me-downs of hers I was always forced to wear. Or if I turn around, I feel I might see the latest partner Mum has looming over me with unreasonable ethics.

'Hiya, Claire. Long time no see.'

I stare at her. My brain is struggling to process this unexpected reunion. Maybe if I had less going on or if life felt more normal then I would be able to deal with this better. But nothing has felt normal since Leah has been gone. Will things ever feel right again?

I know this doesn't. The zeitgeist of my childhood is upon me again, bringing with it a rush of fear, anger and above all, the sense of longing for the mother I didn't have until I was almost too old for one.

Helen is by my side now. She looks curiously between me and my birth mother. 'Is everything all right, Claire?'

Helen must be able to tell from my face that I'm far from OK. She knows me almost as well as her daughter does, or did anyway. I'm still not sure which tense to use in Leah's absence. I've never been more confused than I am right now.

Carole smiles at Helen. Even in this light, it is obvious her teeth are stained from years of goodness knows what; unfortunately, I do know what. My four-year-old self shouldn't have been witness to it all, but she was.

Now Mum smiles as though none of that ever happened. 'I'm Carole. You must be Helen. I'm Claire's mother.'

Now it is Helen's turn to stare open-mouthed at this new arrival. 'Oh.'

Helen looks back at me. 'Are you all right, dear?'

I open my mouth to follow my natural instinct to be polite, to tell a lie and not cause a fuss, especially at this evening's event. But Carole's arrival has stirred something in me. Or maybe it is this eerie vigil-turned-memorial.

In any case, something makes me throw up

my hands instead of slipping into my usual social routine. 'Not really. I think I'm ready to leave. Do you want a hand packing up?'

'Don't worry about that dear. Tony will take care of it. His car is parked nearby. Do you want a ride home?'

'No thanks. I can manage.'

Carole's pale eyes widen. This was obviously not the reunion she had planned. She has apparently accepted one of Tony's t-shirts and has it pulled over a grey hoodie.

Seeing Leah's beautiful face so close to my mother's gaunt and wasted one distresses me. As do all the candles being extinguished around me like this is a funeral.

I have to get out of here.

CHAPTER THIRTY-THREE

Now

My heart pounds after my discovery. Am I kneeling before the skeleton of my best friend?

Lots of people wear Fitbits, I tell myself. It doesn't mean anything. It could be a coincidence. A really unlikely coincidence.

If only I could make out the colour of the strap. Leah's was bright orchid pink. But there is no way to tell down in this corner. I would need to take the watch over to the light. But it must be fastened around the skeleton's wrist.

There is very little remaining on the bones. I can tell that. Could that be possible in two years? The air is damp down here. But I don't know enough about that sort of thing to judge if this is likely to be my friend or not.

The woman in the farmhouse said she saw her. But then she said quite a few things. She had even pretended to be Leah at first. Though she didn't seem to know much about her. It should have been a giveaway when she didn't react to Helen's name. Or Tony's, for that matter.

It takes me a good twenty minutes to work up the courage to feel around for the watch again. The strap feels to be in perfect condition. How long would the battery last down here anyway? It seems Leah always had the thing on charge.

It thankfully comes clean off now when I undo the catch. Yet, I'm in no hurry to take it up to the light coming through the grill.

I take my remaining shoe off at the bottom of the steps. It is more of a hassle only having one.

Watch firmly in hand, I take a deep breath and mentally prepare myself for what I am about to see.

I have gone no further than the first few steps when I hear a voice call out to me.

The silence and isolation I thought I was in, makes me jump and quickly stifle a gasp.

'Hello?' Comes the voice again.

I take a few steps back and look high above me. The speaker seems to be somewhere unseen above my head.

'Are you there? Say something, for fuck's

sake!'

I keep a firm grip on the watch in my hand, as though it is my most prized possession. 'I'm here.'

The farmhouse woman swears again. 'I was worried you'd had it! How far did you get?'

'I made it over the hill. To the boat. I got onto the jetty.'

'Ha! He let you get quite far then? I didn't get to the boat until my second escape attempt. You did better than me.'

I stare into the darkness above me. 'You knew it was an island?'

'Yeah, of course.'

My heart pounds with rage. 'Why didn't you tell me?'

'He made me swear I wouldn't say anything.'

'You're working with him?'

'No! Don't give me that BS! I'm not on his *side*. But he made me promise. He said he would bring me chocolate if I played along for your first time. Do you know how long it has been since I've had a fucking Mars bar?'

'What do you mean you played along?'

It sounds like there is a shrug. 'He wants us to try and escape. That is why we are here. He likes to go hunting. So he got me to tell you the back door was unlocked and to let you think you could escape.'

'But we could have escaped! The keys were

inside the boat. If you had told me where it was in the first place, I could have made it! If I knew it was an island, I wouldn't have wasted time trying to get my bearings. Why wouldn't you tell me everything you knew?'

'I told you. You get treats for good behaviour. Sorry.'

'You should be! If we had worked together we could have overpowered him!'

'That's what he wants you to think. He likes you to try and break free. It gets him off. But it isn't just him you have to get away from, is it? He has that vicious mutt too. That thing is enormous. How do you think I busted my ankle?'

'The dog attacked you when you tried to escape?'

'I don't actually try and escape any more. There is no way out of here. I've known for ages that this is just a game to him. I'm never getting away from this place. But he stopped bringing me food. He told me I would starve if I didn't play along. And he meant it. I know I wouldn't be the first woman to die here. So I do what I'm told.'

My thoughts move to the skeleton down here in the dark with me. 'There's a body down here. Who is it?'

There is a pause. 'I don't know.'

'It is Leah?'

'I'm not allowed to say.'

'What do you mean, you're not allowed? I need to know if this is my friend!'

'Sorry, Claire.'

It suddenly occurs to me how this woman knows my name. If she has some kind of deal with our captor, then who knows what she has been told about me. My driving licence was in my purse. So was my Tesco Clubcard, library card and bank cards too. Then there were the contents of my handbag. The pair could glean quite a bit of information from those things alone.

I turn away from the ceiling above me and ignore the woman's enquiring voice.

At the top of the basement steps, cool air sinks over my face. I take a deep breath and lift the Fitbit clutched in my hand up to my eyes.

My heart plummets when I look at it.

There is no denying the colour, not even in the gloom of this basement or cellar of whatever this place is.

The watch in my hand is a familiar bright orchid pink.

CHAPTER THIRTY-FOUR

Then

What happened at the vigil stays with me. The last thing I expected was for my birth mother to show up and approach me.

I can't shake the uncomfortable feeling off, even after discussing it at great length with Helen several times since. She is fretting about me too much for her own good now. I wish she wouldn't. I hate the fact my past is causing her extra stress when she doesn't need it.

I also hate that I can't tell her everything about my childhood before the care home. I've always insisted that I couldn't remember anything from such an early age. Only Leah knows what is closest to the full truth. Even then, there are bits purposefully left out. I want to tell my friend everything now. But she isn't here. The realisation makes me long for her more than ever.

The feeling of being that oppressed, malnourished little girl again comes over me at random times. Like when I'm at work, or in a lengthy shower at home afterwards where I can't seem to get clean. I'm forced to dwell on how back then, Mum had made no attempt to book me into any of the local schools. Nor was I ever taken out anywhere other than very rare trips to the corner shop. I was left in that flat virtually the whole first few years of my life with no chance of escape and no hope for the future.

Carole was never much of a fan of food, or eating. She certainly never cooked, always opting for other activities. It looked from our interaction the other night that she still isn't a big eater. My whole world was inside that council flat she kept me in for the first four years of my life. And I didn't like one bit of it.

I'm just walking into the Tesco Express on the way home from work one day when I get a call from Helen.

'Hi, Claire.'

There is something stiff in her voice and it immediately makes me tense and forget the salmon ready-meal I had been considering.

I think of the vigil we had at the weekend. Has it garnered some results? 'Hi. Is everything all right?'

'Well, I don't know. I've just got back from work. There was someone waiting on my doorstep when I got back.'

'What do you mean? Who?'

'It was your mother, dear. Carole was waiting when I got back. She's here now.'

'Oh my god. I'm so sorry, Helen.'

'Don't be. I've let her in for now. But she is insisting on seeing you.'

'Tell her … I don't know. I've no idea what to say to her.'

Helen lowers her voice. It sounds like she might be in the kitchen. 'I can call Tony. He can come over and help me with her.'

'What do you mean?'

'Carole doesn't seem to want to leave. It's my fault, I suppose. I asked her inside for a cup of tea when I got back. But she has settled herself on the sofa and says she won't leave until she talks to you.'

I swear without thinking.

'Language, Claire.'

'Sorry.' I drop the ready meal back into the chiller cabinet in front of me. 'I'll come over right away.'

I abandon thoughts of dinner and quickly drive over to Helen's house.

She opens the front door as I approach, leading me to assume she was watching for me out the window.

She takes in my face carefully as I approach. 'I'm sorry to bother you, Claire. Maybe I should have just called Tony in the first place. You were so upset at the vigil. I just thought you had the right to know she was here, that's all.'

I shake my head. 'No, it's fine. I'm going to have to talk to her anyway. This thing needs dealing with. I'm so sorry about her. As if you need all this on top of everything else.'

'Don't worry about that.' She closes the front door behind us before lowering her voice. 'She is in the living room.'

'How does she know where you live?'

'I don't know. It must be all this with Leah. We have been drawing a lot of attention to ourselves, especially online. I mean, that was the point of it all wasn't it, to get exposure?'

I step inside the living room. Carole is settled back on the sofa. She looks around expectantly as I enter the room.

Before I know it, she is on her feet and pulling me into a hug. I half-reciprocate and give her a small pat on the back to hurry the exchange along.

My tough exterior doesn't go unnoticed by Carole, however. 'Don't be like that Claire. I've missed you.'

'I'm surprised to hear that. You barely noticed you even had a daughter when I lived with you.'

She looks down at the carpet. There is a

definite look of regret on her weathered face. 'I know. I'm sorry, sweetheart. I didn't deserve a little girl, especially not such a beautiful one. Look at you. I'm so proud of how you have turned out.'

'I don't think you should take credit for anything good in my life.' I nod at the woman I do indeed credit for this, who now stands hovering in the doorway, watching the exchange. 'Helen has been the one looking after me. She was there when I needed her.'

'Yeah, I'm sure she has been. You were lucky to find such a wonderful home.'

I'm surprised to see tears in Carole's eyes as she acknowledges Helen and gestures around the room. To be fair, it is so much more civilised than that filthy flat Carole had been raising me in. This might be a palace by comparison.

Lately, I've been forced to remember every detail of that flat. Like the permanent layer of rubbish that littered every inch of the carpet. I would have to step over all sorts of debris including half-eaten slices of toast, chocolate bars and needles just to get to the toilet.

I fold my arms across my chest. 'So where do you live now? Are you still in that flat?'

'I've got a new one. In Birmingham. It's in a high-rise block.'

'Oh.'

'It's got good views across the city.'

'Why did you move from the last one?'

'I got evicted years ago. The neighbours complained about me having visitors all the time. Besides, I was doing things I should have been … I know it was my own fault.'

'Yes, I can imagine.'

'I'm surprised you remember the last place at all. You were still so tiny when social services took you away.'

'I try not to remember. But I can't help it sometimes.'

There is an awkward silence. Helen hovers uncertainly in the doorway.

Carole's voice breaks suddenly and she presses a hand to her mouth. Her next words are barely more than a whimper. 'I'm so sorry I couldn't be the mother you deserved.'

Helen moves forward and hands her the box of tissues we have used so much in recent times in this house.

Despite my determination to keep my birth mother at arm's length, I can't help but feel a small tug somewhere deep inside at this. I'd always thought Carole didn't care at all for me. I imagined she was living her life without a second thought about me and my fate. She has no idea what I went through in that children's home. It is hard to imagine that woman can cry about it now.

Helen sits down beside Carole and rubs her back. She glances up at me and I can tell she thinks I'm being too harsh. But she wasn't ever

203

a tiny child at the mercy of this woman, or of the many acquaintances that came and went so often into that dingy flat that it might as well have had a revolving door.

Helen has no idea what those vile strangers were capable of. She couldn't. Leah had a safe and sheltered upbringing that I was grateful to eventually be a part of. My birth mother can't be credited with that happy outcome.

Carole eventually blows her nose and recovers herself. There are heavy mascara marks around her baggy eyes now.

I'm suddenly reminded of the time I'd been frozen in fear in my bedroom listening to my mother's prolonged screams from down the hall.

By the time I had picked up my teddy bear for support and worked up the courage to go and see her, her male visitor had gone. And Mum herself was in a heap with a fistful of crumpled notes on the filthy carpet. Heavy makeup had streamed down her face that day too. I had mused that day she looked like a sad panda.

She had sat for hours smoking and sobbing until she dragged herself to the bathroom to get cleaned up. That memory baffled me for years. When I got older and more clued up, it occurred to me that was just one example of how my mother funded her habit and lifestyle.

Carole looks back up at me with a startlingly similar face now. 'I got myself together about a year after they took you away. But they wouldn't let me have you back.'

My mouth opens briefly in surprise. 'I didn't know that.'

'No, I didn't think you would. They never passed my messages on to you. I bought you presents every birthday and Christmas, sweetheart, but they wouldn't pass those on either. Don't go thinking I didn't care. Because I did. I've thought of you every day.'

Helen catches my eye and gives me an encouraging nod.

I shrug. 'I didn't know any of that. No one told me.'

'They wouldn't have. As far as the authorities were concerned, once a druggie always a druggie. But I changed. I got myself a job and cleaned my act up. I missed you so much. I suddenly realised what I'd lost. The years went on and I thought I was never going to see you again. Then I saw you in that Youtube interview you did talking about Leah.'

My stomach contracts at hearing Carole speak my best friend's name. It doesn't feel right.

She turns to Helen and takes hold of one of her hands. 'I understand what you've been going through. I know what it's like to lose a daughter. I really never thought I would see Claire again. The thought is devastating, isn't it?'

Helen nods stiffly.

'Don't worry though. If today has proven anything it is that you shouldn't ever give up hope.'

*

I'm perturbed by the ambush from Carole. I'm not sure how I feel about her re-entering my life, but we exchange numbers anyway and promise to get in touch again. Carole suggested a meal out somewhere.

Privately, Helen offers to come with us, but I tell her I'm not even sure I want to go at all.

'Part of me says she is bad news,' I say to her.

'That means the other part wants to give her a chance.'

Before I've made my mind up even a few days later, I get a message from Detective Halliwell. When I meet him at the police station, he has bad news. It turns out Holly Thompson's father had an alibi for the evening Leah went missing. Of course, he did. Should I be surprised? That doesn't prove anything in my opinion, despite what the detective says.

'Thompson's wife confirms his whereabouts for that evening. I'm sorry, Claire. It looks like a dead end.'

I shake my head quickly. 'But he could be lying! How could his wife remember what she was doing on a particular night last year? What if she is just sticking up for him?'

The detective nods. 'That can be the case sometimes, however frustrating that might be. But we can't prove otherwise. Nor do we have any proof that Edward Thompson ever set a foot near

Leah.'

'I told you he walks his dog along the route leading to the Fazeley nature reserve.'

'But we can't prove that he did so on the evening Leah went missing. According to him and his wife, they didn't take that route that evening. They watched a film at home instead.'

'That could be a lie. Does Thompson have a criminal record? Can't you look into it some more?'

'I can't tell you that. I have no probable cause for further investigation either. I'm sorry. You will have to let this one go.'

I can't get the detective's face from my mind as I leave the police station and head home. He leaned forward as he spoke, and placed a hand on the desk. It was almost like he was telling me to do something further.

He officially had to tell me to drop it as there was no evidence. But his body language was egging me on. Like a dare. Before I moved in with Leah and Helen, the other kids in the children's home used to dare each other to do all sorts.

Especially one girl, Kylie. She wanted to see who was the bravest, I used to think. Then I realised, she just wanted to see how much trouble she could get the others into.

She was a manipulator. She got off on seeing the chaos she could cause. I sometimes used to wonder what became of her. But what does it matter now?

At least something useful came from my digging at the police station. Detective Halliwell let slip Mr Thompson's first name. Did he do that on purpose?

I load up my laptop, and immediately open Facebook. I scour the many different profiles belonging to people with the name Edward Thompson.

Frustratingly, I can't find one matching his details. I scan the profile pictures carefully, but none of them is him.

I apply the same approach to all the main social media sites and even have a go at plain old Google. But nothing comes back that relates to this guy.

That alone is suspicious in my opinion. Like he is trying to hide. Some people enjoy their privacy. That's fine. People have the right not to be harassed and cyberstalked by old exes and school friends. After the recent trolls I have encountered, I feel as if I should do the same. But I would bet anything that is not the reason Edward Thompson isn't splashing his life details on here.

He is keeping himself hidden for another reason, I just know it. I glance at the time on the microwave; it's past ten. I should probably start working on my nighttime routine of winding down with a hot drink in front of the television. The blue light from the laptop will only keep me awake all night. Instead of putting it away though I end up on Mia's school Twitter feed. I scroll down until I catch sight of Mia's class; it's a picture of them outside near the school pond. I immediately catch sight of Mia and the colourful bow in her hair. It takes me a few moments to spot the other girl in the picture, however. Holly stands near the edge of the group, away from the action.

I notice her hair hasn't been taken care of like the other girls around her; her greasy locks have been pulled back into a basic ponytail. Her uniform doesn't bear the same embroidered badge most of the class adorns, either. She has a general air of being unkempt, just like I was as a young child. I dread to think what could be happening to her at home.

Holly would not remember one night last year, but her mother would. Only she knows whether she is telling the truth or not.

Unfortunately, the police don't share my enthusiasm on this lead. When I think of the cold hard facts, I'm not sure I would either, in their position. I just have the feeling, and not in the same way as when I suspected Tony.

This time, it's different. It's cold and uncomfortable and desperately frustrating, as I know no one else believes it.

But I know this guy was somehow involved in Leah's disappearance. It was him. I just need to prove it. And maybe I will finally find out what really happened to my friend.

CHAPTER
THIRTY-FIVE

Now

To say I'm devastated would be an understatement. In the last twenty-four hours, I've had my hopes raised and dashed so many times.

Now I'm holding Leah's watch in my hand. The clock face is so familiar. It has the background wallpaper and set-up Leah chose. It is all so crushingly familiar. There is no point in trying to pretend this isn't hers.

Still, I clutch it tightly as fresh tears form in my eyes. I don't want to let it go.

'Are you all right?' comes the voice from upstairs.

I ignore it.

'Katrina.'

'My name is Claire.' My voice is so flat. My head pounds with dehydration. It has been so long since I've had something to eat or drink. I don't even know why I'm bothering to respond to her anymore. My world has come crashing down again. 'You already know that.'

'No.' The voice softens. 'I mean my name is Katrina. You asked me what it was before. Sorry I didn't tell you earlier.'

'You told me you were no one.'

'Well, that is true. You know my name now at least. Or what it used to be. My mother chose Katrina after some actress, but no one has called me that since I was sixteen.'

Despite my fury at being lied to, my interest is piqued. This woman is a lot older than a teenager. 'You have been here all this time?'

'Nah, course not. Been here about six years, I think.'

'So why has no one called you by your real name for so long?'

There is a hollow laugh. 'I got called all sorts in my profession. Whatever the bloke wanted. I got a lot of requests to be girls they knew. Nieces, students, colleagues. That sort of thing.'

'Oh.'

'Yeah, that's what everyone thinks, isn't it? That is why he has got away with taking me. No one bothered I was missing, I reckon. I bet no one even batted an eyelid.'

'I'm sure that's not true.'

'Yeah? Have you heard of me before? I bet you must have noticed missing people since your friend disappeared. Your ears prick up don't they, without you realising? I bet you never heard about the disappearance of Katrina Harris, did you?'

I consider all of the missing persons' cases I've researched or heard of in recent times.

'I don't know,' I lie. 'There have been quite a few.'

'Yeah, didn't think so. No one gives a shit. To be honest, I'm not sure I'm that much worse off being in this dump than back there. At least the rent is free.'

She laughs in that empty way again, like she is a shell of a person. She reminds me a little of Carole.

'You're local then? To the West Midlands, I mean.'

'Yeah. Tamworthian all the way.'

'I'm from Tamworth too ... So was Leah.'

My use of past tense stabs me like a knife. My brain must have processed the cold hard reality now.

The woman above me decides to stoke my confusion once again.

'That's not Leah down there, you know,' she says quietly.

I close my eyes. 'Stop lying to me. I have her watch in my hand.'

'It's not what you think. I wasn't lying

before when I said she was taken out of here, but it wasn't a few days before you got here. She got out a while back.'

'Why should I believe you? If it wasn't for the watch in my hand, I might not even believe she was here at all.'

'Because I'm telling you the truth now. He still has her. She lives up in the farmhouse with him.'

'I don't believe you.'

'That's your loss. I just thought you wanted to know what happened to your girlfriend.'

'She wasn't my girlfriend. Why do you keep saying that?'

There is a pause for another shrug before the woman answers. 'Well, she wasn't—but you wanted her to be, didn't you? After a while locked up in here, she regretted turning you down.'

The sound of creaking floorboards reaches me now as I stare open-mouthed up at the ceiling. I try to call out to Katrina again, but it sounds quiet upstairs now.

She has walked away, just when I need more answers from her.

CHAPTER THIRTY-SIX

Then

Helen is following my lead on the Carole situation and doesn't mention it again. Though I can tell she is bursting to. But I have the feeling she wants me to bring up the subject first. I'm still not sure how to feel about the whole thing.

At thirty-two, I kind of feel like it is too late to accept another mother figure in my life. Especially when I already have one so great.

Today we are looking after Mia again. It seems to be good for Helen just as much as it is good for me to be around her. Mia is a delight with her innocent observations and never ending enthusiasm. Somehow throwing ourselves into her care and well-being distracts us and everything else that's going on.

I suppose that was the idea when Helen invited me along for the outing. And it is for that reason that I also agree today to accompany the pair when they go out to the cinema.

It's a beautiful day in the castle grounds in the afternoon after the movie. The sky is a bright blue hardly touched by a whisper of a cloud.

Mia is being spoilt rotten by Helen as usual, I end up carrying her paper bag of pick and mix as she runs on ahead to the swings in the park. Mia seems so small and innocent. I was younger and must have been even tinier at four when Carole neglected me and allowed me to be taken away by the authorities. What kind of a person does that?

Helen pretends to chase Mia up the steps for the slide now as the little girl squeals and giggles. It occurs to me that Helen could still adopt more children if she wanted. I think it would suit her, especially in Leah's absence. But when I suggest this idea to her as we sit on the parents' benches at the edge of the park she shakes her head quickly.

'Oh no, Claire. I'm too old for all this now on a daily basis! Don't get me wrong, Mia is an angel but I don't think I can handle her twenty-four-seven. We will have a good time. But I have to admit it's quite nice to hand her back to her parents at the end of the day!'

I smile. I don't want to admit to her that I

have the same feeling. I know that parenthood is quite a commitment and I just don't feel ready for it. Will I ever be prepared?

I know the biological clock is ticking and there isn't any sign of a partner on the Horizon. As Helen said, I don't technically need one. I just can't imagine being a single parent and doing all this on my own.

I know I could physically do it, but I'm just not sure I want it enough. It is OK though. I can live with that. Maybe it's not traditional but it doesn't bother me. I just hope Helen won't be too disappointed that she won't get to see her would-be grandchildren in the next few years. Maybe ever.

I have the feeling Helen is about to start up a conversation along these lines by the way she keeps glancing at me. She is reading my mind sometimes, I swear.

But then her thought must take a detour when she spots Mia playing with another girl.

'Oh look,' she says brightly. 'Mia's made a friend. It would be nice to connect so easily to people as an adult, wouldn't it? Somehow we lose that over the years.'

'Hmmm. It happens sometime before secondary school I think.'

When Mia emerges at the top of the slide and makes her rapid descent, I spot her being shadowed by another girl. It takes me a moment to realise the other child is Holly.

At first glance, it appears Holly is alone. Then I realise there is a lone woman on the other side of the park watching her more than a stranger should. She must be her mother.

The woman has the same sort of thin figure as the little girl and somehow has the same flattened look to her. Her pale hair is pulled up into a round bun. She seems older than the other mothers scattered around the park, a good fit for Edward Thompson.

Unlike the other mothers, who are all sandals, Mom shorts and t-shirts, she is buried under a long dark coat with ankle boots. It is like she hasn't noticed the weather has turned warm and bright. Or maybe she just doesn't own much else to wear.

In some way, she reminds me of Carole too. What secrets does she carry about what happens behind closed doors?

'That's a girl from Mia's class at school isn't it?' I say to Helen beside me as I keep an eye on the girls now on the climbing frame. I keep Holly's mother within my sight nonchalantly too.

'Oh, I don't know. I don't really notice the other children when I pick up Mia.'

'No, I didn't notice any of the others. But Mia mentioned Holly when I picked her up at the start of the holiday. She says Holly is a bit sad, but she wants to be friends with her.'

'Awww. That's our Mia, isn't it? She can be

really sweet sometimes, can't she? I wonder why the other girl is down?'

'I don't know.' I shrug in what I hope is a casual way. I haven't mentioned my suspicions about Edward Thompson to Helen. The detective was right, there isn't any evidence or anything to connect him to Leah. So I don't dare say anything to her mum now. It would only upset her and it won't get us anywhere. There needs to be evidence first and I have no idea how to get any.

'Apparently, Holly said her father is a bad man. One of her paintings ended up in Mia's pile of work she brought home on the last day of school. It wasn't very nice. Mia told me the teacher confiscated another one for being too graphic.'

'Oh dear. She doesn't sound quite right. She isn't the one whose parents own that restaurant chain is she?'

'No, that's another girl.'

Helen sits up straighter in her seat to keep an eye on the two girls who are now on the other side of the park. 'Perhaps we should move on? We could take Mia to Smyths and buy her a nice toy instead.'

I expected Helen to be more sympathetic to the girl's situation, especially given my own background. 'We only just got here. Maybe we should let Mia release some more steam. She has been cooped up in the dark cinema for hours. It would be good for her.'

'I'm not sure. I don't want Mia to get upset.'

'She won't. She is with the girl in their class all day at school. Holly sits on her table apparently.'

'Oh.' Helen relaxes in her seat again. 'You seem to know a lot about her.'

'Well, Mia told me all this. The girl does stand out a bit. And her painting stuck with me.'

'Did Mia see it?'

'Yes. She knew it was Holly's straight away. She saw the other one at school too. She will be OK for twenty minutes in a public park.'

'I don't know.'

'I'll take a wander over there if you are worried. Keep a closer eye.'

'Thanks, Claire.'

I stroll over to the little seesaw the girls are playing on. Holly's mother is leaning on the other side of the railings, but keeping an eye on her little girl. She isn't absorbed in her phone like most of the other parents.

Mia takes one hand off the handles to wave enthusiastically at me. 'Look how fast we are going, Aunty Claire!'

'Wow, be careful you don't take off, Mia!'

I take advantage of the attention Mia draws to me at that moment.

'You must be Holly's mother?' I ask with a smile when the other woman glances in my direction.

'Yeah.' She nods.

'Holly sits on Mia's table at school, I think. I'm looking after Mia for the day.'

The other woman says nothing in response, so I try and fill the silence as the girls run off to the slide again. 'She seems like a lovely girl. I think Mia brought some of her artwork home by mistake. A painting.'

Still no response.

'Would you like me to drop it over at your house? You live nearby don't you?'

Holly's mother takes her eyes off her daughter briefly to give me a glance over. 'No, that's all right. Holly brought plenty of stuff home. We won't miss it.'

'Oh, OK. I just thought I would check. It was sort of an unusual picture.'

I'm given a sudden enquiring look now. 'What was wrong with it?'

'Nothing,' I say quickly. 'It was just that Mia said the teacher had to confiscate one similar to it. I'm sure was maybe an overreaction though. Holly just seems to like knights and swords perhaps. Does she have storybooks like that at home?'

The other woman's jaw tightens. There looks to be a faint bruise on it, I realise, covered up by makeup perhaps. 'Holly's dad plays on his PlayStation at all hours. So our girl sees Assassin's Creed on the screen all the time. That's probably where the idea came from.' Then she adds quickly, 'She's fine though, no harm in it.

The game is only pretend. Holly knows that.'

I nod. The other woman seems guarded now, but I know I've got a rare opportunity for an answer to the question that has been bothering me recently. 'Does Holly get on well with her dad?'

Immediately, I know I've said the wrong thing. Holly's mother gives me a sharp look and straightens up. 'You what?'

'Sorry, I just meant …. I don't know. Mia says Holly gets upset sometimes in class. She gets the impression she is a bit unhappy with her father.'

The woman stares at me with narrowed eyes. 'What did she say?'

'Nothing really.' I shake my head. 'I just wanted to say that if you want to talk to someone - about anything - then I'm here.'

'You'd better keep your nose out if you know what's good for you.'

'Sorry. I didn't mean to come across as nosy. I just want to help. My early childhood was bad too, I just wanted to - '

'Holly does not have a bad childhood!'

I seem to be digging a deeper hole here. 'I didn't mean anything by that. I just -'

But it is too late. Holly's mother strides across the playground. She grabs her daughter abruptly by the hand she has just placed on the climbing frame. I expect the little girl to protest, have a tantrum maybe, but she says nothing after a look of mild surprise.

Holly sadly seems used to being handled roughly and allows herself to be half-dragged away from the park and her school friend. She doesn't respond to Mia's hurried call of goodbye either.

Her mother storms off with her, exiting through the opposite gate. She throws a furious glance back at me once she is away across the grass.

All of this behaviour deeply troubles me. But afterwards, the thing I can't stop reflecting on is how watery the woman's eyes had become during our talk.

CHAPTER
THIRTY-SEVEN

Now

'Hello? Katrina? Are you there?' It seems like I call out for twenty minutes or more before she finally returns. The creaking of the floorboards overhead gives her away. There must be quite a large gap in the floor somewhere, because Katrina's voice is plenty audible.

'Sorry. He brought food. Do you want a sandwich?'

My stomach continues to burn as it has done for hours. 'Yes. Please.'

'Get ready to catch this, then.'

'Wait, I don't know where the gap in the floor is. I can't see.'

But I hear a small thud somewhere nearby

as the food hits the dusty ground.

'Sorry. I thought you were right under me.'

I get onto my knees and feel around in the filth. Eventually, my hand connects with soft bread with some kind of wet filling.

I take a desperate bite. It turns out to be egg mayonnaise, which normally I hate.

Right now, it is one of the nicest things I have eaten after being so hungry and weary. Even despite the grit as I chew. Or maybe it is eggshell. It is hard to tell the difference in the dark.

Katrina is quiet upstairs. I imagine she is chewing her hard-earned Mars bar.

There is another sound as something heavy drops onto the floor nearby. It makes me jump.

'That's a bottle of water. I didn't hit you, did I?'

I swallow the last piece of my sandwich. 'No.'

'I'll have to try harder next time.' She laughs in her raspy way. 'Just joking.'

I quickly grab the bottle and down almost the whole lot in one go. I hadn't realised how dry I'd become. I've no idea how I managed to gobble the food so fast without any saliva.

When I've finished, I face up to the ceiling again, despite not being able to see anything. 'Did you really have a throat infection?

'I think so. I've had a whole bunch of issues in here. You saw me, I'm a right state.'

My own wrist throbs some more now. I wonder if the dog bite is becoming infected under my coat sleeve. 'You've just been here a while. That's all. Six years is a long time to be in a place like this.'

'It's not that much worse than what I'm used to. I was a mess before I got here if I'm honest. At least the smack is out of my system. Now that's what I call cold turkey.'

'You were a drug addict?'

'Yeah. It was an expensive habit. That's how I ended up in my profession.'

I am forcibly reminded of Carole again. Her habit led her too onto the same path as the woman upstairs. They might have even crossed paths at some point.

'Sorry, your precious ears don't like hearing about that, do they? I bet you don't get that sort of thing in your shiny end of town.'

'I don't exactly live in a palace, just a two-bed semi.'

'Sounds lovely compared to this place. I dream of such things as a bed, or windows, or proper walls even. I've forgotten what normal life is like.'

'We will get out of here. I promise.'

'Yeah, right.'

'I mean it. There are two of us now.'

'Three.'

'There is someone else?'

'I already said, you stupid bitch. Leah is up

in the main farmhouse.'

'You've told me a lot of things. I don't know what to believe.'

'You can believe she really is here. She was locked down there with that poor bitch for a while. She kept misbehaving. The pair of them both fought him. Crystal put a nail through his ear one day. Aiming for his eye, she was. That's why she is in the state she is in now, the stupid cow. She must have known he was going to retaliate.'

I pause and take in this information. 'You're saying this isn't Leah, then?'

'You're a slow one, aren't you? I've already told you that.'

'But you lied. You're working with him.'

'No, I aint!' There is a loud thud and I instinctively flinch as dust gets into my eyes. 'Don't you dare say that again.'

'Sorry.' My already sore eyes stream again. I try to blink out the dust. 'It's hard to know if I can trust you, that's all. You have told me things that weren't true. You even pretended to be Leah.'

'That was a shitty trick, but he made me do it. I didn't want to.'

'So why is Leah's watch down here? It was on the wrist of this skeleton.'

'That's Crystal down there. He came before you arrived and put the watch in the cellar. He wanted you to believe that was Leah.'

'That's crazy. Why would someone do such

a thing?'

'Because he is a nutter. I told you. He likes to mess with our heads. How's the battery doing on that watch? You have to charge those things all the time, don't you? But there it is even years after Leah went missing, still lighting up.'

I glance at the battery indicator on the display. It is almost a full bar. Quite impossible if it really was down here unused all this time. 'How do I know Leah is still alive?'

'Because I told you.'

'What did you mean before, when you said Leah made a mistake turning me down?'

'She said you told her you were in love with her. She was surprised and didn't take it well. But she regretted it.'

I pause and consider this information. Has Katrina really talked with Leah in this place? Or did Thompson torture that information out of my friend?

'You still don't believe me, do you?'

'It's just hard to when you have lied to me.'

There is a long pause where I wonder if Katrina is still there. Then she speaks again. 'OK, here's something else only Leah would know. She told me she wanted to test you and see how you felt about her a while after what you told her. Leah said she made up a boyfriend. She wanted to see if it would make you jealous.'

My breath catches in my chest at the realisation. 'Adam.'

'I don't think she said his name.'

'She kept telling me how great he was, showing me the texts she was sending him. She told me loads about their dates. Then she didn't seem that bothered when she supposedly ended the relationship. The whole thing was invented for my benefit. I didn't realise.'

'How stupid would you have to be though to not notice your best friend is going out with an imaginary guy?'

'Probably as stupid as me.' I nod as my mind continues to whirr in hope. 'OK, let's say I believe you now. When was the last time you saw Leah?'

'You know I can't keep track of time in this place.'

I sigh at the lack of straight answers. It is hard to shake the suspicion that I'm still being messed with. 'How long was she in here for?'

'Almost a year, I think. It was still winter when he took her out for good.'

My insides run cold as I consider the reason Leah didn't come back. 'That was almost a year ago. Did he take her out to hunt?'

'I don't think so. He told me she is in the farmhouse with him. His private pet.'

'So he could be lying.'

'Maybe. But I don't think so. Leah doesn't mean anything to me, does she? It was just nice to have someone to talk to when she was here. There is no reason he would have told me that lie all this time.'

'That doesn't mean it is the truth.' I fasten Leah's watch around my wrist. According to the display, it is almost five in the evening. That tallies with the drop in light outside. I look towards the grill. Orange light glows through the holes. Sunset seems to be approaching.

Despite the fact that Katrina has lied to me before, I somehow believe her now. The detective in charge of Leah's case would say that I was clinging to false hope.

But in all honesty, a little sliver of hope is all I have to cling to right now.

I look back towards the area where I know there is a skeleton lurking just beyond my vision. 'So what happened to Crystal?'

There is a pause. 'She was shot.'

'He has a gun?'

'Yeah. The only time that I ever saw it was the day that Crystal was killed though.'

My insides run cold at the thought of such a powerful weapon in the hands of our captor. It puts a whole new spin on my potential plans to escape.

CHAPTER THIRTY-EIGHT

Then

After the incident in the park with Holly's mother, Helen grills me over what is going on.

I manage to wait until Mia is back with her parents before I break and admit my suspicions. Helen is shocked and has that motherly way of making me feel foolish for not confiding in her in the first place.

She extracts from me what makes me suspicious of Edward Thompson. Which, when I say it out loud to Helen as I had done with Detective Halliwell, seems rather flimsy.

At least Helen doesn't look so sceptical.

'I'm sorry.' I lean back into Helen's squashy sofa and put my face in my hands. 'My head is a mess. It has been since Leah went. I know yours is too. You don't need me dumping all this on you, do you?'

'Don't be silly. I'm glad you told me this.' There is a notable pause in Helen's voice.

'But...?' I prompt her. 'You don't think he was involved.'

She stares at the black screen of the switched-off television. 'We all want to know what happened to our Leah. But I can't see a parent from Mia's class being involved.'

'I know. I wouldn't believe it either. Maybe you and detective Halliwell are right. Maybe I really am seeing things that aren't there.'

Helen nods. 'Like you did with Tony.'

'Sort of.' My head throbs. Despite the heat of the day, I seem to be short on my daily drinks quota. 'There is just something about this Thompson guy I can't shake off.'

A reassuring hand is placed on my shoulder. 'What is it, do you think?'

'I can't place it. He just strikes me as out of place, that's all. Holly says her father is a bad man. Why would a little girl say that in public about her own father? What has he done do you think? I thought I saw a bruise on the mother's face.'

'It's hard to say. We don't know what happens behind closed doors. Best not to get involved. It could be anything.'

I look at Helen sharply. 'I'm surprised you

would say that. You got involved. You adopted me. Look where I came from.'

'Oh, Claire. That was different. I thought you would be the perfect company for Leah. I couldn't face another pregnancy after her. You two made a wonderful pair of sisters.'

'So I was just like a convenient accessory?'

Helen looks at me with her mouth slightly open at my unexpected snap. 'No, nothing like that. I didn't mean … '

'Sorry. I shouldn't have said that.' I rub my fingers on my temples and feel a strong pulse pushing back. 'I'm just so tired. This whole thing has been doing my head in for so long.'

'Yes, I know what you mean.' Helen's eyes take on a watery quality as she stares at the magazines on the coffee table.

'I need a drink,' I say into the awkward silence that I seem to have created. Why can I never keep my mouth shut when I need to? 'I think there is some lemonade left in the fridge. Would you like a glass too?'

'I'll do it.'

Helen returns a few moments later with a single glass of sparkling drink. The bubbles fizz loudly as she hands it over.

'Thanks. Didn't you want one?'

'Not really Claire, dear. I think I might have an early night tonight. I need to summon some energy if I'm to take Mia down to the Snowdome tomorrow.'

'I'm sorry I snapped before. I don't really mean that you know. I don't know where that came from.'

Helen nods. 'Don't worry. This past year or so hasn't brought out the best in us. We both suspected Tony at one point. I think if I'm honest, the police could have told me they had evidence at that point and part of me would have believed them. The slightest thing can make you suspicious.'

'Yes, I know what you mean. This guy's dog … It seemed quite ready to pounce when I walked past. I was wearing Leah's fleece at the time. Do you think … I don't know. Did the dog recognise her scent or something?'

Helen shakes her head and heaves herself to her feet. 'I think the slightest thing can make you question everything. Did Detective Halliwell seem worried?'

'No. I felt like he dismissed the idea before he even looked into Thompson.'

Helen looks troubled by this, but she seems to blink the thoughts away with bloodshot eyes. 'We have to trust his professional judgement. He has seen cases like Leah's before. If this man has an alibi, maybe he isn't involved after all.'

Despite Helen softening after my flare-up, I feel like the evening is over. Will she ever forget my uncharacteristic remark?

I move out into the hallway and pick up my bag from where it hangs over the bannister.

As I turn back around, Helen catches me in an unexpected hug. I give her a reassuring squeeze back. I suppose this is our way of making up. We have known each other long enough not to let a little snap change anything between us.

She gives me a final pat on the back. Then she turns and rummages in her own handbag slung over the bannister. 'Here, take this.'

Helen presses something into my hand.

I look down at the small cylindrical bottle. 'Pepper spray? How did you get this?'

Helen shakes her head. 'Online. It was quite hard to find.'

'Is this even legal?'

'*Don't let anyone know you have it.* It's only for emergencies.'

'But -'

She raises her hands at my protests and shakes her head. 'I don't want to hear any more about it.'

She opens the front door. 'Look after yourself, Claire. You need to start living again. You are too young to spend your days in mourning like me.'

CHAPTER THIRTY-NINE

Now

I shiver in the darkness. It seems colder down here than it was in the farmhouse. 'Is the back door still unlocked up there?'

'No. He locked it up again after he brought the food and water.'

I'm not sure whether to believe her, but I leave it for now. 'What did you mean when you said that Leah misbehaved?'

'She kept coming up with plans to escape. Like you, she thought if we all went at him at once, we could take him down. But I know what he is like when he gets wound up. I didn't want to make him angry. So I stayed well out of it.'

'So you sat back whilst they risked their lives? If you had tried to help them - '

'Yeah, yeah! It probably would have worked. Do you think I haven't thought that the whole time since?'

There is a thud as something is kicked or thrown upstairs. 'I know I'm a worthless piece of shit! I don't need you to tell me that. It's all I have ever been told by anyone.'

'I wasn't going to say that. But we increase our chances of getting out of here if we combine our efforts. Come on Katrina, I need your help.'

I feel in the air above my head, but can't quite reach the ceiling. I sense it is just beyond my fingertips. 'If we can make the hole in the floor bigger, maybe I can get back up there. Then when he next brings food, we can surprise him.'

'Great idea and all, but there isn't anything to use.'

'What if you just stomp? The floorboards are so rotten, you should be able to make a difference. How big is the hole now? I can't reach it.'

'You could probably squeeze through. But if you can't even reach, then what's the point?'

'Maybe you can lean down and pull me up?' As soon as the words have left my mouth, the look and feel of Katrina's skinny body are re-impressed upon my mind.

'You're too heavy.'

'You only have to get me up so far. Once I can grab hold of something else, I'll pull myself up. Come on. Let's try while we still have some energy from the food. It was only one little sandwich. How long will it be before we get more?'

Katrina doesn't respond.

I look uncertainly towards where her voice sounds closest. 'Was there more food?'

'Some.'

'How much?'

'It has to last until he brings more. I don't know when that will be.'

I have the feeling Katrina doesn't want to share whatever bundle of rations there might be upstairs. I am in no position to accuse her, or even negotiate right now. 'Then we definitely have to get out of here.'

'You're not getting it, are you? I've been trying for years. So have the others. They've tried everything. There is no way out of this fucking hellhole.'

I put my fur-lined hood up around me as the chill really sets in. 'Then what do you suggest we do?'

'We keep trying to survive. We can wait. As you said, we will go at him when he isn't expecting it.'

'What if he never lets his guard down?'

'Then we die.'

CHAPTER FORTY

Then

Are we mourning Leah? Or is she hiding out there somewhere? I find the latter hard to believe, no matter how much I want to. We would all be furious if it turned out Leah staged her own disappearance, but completely relieved at the same time; I wish more than anything that was the case.

At the same time, I know there is no way my best friend would put us all through this. She could never walk away without saying goodbye. That just isn't her.

There was a brief moment of hope just before Leah's birthday when a sighting was reported on the missing persons Facebook page we set up.

It turned out to be a false lead; barely a lookalike.

One day, Detective Halliwell tells us cases like this often run cold. So is that it? Does he not expect to hear anything else now? Maybe that was his way of saying we shouldn't get our hopes up any more.

I don't know what is worse, no leads at all, or having our hopes raised and dashed. It's all very trying for Helen and I. The toll it is taking on her is obvious. If she wasn't throwing herself into keeping busy, I don't think she would be coping.

At least, I assume she is busy. It seems she has slipped away from me since that last real talk we had. I'm having flashbacks to when I told Leah about my true feelings. Have I forever tainted my relationship with my would-be mother now too?

I'm walking to my car after a busy day at work. It's been another scorcher. It won't be long until the summer holidays when it will be tough navigating through the park due to the growing throngs of people.

My body aches and I'm starving. Helen hasn't been over for weeks with trays of food or even nagged me via text to eat well. This is the first time in a while I have really noticed her absence. I'm just contemplating the warm bottle of orange juice I bought but didn't get around to drinking at lunchtime when someone calls my name.

It's James. He is leaving work for the day too. 'Hiya. Busy day, eh?'

I roll my eyes. 'Awful. I'm boiling hot. I've had four lost kids to deal with today.'

He laughs. 'How could someone lose four of their children?'

'They were all from separate families.'

'Oh no. It's been a tough one for me too. Some toddler had a tantrum and threw his mum's phone into the tiger enclosure. We had a job to get it back.'

'Oh yeah, I heard about that. I think I'll be glad when summer is over this year.'

'I thought you loved this job.'

'I did. But then … I don't know. I think I've just had a bad day. I've got low blood sugar too, which doesn't help.'

'Why don't you come over to mine for dinner? You'd be proud of me. I've got a stew in the slow cooker you got me. There's plenty of it.'

'Slow cooker stew? In this heat?'

He shrugs. 'I usually let it cool down a bit before I eat it. If I didn't prepare dinner the night before, I probably wouldn't bother cooking at all. There doesn't feel like much point if it's just me at home. I suppose you will be the same now, won't you?'

The thought catches me off-guard. 'Yes, I suppose.'

'Sorry. I know it's been hard on you since

Leah has been gone. You two were close. She said you always used to do the cooking, but I don't know if you would be into it if you're alone. I mean, I don't know if you do live on your own.' James reddens. Sorry, I'm being nosy now. It's none of my business any more I guess.'

'No, it's OK. It's still just me at home. I haven't really … you know … met anyone since you.'

James's eyebrows flicker. 'Wow. I didn't realise that. I never thought you were that into me at the time.'

'I sort of was. It was Leah who thought my heart wasn't in it. I guess you got the same impression.'

'No, I thought things were going well with us. I mean, I really liked you. I still do, to be honest.' He laughs awkwardly and kicks at some gravel with his boot. 'But it was Leah who told me she didn't think the thing was going anywhere. She said you were thinking of breaking the thing off.'

'Oh, that's strange. She told me the same thing. When did you get the chance to talk to her?'

'I ran into her in town one day. She worked at Ventura Park, didn't she?'

'Yes.' The use of past tense still cuts at me every time. I want to scream at people and tell them we don't know Leah only exists in our memories yet. We just don't know either way for sure. Will we ever? 'I wonder why she said that.'

'I don't know. I probably shouldn't say it with her being gone and all, but I don't know … '

'What is it?'

'Leah always seemed sort of attached to you. I mean, you two spent a lot of time together. I always got the impression I was intruding. Or I was a third wheel or something.'

'No, I don't think so.' I shrug. It seems like an odd thing for James to say. But I know him. He isn't the type to make things up. If anything, he was always too honest in our relationship, always admitting a discount he had obtained on a show ticket, or telling me too much about his ex-girlfriend's bedroom preferences.

'Maybe I got it wrong then. I just wonder sometimes if we made a mistake ending things.'

'You were the one who called time on it in the end,' I remind him.

'What if, I don't know, we gave things another go? How about we start with that dinner tonight?'

I smile in surprise. Has James been harbouring these feelings for me for a while? I've often thought there was something in the way he looks at me sometimes. Then I would remind myself he was the one who ended it last time.

I can still picture the pregnancy test I took in those first post-split weeks perched on the side of the bath as I waited for the results. My prayers were answered that day when I got a negative reading. Now it seems that stress might not have been necessary at all.

I'm about to say yes to James's offer. Then I get a phone call that makes me forget my horrible day served with a garnish of a chance with my ex.

It is the police on the phone. What they tell me makes me finally realise why Helen has been so withdrawn lately.

'Hello. Is this Claire Evans?'

'Yes. Speaking. Who is calling?'

I'm immediately put on alert when I'm told it is an officer from the local police station. 'What has happened? Have you found Leah?'

'No,' the female officer says flatly. 'We have Helen Bayliss here at the station.'

'Is she OK?'

'It's not good news. Ms Bayliss has been arrested.'

'Arrested? That must be a mistake.'

I even feel the tension in my shoulders relax slightly. I imagine I'm dealing with a woman at the front desk. She must have got the details muddled up. Helen has never so much as had a parking ticket in her life. She accidentally shoplifted a packet of sugar from the supermarket once and drove back to make sure it was paid for.

'There is not any mistake. Helen Bayliss was arrested this morning. She requested that you pick her up from the station.'

CHAPTER
FORTY-ONE

Now

My stomach rumbles as consciousness comes back to me. I've slept so lightly that I wonder if I have even been asleep properly at all. Nevertheless, it takes me a few moments to come around. When I do, I realise that I can see more than I expect.

I blink. Light is flooding into my cellar prison. Crumbling concrete steps come into focus.

I sit up and look around.

A gasp escapes me when I see the full horror of the nearby skeleton. It's not entirely as I pictured. It isn't pristine white or as clear-cut as I would have expected; a far cry from the classic representations I've seen in films and the secondary school science model.

Long ginger hair flows from the head. There is still clothing hanging from the shrunken torso and limbs. I look away quickly.

It definitely isn't Leah. Katrina was telling the truth about that at least. Does that mean my friend is up in the farmhouse as she said too? We only have Thompson's word for that. Is he lying? Has he set the whole thing up as a lure to get me to trap myself in the other farmhouse instead? That sounds like the sort of game he might enjoy according to Katrina. Though I can't say for sure.

Grey sky awaits up the stairs. Dark clouds move slowly across the canvas of it.

Why is the door open now? Is my captor lurking on the other side watching me to see what I will do next?

As though reading my mind, Katrina answers my question. 'It's a trick you know.'

I jump. 'I didn't realise you were awake.'

'Are you going to make a run for it?'

I look back towards the promise of fresh air. 'Will he be waiting out there?'

'Somewhere. You never know how much of a head start he is going to give you. Or how far he wants to push things.'

'What do you mean?'

'Sometimes he gets too excited. It is hard for him to get new women, so he doesn't usually take risks. But he loses his head sometimes. Crystal got really hurt one day when he was

245

hunting her.'

I get to my feet. My socks make no sound as I move towards the steps. I take each one tentatively and peer out, halfway up. There is nothing but grass and the slope of the hill in sight.

'Are you going for it?'

'I have to. I can't stay in here and wait. You really think Leah is in the other farmhouse?'

'What? I don't know. I thought you wanted to escape. You have to find a way off the island.'

'I do want to escape. But I want to know where my friend is first. Not knowing what has happened to her has killed me. Her mother too. I can't leave without finding out.'

It is eerily silent outside, even the wind has dropped this morning. According to Leah's watch, it's 9:34 AM. Apparently, I've taken seventeen steps too.

Halfway up the concrete steps, I stop still and listen intently. My eyes dart all around, but I don't take another pace.

'Are you still there?'

'Yes.' I keep my voice low, unwilling to alert Thompson of my movements more than I have to. I don't know how far away he is, or what weapons he may be carrying upon his person ready to unleash upon me. Is there still pepper spray left in that little bottle he confiscated from me?

'What are you waiting for?'

'I don't know. I just want to try and figure out where he is before I leave.'

'You can't. That's the point. He wants to take you by surprise. Stoking your fear is what makes it fun for him.'

I want to say I'm not afraid, but I'm trembling beneath my coat and not just from the cold. 'I just need a minute.'

Katrina laughs. 'You will only make it worse for yourself the longer you wait. Trust me. Best to just go for it, face the music and be put back in here.'

'I don't want to end up back in here.'

'Of course, you don't. But that is the only place you can get. We are on a fucking island.'

'I told you. The keys were in the boat.'

'They can't have been.'

'I saw them.'

'Bullshit! He wants you to think you can make it. He's smart. He knows all the tricks to make you think you can get away. But you can't. Not ever. You were either imagining things, or it was a trap of his.'

'The keys were definitely inside the window of the boat though. I'm sure I saw them. So that's what I'm going to go for once I've checked the farmhouse.'

'Don't be stupid. He is usually always in the farmhouse, especially to start with. I wouldn't bother. Maybe I was wrong about Leah. I haven't seen or heard her for ages. She is probably dead.'

'Please don't say that!' I shake my head to dismiss Katrina's words, but they ring in my ears regardless. I say my plan out loud again as if to reassure myself. 'The boat is our only way off this island. And I'm not leaving without Leah.'

As soon as the words have left my mouth, I feel a deeper sense of panic. 'There isn't recording equipment down here is there? Thompson can't see or hear us, can he?'

'No. Never seen any, anyway. I mean, look at the place. It's amazing this building hasn't fallen down yet.'

'I guess you're right.'

'So are you going or what? I told you, you just have to go for it. Look, there is another chocolate bar up here. When he locks you up again, we'll split it, eh?'

'I'm honoured, but I can't be locked up again.'

'It's nice you still think that. Just shows how new you are here.'

The resolution in Katrina's voice unsettles me. She really has given up all hope. I make a promise to myself to never become like her. I can't fail.

I take another step and deem the coast is as clear as it could ever be. 'That's it. I'm going.'

Katrina lets out a low breath. 'Good luck. You'll need it. I hope he doesn't hurt you too badly.'

CHAPTER FORTY-TWO

Then

'**I**'m so sorry Claire. What must you be thinking?'

'What's going on, Helen? They told me you were arrested!'

'I was.' My would-be mum doesn't elaborate at first. She puts a hand to her forehead and leads the way outside of the air conditioning of the police station and into the June heat.

I follow, fed up with the hot weather by this point. I am still weary and longing for the shower I've been thinking of after being at work all day.

I open the passenger door for Helen, but she leans against the hot metal instead, looking up at the bright blue sky overhead.

I get a bottle of water from the boot and hand it to her. 'So you were arrested.'

She nods, swallowing down a large gulp. 'That's right.'

I feel my eyebrows raise. 'What for? And why did they keep you in there for so long? I was told you were taken in this morning.'

'It was just before lunch when they picked me up. We were finished not long after that. I didn't want to go home or to work. It didn't feel safe.'

I look at her sharply. 'Why not?'

She ignores me and carries on. Helen still seems to be riding some kind of adrenaline rush. 'I didn't want Tony to find out what I'd done either - don't tell him. I'm so sorry, Claire. I didn't want to disturb you at work. I just wanted you to know what has been going on.'

'Which is what?'

'I broke into Edward Thompson's house earlier.'

I stare at her, the woman who told her daughter and I off for eating strawberries straight off the plants at the pick-your-own farm. 'You did what?'

'I couldn't stop thinking about what you said about this bloke. Your words kept coming back to me in the middle of the night for weeks. I couldn't sleep thinking about it all. Then I thought, well, if he has done something to my Leah, then I have a right to know. You were right, he is dodgy as hell. I've been following him around every chance I've had. June has given me a verbal warning at work for being late too many times. It hasn't been easy keeping tabs on him. He disappeared one day and I still don't know where he went to. I lost him at the petrol station when I had to refuel.'

'Helen,' I say warningly. 'I didn't realise. Why didn't you tell me all this was going on?'

'I didn't want you getting involved. You've got your whole life ahead of you. But I need to know if this bloke hurt my little girl. Though I couldn't find anything out about him other than the fact he is a creep.'

'What do you mean?'

'He drives around the streets at night. You know, the dodgy estates, looking for … I don't know what I would call it. Company, I suppose.'

'Oh. I didn't know that.'

'He is a deviant all right.'

'But that doesn't prove he ever went near Leah.'

'No. It doesn't. There wasn't anything in his home that does either.'

'Did you really break in?'

Helen nods, looking half-distressed, half-exhilarated. 'I waited until he went out. Then I went in through the back door which he leaves unlocked.'

'What about the dog?'

'He took it with him. You told me he does

the circular walk from the quarry to the nature reserve. You were right. I know his routine now. He doesn't seem to work, he seems to let his wife earn the money. When he leaves the house, he drops Holly off at school in the morning. Then he goes home for an hour or so. I have no idea what he does all day when he is alone in the house. Plays games on his console, I suppose. There was a violent game on pause when I went inside. Anyway, around ten-thirty he does a dog walk. Usually, it is a local one around his housing estate at that time. Later on, he does the big walk you saw him on. I can tell which outing he is going for because he always takes a ball for the dog for the shorter one. This morning he didn't, so I made my move. I wouldn't have been caught if it hadn't been for the neighbour that saw me. Nosy bugger, peering out his window.'

She exhales deeply.

I stare at Helen. I'd had no idea she was up to all this without me knowing. 'So you didn't find anything?'

'Just some unsavoury materials in the bedroom that I assume he uses with his wife. And some disgusting magazines. Nothing illegal, or anything to do with Leah. I don't know what I was looking for really. I was just going crazy not knowing. It just felt like I should do something, you know?'

'I know what you mean. But don't do things like this without telling me, OK?'

'Hmm.' She avoids my eye.

'Helen? Please don't put yourself in danger. If you suspect something, either tell me or the police.'

'The police weren't doing anything! You heard Detective Halliwell's last update. They have pretty much given up by the sound of it! And you were fobbed off when you tipped them off about Thompson. We might never know what happened to Leah if we leave it up to them. I can't live my entire life not knowing where my little girl went … or if she suffered.'

Helen's chin dimples as she takes a determined swig of water. Her eyes reflect the bright sky above as she tips her head back.

I rub her shoulder firmly. 'You can't think like that. We will find out the truth. I just don't know when. Please stay strong. And don't go off doing crazy antics without me, OK?'

Helen smiles weakly back at me, tears wetting her eyelashes. Somehow I get the feeling she can't commit to a promise to me she is already planning to break.

CHAPTER FORTY-THREE

Now

I take each step in my socks until dust and concrete become fauna. The wet grass soaks through to my already numb feet.

Now I wish I had my shoes. It wouldn't make running any easier, but I feel so weak and exposed. It feels so ridiculous to be roaming around this rugged landscape without anything more on my feet than the plain black socks I was wearing during my evening out to the pub.

The knowledge that there is something much worse than sharp rocks and thorns to contend with nags at me. I keep turning my head every chance I get and staring around. At any moment, I know there will be a pair of dark figures emerging from over a slope, or from the farmhouse.

Last time they came from the farmhouse building. I stare up at the windows. Could Leah really be in there? Muffled barks and yelps erupt from inside the craggy, moss-covered walls. It settles my decision.

There is no way I'm going into that building if that dog is raring for blood inside. I'm going to have to try for the boat again. It is my only option. I'll get away and bring a ton of trouble down on this place.

The police will have no choice but to see Thompson was guilty all along. Then we will find out if Leah is still here somewhere, whatever state she may be in. Is she as starved and thin as Katrina? I shake thoughts of Crystal out of my head. What conclusion has that poor woman's family drawn about her disappearance? Do they still cling to the hope they will see their daughter, niece or sister again?

I don't want to analyze my thoughts about Leah right now. I'm still not sure what to think. Can Katrina be trusted? Or has she been ordered to give me false hope, like that horrible trick Thompson played with the watch?

I move around the other side of the slope, as far away from the occupied farmhouse as possible. The distant mainland is visible. A scrap of sunlight poking through the clouds illuminates the green of the coast. Too far off to reach, but just visible. Thompson couldn't have picked a better place to play his twisted games.

Over here on the island, it is completely clouded over.

I keep my body low this time. The boat is my target. I know I can get to it before I'm caught. Before the farmhouse disappears out of sight, I turn my head and catch sight of a large dark shape moving in front of a window. It is too big and tall to be the dog, so Thompson must still be inside. Yet, the curtain is drawn. He hasn't seen me.

Yes, I think. I know I can make it.

I've never piloted a boat before. Growing up in the West Midlands, the closest experience of the sea I've had is going down the chippy for dinner on a Friday evening. My biggest worry right now is hoping I can figure out the controls in a hurry.

When I reached the boat last time, my mind took a frantic sort of snapshot of the jetty.

The boat was tethered by a single rope, I believe. So I'm confident I can cast off the vessel quickly. Once I'm adrift, I will have time where I'm out of Thompson's reach to figure out how to sail. The little boat is tiny. It can't be that hard to control.

Thompson has been doing it all this time, back and forth. And he was stupid enough to pick me as a target. Big mistake.

Once I'm nearing the patch of land near the jetty, I take another glance over my shoulder.

Still nothing in sight. Yes, I'm getting away with this. Is it really possible Thompson didn't see me leaving the cellar? In that case, I definitely will definitely be able to escape. I take the last bump in the landscape at a jog, success pounding in my ears.

Then I see the jetty. And my mouth drops open.

The boat is gone.

I stare at the scene for a few moments in horror. This can't be happening. Has Thompson left the island? He can't have. I just saw his silhouette in the window and the dog is still here. That animal seems to be the only thing he cares for, more than his daughter, or his wife.

I move down the rotten old jetty, in case the boat is in sight somewhere. I wonder if Mrs Thompson knows the full extent of what is happening here. Does she know anything at all? She might just think her husband's absences are down to a simple affair. If she knew any of this, would she have the strength to take herself and her daughter away from it all?

The dog still being here gives my captor away. He wouldn't leave it behind. Plus the cellar door was opened whilst I was asleep. No one else could have done it.

Unless it was Katrina. No, she can't have. Then I remember what she said to me less than ten minutes ago. *He wants you to think you can make it. He's smart. He knows all the tricks to make you think you will get away. But you can't.*

This is a trick then. The boat has been moved, that's all.

This is just one of his games, I tell myself even though I'm trembling from head to foot now in terror.

I turn back from the jetty and face the island behind me. 'I know your game, you miserable shit. You can't fool me like the others.'

Muttering these words to myself makes me feel braver than I am. I need it because right now, I'm terrified. My plan has gone awry. The only thing I was sure of was that the boat would be here and now it isn't. That was all I had. I've never felt more alone than I do at this moment.

The boat must be here somewhere. I have no choice but to go and look for it. There is still time to find it. Will the keys still be inside?

I don't even make it to the brow of the hill when it happens.

The barking has started. The sound cuts through me like a hot knife.

For a moment, I'm frozen in fear. Another growl. The sound is too close. The hill peak is too far away. I won't make it.

So I do the only thing that seems logical at the moment. I turn and run, my legs almost giving way beneath me as I make the descent back down the slope.

I race for my life, Katrina's words about Thompson getting over-excited and letting things go too far sometimes throb in my ears. Is he armed with the weapon she warned me about?

The terror is real now. I hate letting my captor get what he wants, but my breath comes in ragged in my chest. I'm not so unfit that all my frantic panting can be blamed on years of shirking exercise.

The farmhouses come into view now. Part of me wants to push on to the building in a better state of repair and see what is inside. Could I barricade myself in there? What would I find if I did?

I'm about to make the directional change towards it, but the dark figure of the dog comes into view nearby. Terror gets the better of me. I can't imagine there are any door locks on the property on an otherwise uninhabited island. Even if there were, they would be too flimsy to hold back a man with dark desires and his faithful companion.

Somehow, I make it to the cellar before my pursuers.

I'm ashamed to say I whimper in fear as I stumble down the steps and hit the concrete floor again.

I retreat into a dark corner, half-scrambling. Did I really think I was in control just minutes ago? Now look at me. Katrina was right.

A shadow moves across the doorway. For a moment, I long for the relief of hearing the cellar door slam. To be plunged into darkness and isolation would be preferable to the fear coursing through me now.

I have nothing to defend myself with. All I can do is wait for my punishment.

CHAPTER FORTY-FOUR

Then

I t is my turn to find excuses to drop in on Helen over the next month or so. I don't trust her one bit. This recent episode has me worried she will do something rash again in her pursuit of the truth. I regret mentioning Edward Thompson to her at all now.

What if I was wrong?

But then, in the first week of the summer holidays, something happens that reassures me my suspicions weren't that unsubstantiated after all.

Helen looks after Mia for the day when her parents have to work. Usually, a bundle of energy and excitement, today she seems a little down.

Helen sets a glass of raspberry lemonade in

front of her as she sits unusually still at the table and chairs in the garden. 'What's the matter, dear?'

Mia shrugs. 'Mummy said I could ask Holly to come over to my house for the holidays. But Holly couldn't come to school in the last week so I didn't get to ask her.'

'Oh no, that's a shame. Was she poorly?'

'Sort of. Mrs Davies said she was bitten by a dog. We had to do a worksheet on how to handle pets afterwards.'

Helen exchanges a horrified glance with me.

I put my own glass of colourful drink down on the table. 'How did Holly get bitten by a dog, Mia? Was it her own pet dog?'

'No. Mrs Davies says it was a dog in the park. But I thought dogs weren't allowed in parks, so how could it get her through the fence?'

'I don't know, sweetheart.'

Helen rubs Mia on the back. 'We have to watch out whenever we go outside, don't we? Sometimes people break the rules.'

She raises her head and gives me a meaningful glance.

When Mia is exerting herself on the small trampoline Helen bought for the holidays, we are free to descend into speculation over her classmate.

I run my fingers through my hair. 'Do you think it was her father's dog that attacked Holly?'

'It must be, for goodness sake. It would be quite unusual for a dog to get into a child's park. I mean, these days, you never know. All sorts goes on, doesn't it? But it would be highly coincidental if that were to happen when you said there is a dangerous dog in the home of that poor little girl.'

'I wonder how badly she is injured?'

'It must be quite bad if she couldn't go to school.'

'I suppose the parents wouldn't have admitted it if her injuries were minor. They would have passed it off as a cold or stomach bug or something instead.'

Helen presses a hand to her mouth. Her eyes crease at the sides.

I pass her my napkin. 'Here. I'm sure Holly will be all right. If it was that serious, it would be bigger news. The parents would be in trouble.'

She shakes her head. 'I just feel so bad for that little girl. You didn't see her bedroom. There were bunk beds in one room. I think the mother sleeps in there with her. It looks like the dad has the back bedroom to himself. There is only one pillow and his things are strewn everywhere. Nothing of the mother's at all in there. Why do they have to live like that? What is Thompson like behind closed doors? We already know he is up to no good when he is out and about. And now this happens.'

'It's not your fault. As you said before, we

probably shouldn't get involved.'

'Oh, I didn't mean that. Of course, I didn't. I'm sorry we had a little falling out over it, really. I just wanted to ward you off so you don't get dragged down and into trouble with me. Keep yourself clean, Claire. You have so much ahead of you.'

Her comment gives me pause. 'Why are you talking like that? You aren't planning to do anything else, are you?'

'No. And even if I was, I wouldn't tell you. You've got so much I want to see you do.'

*

My last visit to Helen troubles me. I have the feeling she is planning something else, but I can't imagine what. She just shuts me down whenever I try and ask her via text or phone.

Carole has been nagging me lately too. Her texts and invitations for that meal out are becoming harder to ignore. In the end, I relent. Perhaps it is because I'm missing Helen, that I agree. Or maybe that softer part of me that is curious about Carole speaks up for itself now.

In any case, I agree to lunch one Saturday at my local pub.

'This is nice,' she says as she settles herself across the table from me at a table outside. It is as hot as it gets in Britain today and a wasp hovers interestedly around my bottle of Coors Light.

Carole is dressed in a pair of jeans and what looks like the same grey hoodie from the vigil.

Her eyes are bloodshot. Has she been crying this morning, perhaps dissolved in thoughts of the past?

Today might be harder for her than I realised. I've been so busy caught up in my own feelings about all this, I haven't really thought about Carole's. I'm still getting used to the idea that she isn't the villain I thought she was. Perhaps she thinks me heartless?

Leah has always told me I can come across as cool and uncaring to some people sometimes. Only she and Helen saw my softer side.

'Yes, it's a lovely day, isn't it? Summer is the busiest time in the theme park where I work.'

'Look at us, talking about the weather!' Carole laughs, exposing those yellowed teeth again. 'I've missed you so much, Claire. Thank you for agreeing to see me today.'

She takes hold of my hand on the table and strokes it briefly. 'So you work at Drayton Manor now?'

'Yes.'

'That must be exciting. Better than the used furniture centre I work at.'

'It has its moments. I prefer it when the park isn't so busy though.'

'You were always such a clever little girl. I imagined you had maybe made something more of yourself. I was surprised when I found out where you worked.'

I take my hand from hers. 'I … I don't know.

You can't judge someone by how they were at age four. I'm happy with my job. I just prefer it when it is a little quieter, that's all.'

'I didn't mean anything by it. I just dreamed of you being wealthy and living in a big house with a gorgeous bloke.'

'My job pays plenty for my lifestyle.'

'Yes, it must.' She nods, seeming heartened by this.

Part of me relaxes. Even though I'm trying not to care, part of me deep inside wants this woman's approval.

'Helen says you have your own house in Fazeley. That won't have come cheap the way house prices are these days. It's like winning the lottery, isn't it? You have your own car too. You are doing much better for yourself than I ever have!'

'Well, I don't own the house. It belongs to Helen's brother. You must have misunderstood her.'

'Oh, my mistake.' Carole seems thrown off by this and I'm disappointed to have to dispel her brief illusion.

'I thought you were proud of me.'

'I am,' she says quickly. Yes, I really am, Claire. You've grown into such a beautiful lady. You have everything so together. No thanks to me.'

I take a sip of beer. The outside of the bottle is dripping with condensation. 'It's fine. I had to get over that a long time ago. I was happy with my life until … '

'What happened? Did you have a bad breakup?'

'I mean, you know, I was happy before all this with Leah happened. Everything was going well before she went missing.'

Carole tilts her head as she considers me. 'You seem really upset about your friend. You two must have been very close.'

'We were. I mean, we are. I don't even know whether to speak in the past tense or not. We just don't know what happened to her. We might never know.'

My mother nods, as though to prompt me. 'But she was just a friend. It must have been quite a while now since she disappeared as well, eh? You have to move on.'

'Just a friend?'

'Yes. Think of the future.'

'You sound like Helen.'

'Exactly. We mothers only want what is best for you, sweetheart. Helen has lost her little girl and she seems to be taking it better than you.'

'You haven't seen how upset she has been. And you don't understand how Leah and I were when we were together … '

'What do you mean?'

I don't say anything more, but should I? Would it be easier to spill my heart out to a relative stranger? She might be able to understand from a more distant perspective. On the other hand, she is my flesh and blood. Could she know things about me I don't even understand?

My heart pounds in my chest. The other pub-goers around us talk and enjoy the hot sunshine.

I take a deep breath and voice my inner thoughts, something that feels alien to me. 'I have feelings for Leah. I mean, I did, when she was here. That's the reason I can't just let her go. I'm sort of in love with her.'

Carole's pale eyes widen. I can tell my answer was the last one she expected. She nods politely. I can tell that if we didn't have the advantage of unfamiliarity, I would be getting a different response. But as Carole is compelled to be on her best behaviour, she nods. 'I see.'

'Do you?'

'Yes. I mean, that was a little unexpected! I suppose that explains why you aren't married.'

'Not exactly. I've been out with blacked before. There is technically still time to find someone too. Leah wasn't married either and she wasn't interested when I told her how I felt.'

'That must have been hard for you.'

'Yes, especially now she is gone. I'm starting to think I'm not going to get any closure on the situation. It's approaching two years and we still know nothing more than we did at the beginning.'

I was right, talking to someone I don't know so well but still has my best interests at heart is easier.

'You have to move on though, Claire. You have a good life, you know. Better than most. You live in a nice house in a nice area and you have a good job. Have some fun.'

'It's not that simple. Nothing feels fun without Leah.'

'If she wasn't interested in you, then you haven't lost as much as you think. I know you will find happiness again, sweetheart.'

'I know I should. But it is just hard.'

'I get it. I honestly do. Picking yourself up when things have gone wrong is the hardest thing you will ever have to do. But you aren't alone. You have Helen and now you have me too.'

'Thanks.'

'You're welcome.' She takes a sip of her drink. 'Thank you for telling me this. I feel like we have really bonded.'

'Me too.'

'I'd like us to do this again. But I'm moving out of the area in a bit.'

'I thought you had a flat in Birmingham?'

'I do. But I'm being evicted soon.'

'Why?'

'Nothing like last time, I promise. It's just rent arrears. The council have been on my case like there's no tomorrow. You know what it is like when a company decides they owe you money, they can get pretty nasty.'

'Why didn't you pay your rent? I thought you had a steady job.'

'I did. I mean, I do. But I was short on one rent payment a few months ago. I had most of the money, but I couldn't just pay part of the bill, so I kept hold of all the cash.'

'Then what happened to it?' My heart is sinking, even as I ask the question.

'It just got spent on other things. You know how it is. My fridge broke down and a girl has got to eat, hasn't she, eh?'

There is silence for a few minutes as Carole takes another sip of her drink. The pie and chips she ordered lay mostly untouched on her plate. It seems her appetite is no greater than I remember.

'Where will you go?'

'That's just it. I don't have anywhere else to go. The council say there is a flat available up in Milton Keynes. That's near where your Aunty Cathy lives. But I can't apply for it if I'm in arrears. The housing won't allow it. So I'm in a bit of a bind, I suppose.'

'When did this happen?'

'Oh, it's all been playing out for a while. They gave me sixty days of breathing space where they didn't charge me any interest. But that's over now. They have whacked on loads of interest and penalties since then.'

I think back to the first tentative message

I received from Carole on Facebook. The timing couldn't have been more coincidental. 'That's when you first contacted me.'

'No.' Her response is too casual and her eyes widen too much. She looks over into the distance before she responds. 'I don't know. Was it? I didn't think about it.'

'I'm sure you did. That's why you got in touch, wasn't it? You want money from me.'

'No! Course not! I just want to get to know you, Claire. It's just bad timing this eviction thing is going on in the background. It means we don't have much time … unless you help your poor mum out.'

She looks at me expectantly now, drawn-on eyebrows raised in hope.

I hesitate. Part of me wants to help her. My hand even twitches for my phone with thoughts of a bank transfer. But then I consider what would most likely happen if I give my mother money. And what she would spend it on.

'I can't help you, Carole.'

'But you have so much! You have your good job and you are living rent-free in that nice house. You wouldn't even miss the money.'

'You've never even seen my house. And I'm not rich, you know. Yes, I could help you. But what are you really going to do with the money if I handed it over to you?'

'Nothing, I swear! It's only for the rent. I just need to get these vultures off my back.'

'I wouldn't exactly describe the council like that. I'm sure there will be something that can be done. Can't you appeal, or something?'

'Well, to be honest, it isn't just the council that wants money off me. I've run a couple of other bills up too.'

This gets better. 'What kind of other bills?'

'Just some debts.'

We both know what she means by that statement. She looks at me from beneath mascara-laden lashes and understanding crosses the table between us.

I sigh. 'I can't believe I fell for this. You never cared about me ever, did you? This was all about money the whole time.'

Carole shakes her head adamantly. 'No! I love you, sweetheart.'

'You don't even know me.'

'It's just bad luck that I've fallen on hard times when we have met up again, that's all. Let's not ruin things, eh?'

'You've already ruined things. My whole life could have been ruined if I hadn't been confiscated from you when I was.'

I stand up. 'You were right. I was lucky to have been adopted by such a nice family. I owe them everything, and you, nothing.'

I throw some money down on the table to pay for the lunch.

Immediately, Carole's gaze is fixed upon the notes. But a waitress swoops out of nowhere and collects the money with a smile as she clears our table.

Carole looks visibly gutted at the loss of the money. She looks back up at me as I pull my handbag over my shoulder. 'I really did miss you, Claire. If you knew what was good for us both, you wouldn't leave me in the shit like this.'

'I do know what's good for me. That's why I'm leaving.'

'There are so many things I want to tell you.'

'Like what?'

She casts around wildly. 'All sorts.'

I have the feeling my birth mother is just trying to stop me from leaving.

'Goodbye, Carole,' I say as I turn out of the beer garden.

At the main road, I squint in the sunshine back towards the pub. Carole has made no attempt to come after me. She knows the game is up now. She won't get any money, so there is no point in pursuing me.

Unwanted tears leak from my eyes as I walk back home. My birth mother never cared, yet I allowed myself to be taken in. Carole hasn't changed, she has simply got better at acting.

CHAPTER FORTY-FIVE

Now

The shadows move in the doorway and I can see daylight again. The only problem is the figures causing the shadows are coming towards me, as they descend the steps.

I want to scream, *"Go away!"* but I don't want Thompson to hear the fear in my voice. I don't want him to think he has won, not even for a second.

The dog gets here first.

Thompson clucks his tongue at his companion quickly. 'Wait!'

The animal raises his head and wags his tail cautiously at his owner. It looks at me expectantly, licking its lips. I scramble backwards slowly, unwilling to turn my back on it.

At this moment, I feel hopelessly sorry for little Holly. She is only six years old. She must have been terrified as the beast pounced on her. I wonder what she possibly could have done to set it off on the day of her attack.

His master turns to me. 'What do you think you are doing?'

'I don't know what you mean.' My back hits the wall and I try to slide myself up it and look more composed.

I don't suppose in the dull light, the sweat beading on my face is particularly obvious, but my expression and breathlessness must give me away. My body language too, but I don't dare make any bold movements with that animal in here.

'Why did you come back down here?'

'I don't understand.'

'Didn't that whore up there tell you?' He jabs his finger at the ceiling. 'You have to be caught before you are allowed back in here. You have to earn your lodgings. There is no point in me letting you stay unless you play along with the hunt.'

'I did play along! I ran. You chased me. That's it. It's over.'

'It is not over until I say so!' His voice rises erratically and echoes around the dismal room.

'I'm sorry. I'll do it better next time,' I lie. All the while I'm thinking, "*There won't be a next time, you miserable shit.*" When this cellar door opens again, I'm determined it will be for the last time. Even though I have no idea how to go about orchestrating it at this moment.

Upstairs there is silence. I have the feeling Katrina is listening.

'There won't be a next time at all if you don't do as you are told now. Get up.'

'What?'

'You heard me you stupid bitch. Get on your feet!'

'No.' I fold my arms resolutely across my chest and press myself firmly back into the wall. 'I'm not playing. I want to know what happened to Leah.'

'What happened to her is the least of your worries.'

'Why are you speaking in the past tense? I just want to know the truth. Tell me! Then maybe I will cooperate.'

He actually laughs. It's an open-mouthed laugh. He even turns his head as if to share the joke with someone else. But it is only him and his dog and myself down here.

The remains of Crystal stay motionless. The dark cavities of the eyes stare into my soul from this angle, and I wish I could avoid the burn of her gaze.

When Thompson turns to me again, there is a rigid look about his unshaven face. His dark eyes are wild with an energy he hasn't had during our encounters around town. He seems free to let himself go on this island. 'Your friend is dead. I killed her after she stopped playing along.'

'Where is she now?'

'You mean her body?'

My own mouth sets in a grimace at the thought. 'Yes.'

'She was dinner.' He jerks his head down to the dog at his heels. 'Any rubbish left after that, I dumped in the sea. There is no chance of evidence getting out with these tides. Whatever you throw in always comes back onto the rocks.'

I shake my head. I want to retort something back at Thompson, but can't open my mouth. If I did, I think I might be sick.

'Now, Claire. You will get up and go outside. I know you can be a better-behaved pet than Leah was. I'm not saying she didn't have her uses. But she couldn't follow orders like I know you can.'

'I'm not doing anything you tell me.'

'Yes, you will. Do you really want to end up like Leah? Or Crystal?'

'I don't care!'

The horrible images Thompson has conjured up in my mind regarding Leah's fate won't leave me alone. They are all I can think about. At his words, something inside me has broken. I have suddenly lost the will to run, no matter the consequences.

'If you don't care about yourself, then at

least spare a thought for poor Katrina.'

I look back up at him. 'What do you mean?'

'If you aren't giving me any fun, then she will.' He looks up at the ceiling. 'Won't you, you fucking slag?'

He looks back down at me. 'You can stay locked in here and listen to it. It's been a while since we played. I'm sure she will give me a good time.'

It isn't a conscious decision, but I find myself on my feet all of a sudden.

'Good girl.' Thompson senses his victory and gives a nod. He seems to suppress a smile. 'I'm going to go back outside. You wait for a minute and then you come out too. By now you have realised the boat is gone. You're a smart one. You know that is your only way off the island. So you are going to have to find it.'

'Why don't you just tell me where it is? I can head straight for it and get it over with.'

Thompson turns back to me from the steps. 'The game is over when I say it is. Not a second before! If you don't cooperate, there won't be any more food for a month. That means for both of you.' He jabs his head at the ceiling. 'She will tell you I mean my promises.'

He heads up the steps before turning again and calling back. 'We will start again. You have a sixty-second head start. Then we will play.'

CHAPTER FORTY-SIX

Then

I don't hear from Carole again. It confirms what I suspected. She only got in touch to try and squeeze money out of me. Now she knows she won't get anywhere, she has apparently disappeared back under the grimy stone she crawled out from. Part of me is surprised that she allowed me to walk away so readily. I had half-expected her anger to flare up as it often used to.

Despite my determination to shut her out, part of me feels guilty about what her fate might be. Should I have handed the money over to her anyway? I could have done it as a parting gift. But that might have been the straw that broke the camel's back. What if she overdosed because of me?

I don't need that on my conscience as well. It's already overloaded with things I could have done to prevent Leah's disappearance. I do hope Carole doesn't say anything to Helen about what I have confided in her. My stomach contracts at the thought. Her silence seems slightly ominous, as though she might spring out and catch me unawares. She knows where Helen lives after all, but I'm sure that's just my own paranoia.

Helen still hasn't been in touch for a while, but there might be other reasons for that. I don't trust her not to do something she shouldn't with regard to this Edward Thompson situation. So I learn from my mistakes and continue dropping in more than I probably should.

'I know what you are doing,' she whispers in my ear when I take over a package of cream cakes one day towards the end of the summer holidays. To my relief, however, she seems to be behaving herself.

At work, the atmosphere between James and me feels different since the brief talk we had in the car park. The air is charged and something untapped hangs in it. It is like he wants to make a move or nudge me into making one.

The only problem is, I'm not sure how I feel about him. Do I have enough of a tug towards him to give things another go? If I have to ask myself the question, I think I know what the answer is.

But perhaps I should make some attempt to get my life together. If my interactions with Carole have taught me anything, it is that I probably should move forward. Despite her nefarious intentions, she advised me to move on the same as Helen did. Perhaps I should start listening.

James and I end up in the same lunch queue one day at work. The line is bustling and the tea room is noisier than ever so we don't exactly get a chance to talk. Today I have the feeling that he is trying to casually prompt me into spilling my weekend plans.

I'm on the verge of doing so when the phone I have out and ready with GooglePay buzzes in my hand.

I see Tony's name on the screen and my stomach immediately clenches. Tony never calls me. If he gets in touch it is always a text or a ring on the doorbell.

I press my phone to my ear. 'Hello? Tony? Is everything all right?'

'Claire.' His tone is short as always. But there is something else in his voice. Something I haven't heard since the time shortly after Leah went missing.

'What is it? What's happened? Have they found Leah?'

'No, nothing like that. It's Helen. She's … I don't know how to say it.'

'Has she been arrested again?'

'Eh? Arrested? No, of course not. I've never known anyone more honest, like. Do the police suspect her of having hurt her own daughter?'

'No, not at all. So what is it?'

'She's been in an accident.'

'What kind of accident?'

'Well, I don't know if that is what I would call it. Someone hit her with their car as she was leaving work. They didn't stop.'

The room seems to spin around me. 'A hit and run?'

'Yeah. June from work heard the whole thing and went running out to see her lying on the pavement - ' His voice cracks unexpectedly.

I feel something tug deep inside of me too. My heart pounds in my ears. 'Is she OK?'

Uncle Tony clears his throat. 'She was rushed to hospital. Apparently, she is conscious. I mean, I don't know about this sort of thing. I haven't got there myself yet. I'm on my way now. They think Helen might have a broken hip and a concussion.'

'Oh my god.' A million questions run through my head. 'I'll come to the hospital right away.'

'Yes, you do that. I'll see you there.'

I leave my place in the queue of the tea room, barely noticing James's look of surprise when I explain what has happened.

All I can think about now is Helen. I need to be there for her now no matter what.

CHAPTER FORTY-SEVEN

Now

'For fuck's sake! Why did you have to argue with him? Didn't I tell you, just do what he says? You'll get an easier life.'

'I don't want to spend the rest of my life here! I just wanted to know what happened to my friend.'

'You've got thirty seconds left. You had better get going.'

'What? I can't!'

'Yes, you can. You heard him. He will starve both of us if you don't get out there right now!' There is a pause. Then Katrina's abruptly softer voice scares me. 'Please, Claire.'

Guilt stabs at my insides. I don't want Katrina to suffer. Having a fellow inmate is actually a disadvantage here. That creep can play us against each other, even if we have given up caring for ourselves, we can't stand to hear the other one tortured.

Katrina is already so thin. I've probably got enough reserve on me to take a hit. Would he really starve us for a whole month?

'Come on!' Katrina urges. 'Get going. He means it!'

My thoughts are jumbled with news of Leah's fate and what it means. Along with the possible locations of the boat on this island that I'm not overly familiar with. Katrina's pleas only add to the chaos.

'Katrina, just be quiet for a minute and let me think!'

'You haven't got a minute. It's been sixty seconds already! Just get out of here and start running!'

'I can't! If we keep doing what we are told, then we will never get out of here. We have to break the cycle.'

'What about waiting for him to slip up?'

'We can't wait. Besides, how do we know something won't happen to him whilst he is away? He could have a heart attack or crash his car. He could even fall off the boat in between here and the mainland. We can't rely on him forever to survive. You know that!'

'You're wrecking my head with all this! Just get out, you stupid cow! Please!'

I grab panicked fistfuls of hair before I think of what to do. I turn and blink up at the ceiling.

The increased light pouring in from outside allows me to see the gap through which Katrina has been talking to me. The hole is quite big, by the look of it. I must have done well to avoid it when I was stumbling around in the dark kitchen upstairs. There is just a thin strip of wood in the way. I'm guessing it is a rotten floorboard.

I jump up and my fingers grasp the wood before I slip off again. I try again.

'What are you doing now, you crazy bitch?!'

'I need to get this wood out of the way. You have to help me!'

'What? No!'

'Please. Just give it a good stomp or tug. Please!'

'I can't. Just go away! Why can't you just do as you are told?'

'Because this is our chance. We have to strike at him when he isn't expecting it. When I don't come out of this cellar, he will come back down here. We can attack him from above. Remember that broken plate? We can take a shard each. He won't know what has hit him.'

'But - '

'And the dog can't get us from down here. It's the perfect plan.'

Katrina swears, I hear her shift and move around. At first, I think she has started pacing around in frustration. Then the wooden floorboard slides easily out of place.

She appears to flatten herself against the floor upstairs and reaches out her arms. 'Give me your hands.'

I stretch up gratefully and her thin hands cling onto my forearms. Despite her lack of body fat, she is surprisingly strong. But not strong enough. She doesn't have the ability to move me more than a few inches off the ground.

Barking erupts outside. The pair of hunters are wondering where I am, no doubt. I bite my lip, not wanting to panic Katrina further. I'm relying on her cooperation. My life depends on it.

She lets go of me and I land in my socks on the concrete floor again.

'I can't do it,' she pants, defeated, rolling onto her side. Her dirty hair clings to her forehead. 'Please just run!'

'No! I think I can see a pipe. Is that what the dark shape is to your right?'

She shrugs. 'Yeah.'

More barking pierces the air outside. This time, it echoes around the cellar. I know Katrina can hear it too. I can just about make out the whites of her eyes as she stares down at me.

I look back at her imploringly. 'Please try. This is our only chance. We might not get another one.'

She rolls back over again and slides her arms back through the gap.

'That's it!' I wait for the advantage she gives me in height. It's a little more this time. She groans with the effort of clinging onto me and there is a horrible crunch, but I manage to swing my arm out and grip hold of the pipe. It is thinner than I expect and it bends and swings down unexpectedly.

There is a metallic twang somewhere, but I grab more of it with my other arm. Katrina rolls over and disappears out of sight.

Then I see her silhouette throw all her weight against something in the darkness upstairs.

Now I am elevated enough to find a grip in another gappy floorboard. I heave myself up. My muscles burn and scream at me, but I push through it. Katrina's thin arms grab me around the waist and it is just enough for me to slide my legs up into the darkness too. My knees connect with the rotten floor confirming my success.

Katrina's voice is close to my ear now. 'Come on! Get up!'

I scramble to my feet. I think I hear the dog's bark echoing around the cellar below. But I can't see it. I must have clambered out just in time before I was spotted.

Katrina presses a shard of ceramic into my hand.

'There,' she breathes in my ear. 'Make sure you get him in the neck. Or the eye if it is a good swing. Just don't mess this up. He will make us both wish we were never born. Even more than we already do.'

I nod, then realise, she might not be able to see it. I lower my body flat on the floor, just as she must have done moments ago.

There is a good view of the cellar from here. I must be right above where Thompson was when he was talking to me before.

As soon as he reappears to come and punish me for not running, I'll take my shot. It's going to be a very small window of opportunity. I'm frustrated with Katrina for not thinking to try this when he was talking to me and distracted.

It is going to be harder for me to get away with this now. But I can probably put more force into the attack than she could have done.

'Come on,' she whispers close to my ear again. 'Where is he?'

'Shhh,' I breathe back at her. 'He'll hear you!'

'He isn't coming! He knows what we are planning to do!'

'Don't be silly. He can't know. He will come down to see where I've gone. He will have to check I'm not hiding in the corner or something!'

But Thompson still doesn't turn up, nor can I see or hear the German shepherd. The minutes tick by at a painfully slow pace. My anxiety grows with every passing moment.

Katrina swears. 'You shouldn't have done this! He is going to have at us both now! What have you done? I'll tell him it was your idea!'

I shake my head and hope she will quieten down. 'This won't work if he hears us!'

It turns out Katrina may have been right however when the front door of the farmhouse suddenly opens, illuminating us both.

CHAPTER FORTY-EIGHT

Then

I pick up some obligatory flowers when I pass the Asda in Ventura Park. It seems like the right thing to do. My world seems to be in turmoil at the moment, so I take the rest of the day off work. I tell my boss there has been a death in the family. I just hope by the time I make it to the hospital that my lie hasn't somehow become the truth.

I'm forced to ditch my colourful floral offering before I even make it past the main desk though as Helen is in intensive care. Instead, I hand the bunch to an elderly lady with long brittle hair being wheeled towards a taxi outside.

She beams at me and inhales the scent. 'Oh, carnations, how lovely. Reminds me of my wedding bouquet. Bless you, girlie.'

In a ward upstairs, I find Tony hovering awkwardly near a vending machine.

'Claire, love.' He pulls me into his idea of an awkward one-armed hug, which is mainly a pat on the back. 'You came straight over.'

'I did. I couldn't stay at work and worry about her all day. How is she?'

'The doctor is with her now. I haven't seen her yet either. I don't know what kind of state she is in. They just said she was stable and awake, but I wasn't allowed to bring flowers.'

'Same with me.'

He sighs and looks up at the strip lighting overhead with watery eyes. There aren't any windows in this area. 'First Leah, now Helen. What's going on, eh?'

I bite my lip. From his surprise on the phone, Tony knows nothing of Helen's arrest or her private investigations. I'm not sure now is a good time to fill him in. I just hope what has happened is a random coincidence and unrelated to the person Helen has held firmly in her sights. 'I don't know.'

Tony sinks down onto one of the well-worn chairs nearby and I join him. 'We've never had a big family, me and Helen.'

'Yes, I know.' I want to tell Tony I can relate and I feel his pain just as much as him, but I can't find the words. My head is a mess. All this seems surreal.

'It was always just the two of us growing up. Our parents went young. You know that already, don't you? You just don't expect something like this to happen. A hit-and-run is something you expect to hear about on the news, not down the phone. Like our Leah. It's like living in a nightmare you can't wake up from.'

My own chin wobbles now and I try to bite down tears.

A flurry of black in the corner of my vision leads me to turn and see two police officers appear beside us. We both scramble to our feet.

The male and female officers take basic details from Tony with interjections from me too. Tony tells them that Helen was leaving work when the incident happened. The sandwich shop she works at is a small business. No, he doesn't know whether there is a surveillance camera.

A pencil darts across a notepad the whole time. It seems so meagre to see Helen's routine and movements condensed into a few notes jotted down on a small piece of paper.

When it comes to the part where the police ask for any known enemies Helen had, Tony gets a little agitated. 'She didn't have any enemies. She was the nicest lady you could ask to meet.' He jerks his head at me. 'Tell them, Claire.'

I look from Tony's adamant face to the police officer with her poised pencil. 'I don't know. Can I talk to you alone for a minute?'

Tony blinks at me. 'Eh? What's going on?'

'I'll tell you later,' I lie.

When we have moved down the corridor where Tony can't hear us, I reveal my suspicions to the officers about Edward Thompson.

The female officer jots down the details hurriedly. Her name escapes me. Today has been such a whirlwind and I seem to have dealt with the police a lot in the last couple of years.

She looks up at me now. 'You said you told Detective Halliwell about this person already, yes?'

'Yes, I did. But he didn't think there was anything in it. So Helen went off and looked into it herself. She ended up breaking into his house. I wish I hadn't opened my stupid mouth about the guy now.'

'You don't know it was him who was responsible for what has happened today. Hit-and-runs are quite common, sadly. It usually is an accident, even if the person doesn't come forward right away. We will take a look into this further. Hopefully, the person will hand themselves in.'

I nod, feeling completely frustrated and helpless. 'Is there anything else I can do to help?'

The male officer speaks up now. 'Not unless you can think of any other individuals who could hurt your mother.'

'Helen's not my real mother. She adopted me when I was twelve. My real mother is ... '

I pause all of a sudden. Could Helen's visit to

the hospital have anything to do with Carole?

The officers glance at each other briefly. The female officer prompts me along. 'Your real mother is what?'

'I … I don't know. She contacted me recently and tried to get involved with my life. I hadn't seen her since I was four.'

This gets jotted down. 'And your biological mother got in touch when?'

'A few months ago.'

'What do you mean, she tried to get involved with your life? Did you not want her to be?'

'I don't know. I was starting to give her a chance, but then … she let me down.'

'Let you down how?'

'She wanted money from me. That was all she wanted the whole time. I thought she had changed and regretted letting me go.'

'Did you give her any money?'

'No.'

'How did your birth mother react when you said no, Claire?'

I shrug, thinking back to that sunny day in the beer garden. 'She wasn't happy. She tried to get me to stay. But I told her I didn't need her and that I was lucky that a better family that took me in.'

My heart sinks. I don't know Carole well enough to know what she is capable of. Did she hit Helen with a car as revenge for me not helping her out? Or because she was angry that I have another mother I truly love. I don't even know if Carole can drive. I'm sure she is in touch with questionable people though, any of whom might have been willing to help their companion if she asked them for a favour.

The officer takes notes as say everything I know about Carole. I realise I don't even know her address.

I return to Tony feeling numb and slump down on the seat next to him.

'What was all that about then?' he asks, nodding at the uniformed officers as they walk away.

'They just needed some details. They are exploring all possibilities, even small ones. As you said, Helen is so nice to everyone. She doesn't have enemies. The police just need to find who did this.'

He nods, his eyes watering uncharacteristically. 'I just need her to be OK, Claire. I don't know what I will do if she isn't.'

'Helen is the strongest person I know, Tony. She will be fine. She has to be.' I try to sound convincing but the doubt in my own voice is palpable.

The two of us sit in mutual silence for while pondering various possibilities.

Eventually, Tony seems unable to take any more. He tells me stories of himself and Helen growing up together. Most of them are tales Leah and I have heard many times before. But he shares a new one of the time he and Helen went rock pooling with their parents in Dorset. It all sounds idyllic.

As he talks, guilt sinks into my insides. Tony might lose Helen because of me. Whichever way I look at it, this is my fault; whether it was because I told Helen about Edward Thompson, or because my birth mother wanted to get back into my life, I'm the one to blame.

I can't help but feel a pang of jealousy. Their sibling bond is so strong. You only have to see them together to know that. I've had a taste of it with Leah. I just hope Tony doesn't lose his sister now too.

Because if he does, I'll never be able to forgive myself.

CHAPTER FORTY-NINE

Now

L ight illuminates the scene. For a moment, I see the ridiculousness of the situation as though we are in suspended animation.

I'm lying on the floor above the hole, waiting to slide my arms through. My piece of plate is gripped in my hand; it is now that I see it is a fragment of one of those white and blue-patterned old sorts, probably an antique.

Katrina crouches beside me. Her thin and terrified face is turned towards the front door where Edward Thompson and his dog are silhouetted.

Her expression is a stark contrast to that of the man. He looks furious.

Thompson strides into the room. His

walking boots make a dull thud that echoes menacingly. I suppose he does it on purpose to elicit as much fear as possible, but it is effective, nevertheless. The sound is accompanied by claws on the stone floor.

I struggle to scramble to my feet.

Katrina manages it before me and shrinks towards the nearest wall, as though keen to demonstrate her opposition to me and my plan. 'She did it! It was her idea! She climbed up by herself!'

Thompson doesn't even glance at her. 'Shut it!'

His eyes are fixed on mine. I hate to consider it, but I fear my expression is just as obviously afraid as Katrina's.

He stops just short of me, level with her. 'Didn't I tell you this would be made harder? All you had to do was do as you were told. Why didn't you run?'

'I'm not going to. Not after what you did to Leah. I'm not going to be another one of your victims. I only wanted to find out what happened to my friend. Katrina said she was still alive.'

Thompson seems to cringe at the use of names. Perhaps he doesn't like thinking of his pets as human beings. 'And now you know. It's a shame you let this worthless piece of shit get your hopes up. She used to lie for a living. She made a career out of it. Why would you listen to her?'

He gestures towards Katrina who keeps quiet, as though hoping to be forgotten if punishments are being doled out. 'Your friend was alive, and certainly kicking. But then she became difficult. Suddenly, doing what she was told was too good for her. So she became boring. We had our fun together then she was finished.'

'No,' I whisper.

Out of the corner of my eye, Katrina's form seems to slump in on itself. This news is a shock to her too. She had genuinely believed Leah was still alive.

Thompson's lips pull themselves into a smirk. 'If you behave yourself and do as you are told, I can take you out as a reward and find a piece of her you can keep. I see you found her watch. How about a shoe? Or the pair if we can find them. Looks like you could use something on your feet. It might make you run better when we go hunting.'

Fury causes my face to spasm. It is now that I realise the sharp shard of the plate is still in my hand, mostly tucked out of sight up my sleeve. I grip it tightly. It is more than obvious that one false move will see me attacked and injured, whether by this man or his dog. But the thought of Thompson hurting Leah and desecrating her remains afterwards is too much to bear.

'I'm not going to do a single thing you tell me! You killed my best friend.' My voice breaks despite my fury. The dog is still, watching me shout with a stiff tail. 'I won't play your games!'

Thompson's expression darkens. He can tell by my resolve I am serious. He gives a brief nod and then glances at Katrina. 'OK then. This one can take your place. Anything that happens to her next is on you.'

He gestures towards the door. 'Start running.'

Katrina doesn't need much instruction. Her mouth has become a tight thin line. Her hollow eyes look back at me fearfully as she stops leaning against the wall and her bare feet take her weight again.

I shake my head at her quickly. 'No! Don't do this!'

She ignores me. She allows her filthy duvet to slide off her shoulders, revealing her painfully thin body now in the light of day. She is dressed in what was obviously once a form-fitting red dress. Now it is stained and bulges loosely over her stomach and hips. Katrina's collarbone is especially visible beneath the thin straps of her revealing garment.

Her bare feet slap against the concrete until she reaches the doorway and slips out of sight in silence. The dog wags his tail a little as he sniffs the air after her.

The pair watch Katrina through the doorway. Thompson keeps his back to me as he watches the woman's figure move into the distance. The dog ventures out and sniffs the grass, head low. He is raring to go.

Neither notice as I creep forwards with the shard I've slipped out of my sleeve. There is a bare area of neck beneath my captor's coat collar. I raise my hand to strike.

Unfortunately, he turns at the last minute and spots me just as I am inches from my target.

He gives a muffled roar as he turns and swiftly grabs my arm. He twists my wrist with ease. My bones are compressed under his vice-like grip and I fear they may break.

His fingers dig viciously into the recent teeth marks left behind by his companion on his last attack, reopening the little wounds.

An involuntary groan of pain leaves me. At this, the dog appears at his master's side. Now I scream out as sharp teeth dig through the denim around my ankle.

The shard of ceramic slips from my hand in shock and I know it is all over.

CHAPTER FIFTY

Then

I t is a good month before Helen is allowed home from the hospital. Even then, she has to use a crutch to support herself. Tony insists on having her live with him until she has fully recovered.

Part of the reasoning behind that is so he can protect his little sister from anyone who might wish her harm, even if he doesn't understand who that might be.

He has asked me once or twice about what I said to the police after they left the hospital that day, but I didn't tell him the full truth. I couldn't bring myself to when Helen made me promise not to tell him about her arrest.

Tony goes out to collect some groceries to

stock up his fridge. Helen uses this opportunity to admit what really happened just days before she was hit by the car when

Helen reveals she made a call to social services and explained her suspicions about Holly to them.

'Oh, Helen! Why didn't you tell me you were going to do that?'

She shrugs. 'I couldn't just sit around and feel sorry for that little girl when she could be in danger. We both know her parents were lying about what really happened to her. I didn't want to drag you down too.'

'But we didn't know that for sure.'

'That is what child protective services exist for. They can make their own investigations and come to a conclusion based on what they see and the evidence in front of them. I had to call them.'

'But that is probably what almost got you killed.'

'That is why I told you to stay out of it, Claire. I'll handle this.'

'But look where this has got you - a stay in the hospital. Meanwhile, Thompson is sitting pretty. The police couldn't get anything on him you know. He has a watertight alibi for the day you were struck.'

'I know. Detective Halliwell told me. He was caught plain as day on the CCTV camera at McDonald's with Holly. There is no way he could have been in two places at once. He obviously put a friend up to it, but June only has a CCTV aimed at the till. We will never know who was driving the car.'

'Are you sure you didn't see them?'

'Positive. I was facing the other way. Never saw them coming. I blacked out straight away. You don't expect a car to mount the pavement in the middle of the day, do you?'

'No, you certainly don't. Did the police say anything about Carole?'

Helen nods. 'Yes, dear. They don't think she was involved. It looks like she was in Birmingham that day. It couldn't have been her. I'm a little surprised you mentioned her in that context to the police. Do you really think she would have been capable?'

I lean my head back on Tony's leather sofa and sigh at the ceiling. 'I don't know. I thought she had changed. But she just wanted money. She is quite a good actress. For a while, I thought she might actually have had a change of heart and care about me. But it was all a lie. I really had no idea how she was going to react.'

'Well, she seems to be out of the picture again. Are you sure that is what you want?'

'Yes, definitely. So you haven't heard from her then?'

Helen looks puzzled. No, of course not. I would have mentioned it.'

'Good. And promise me you won't play investigator on this Thompson thing. I mean it,

Helen. Please. I can't lose you too.'

Much to Helen's complaint, I find myself finding ways to take care of her over the next few months, supplementing Tony's efforts as much as I can. She isn't used to so much fuss. I know it hurts her to be the one waited on hand and foot when normally she is the mother hen clucking around after everyone. Her broken hip is improving, but it is a frustratingly slow process, most of all for her.

I cook for Helen and Tony one day after work at the beginning of October. It's a quick dinner of sausages and Yorkshire puddings, but I know it will go down well. It is one of their childhood favourites they have been reminiscing about lately. I just hope they don't mind the store-bought shortcuts I've made.

I haven't had much time after work today, even though the quiet season is upon us at the park. I've been running around taking care of maintenance issues; wear and tear mainly after a hectic summer.

Tony is outside in the back garden, sweeping leaves from his neat path.

The food is almost ready. I tip some frozen Yorkshire puddings onto a tray and slide it into the oven.

I hear the toilet flush and go through to check Helen has made it downstairs and back to the sofa OK as is my habit these days. When I peer around the door, I see she has made it upstairs, down again and across to the place she has adopted on the sofa. But she seems stuck on her crutch before she is able to settle her weight on the seat.

I rush over and put my arms out to support her. 'Do you need some help?'

'What's this?' She points down at my phone I've carelessly left on the footstool.

I look at it in confusion for a second before I realise James's name is on the screen. Helen isn't stuck at all, she has just paused to read the contents of the text notification.

I snatch it up and see the snippet of the message she is referring to. My cheeks redden. 'Oh, nothing.'

'It looks like an invitation for a date. You didn't tell me you had a bloke interested in you.

'I don't. I mean, we already dated. I don't know if I want to get back together with him or not.'

'James,' Helen says thoughtfully. 'He is that bloke that came out for your birthday drinks one time wasn't he?'

I help Helen down into her position on the sofa. 'It's amazing how good your memory is for things like that.'

She means business when she mutes The Chase on the television and looks at me seriously. 'Claire, it would be nice for you to have some company. Don't you think it is about time you moved on?'

I don't ask what or whom she is asking me to move on from. It must be obvious by now. 'I'm too busy,' I lie.

'Claire. Don't put your whole life on hold because of me. Or Leah. I think we have to admit certain truths now. We have to be honest. She isn't coming back.'

The sudden harshness of Helen's words paralyses me where I stand.

We have skirted the subject for a while, talked around it, and left it unsaid in the air between us. Now we are finally having the conversation I've been dreading.

Helen gives a single nod as she blinks back tears. 'It's been almost two years now. I don't know what happened to our Leah. But if she was still alive she would have come back to us by now. We all now know that.'

I open my mouth to argue. I want to throw up all the examples of missing people who have returned years, even decades later. But I can't. I know none of them are truly relevant now. Helen is right, her daughter would never leave us like this.

Something terrible must have happened to her, whether Edward Thompson is responsible or not.

The hit of reality makes my breath catch in my chest. I sink down onto the sofa too.

Tears continue to form in Helen's eyes. She smooths out a crease in the knee of my jeans unnecessarily. 'It breaks my heart to say it, but Leah can't be alive now, no matter who did it or what happened or why. I just hope she didn't suffer too much.'

Helen's voice fails her now and I feel my own face tense. I forget trying to swallow down the lump in my throat and pull the closest thing I have to a mum towards me.

We sit like that for I don't even know how long. Eventually, Helen pulls back and dabs at her eyes with the heel of her hand.

I get up to fetch a box of tissues from the kitchen. It is then that I see the smoke filtering from the oven I'd completely forgotten about. I slide the tray out. Judging from the state of it we might be having a takeaway when Tony gets back inside.

Back in the living room, Helen takes a handful of tissues and works on sorting her mascara. Leah never framed those inherited eyes with much makeup. She didn't need it. She had such dark lashes I always assumed she got from her father.

There I go again, thinking in the past tense. 'It's a scary thought, suddenly thinking that all my experiences of Leah are in the past. It is hard to imagine there won't be any more of her in the future.'

'It's what is still left to come that you need to think of now, Claire. You have to let Leah go.'

'I wouldn't know how to do that. She has

been the most important part of my life for so long.'

'Same here. But the difference between us is, you are still young. I know it's hard. Leah would want you to go on living your life.'

'What about Edward Thompson? He is dangerous. I don't want you being under threat.'

'Tony will take care of me here. I don't plan on doing anything to put either of us at risk. I don't want to lose him too. I'll keep my eyes open though, the last thing I want is to go before I find out the truth, whatever it might be. Bad people slip up eventually. We just have to watch and wait until they do.'

CHAPTER FIFTY-ONE

Now

It's dark again. I break out in a cold sweat as I lie on the concrete floor. My cheek is pressed against the dusty surface. I'll get up in a little while. I just have to breathe through the pain first.

Then I'll try my leg to see if I can put my weight on it. I can't see the damage in the dark. I know Katrina had an ankle wound inflicted by the animal. Hopefully, mine won't turn out to be much worse than hers. She said she has suffered through various maladies in this place. If she can make it, so can I.

Thompson called off his mutt after it tore into my leg enough to subdue me. It was a punishment and a warning. 'Next time, you won't be so lucky,' he told me as he slammed the farmhouse door shut behind him.

The sound of the dog barking is audible in the distance. I hope Katrina is OK. It sounds like she is being given a generous head start. Thompson is stoking her terror just for his amusement. Perhaps he will play a longer game now, to make up for the disappointment I caused him.

The hound is already in a frenzy because of me. The taste of blood is on its tongue. Whatever happens to Katrina now will forever be on my conscience. I've brought this punishment on her. I hope she realises I was only trying to liberate us both.

After a few moments, I heave myself into a sitting position. My ankle throbs. It's frustrating not being able to see how bad the injury is. My hands work down my leg, squeezing and exploring tentatively.

The pain seems to be mainly on the surface. As long as there isn't an infection, I suppose I'll live. But for how long in this place, I just don't know.

My heart breaks for Leah and I feel my face give way to a wave of grief. The image of the violent waves near the rocks springs out of the darkness before my eyes. Was my best friend down beneath the churning water the entire time I've been on this island?

The false hope of having found her watch

stings me, as does Katrina's suggestion Leah could still be alive. I grip the wristband of the watch and stroke it with my thumb. This is all I have left of my best friend.

I'll never have the chance to be close to her again. What were her last moments like? Thompson neglected to tell me how he killed her. Perhaps if I play along next time, I can barter the information from his vile lips.

The farmhouse seems marginally more welcoming in comparison to the cellar. I was locked down there in isolation for breaking the rules. At least when Katrina gets back, it will feel more like company if I'm not having to talk to her through a gap in the floor.

I just hope my new friend makes it back. I can't imagine being like her, living in solitary confinement for so long, aside from brief episodes with Crystal and Leah. The experience has worn her down. She now believes there is no escape from this prison.

Like a caged bird that has seen others of its kind hit themselves against the bars too many times. Despite Katrina's initial yearning for freedom, she has resigned herself to the fact that her confinement is permanent. She didn't even react when she knew the back door was unlocked.

The thought starts a fire in my brain. The back door. Could it still be unlocked? Would Thompson have overlooked it with everything that has been going on? Had he locked it again as Katrina had said, or was she lying to me as I suspected at the time?

I force myself first onto my knees and then my feet. My ankle throbs as my blood surges, but the injury doesn't seem as deep as I first suspected.

At least I can walk. Gratitude fills me at this small win.

I reach out blindly and move to the back of the property. My feet stumble as I reach the kitchen doorway. There is just enough light coming from the hole in the floor to avoid stepping into it.

My fingers grip the door knob. I throw my weight into it and give it a good shove. To my amazement, it opens. My bloody hands come into view, gripping the tarnished brass knob.

I push it out all the way and step out onto the grass. My feet are cold and wet again, but the feeling of illicit freedom is intoxicating.

Thompson is occupied and I suspect he didn't have the gun he supposedly owns on him. I have a short window with which I can take him by surprise.

This time he will never see me coming.

CHAPTER FIFTY-TWO

Now

The pain in my ankle slips away as a new wave of adrenaline kicks in. I don't have much time. I've shut the farmhouse door behind me, but it won't take long for Thompson to realise I'm not in the building as he expects.

Or will it? Will he simply open the front door and throw Katrina's injured form inside? I could have more time than I realise. But my captor will figure out soon enough that I'm not locked away. Surely the first thing he will do is head back to the farmhouse. And that is right where I am heading now.

There will be weapons, makeshift or otherwise. I wonder what happened to my pepper spray; there might still be some left inside. Besides, Katrina said Crystal was shot. That gun must on this island somewhere too. I can't imagine Thompson taking it to the mainland where he could be caught with it. This place is the perfect hiding place for a weapon like that, along with anything else he wants to remain hidden, like us women.

Thompson doesn't seem to take the gun hunting with him. He doesn't want his pets to get too badly injured unless they really misbehave.

It sounded like he made an example of Crystal because she was too disobedient. I can imagine my fate may be similar and perhaps even closer than I think. What will my captor do when he realises I have escaped without him realising? It could be what finally pushes him over the edge. Is that what Leah did? Perhaps that is the crime that required the sentence of her life.

I keep my body low as I jog through the matted grass over to the other farmhouse. There is no eruption of barking as I approach the old stone building. I snatch at the flimsy handle and push it open.

It is almost a surprise to find the door isn't locked. Didn't Thompson expect his women to head for this place? Or were they all expected to head straight for the boat instead?

I fear this is a trap, that I've been led here on purpose. But that is the kind of thinking Katrina falls into. Unless she is still in league with our captor. Perhaps the two of them cooked this up together.

I shake the thoughts away. The fear in Katrina's eyes as she left to be hunted was real. She may have relied on her ability to act for a living once, but she couldn't fake terror like that.

Inside this farmhouse, it's terribly damp. Worse than the building I just left, slightly warmer though. The faded wallpaper is spattered with green and peeling from the walls in places. The tiny sofa and chair are flattened with age and the lace draped over the back is black with mould.

Oddly, the old porcelain ornaments of animals on the mantelpiece are free from the dust that is everywhere in the other house. Does Thompson actually take care of cleaning them? He has done a half-hearted job if he has. I wonder why he has bothered.

The main difference in here is the light. Not only from the small windows but also from the fireplace. The low flames hiss and crack loudly, as though they know I shouldn't be here and want to call me out.

I'm aware I'm running out of time, so I quickly scan around for something I can use. There is a stand of brass tools beside the fireplace. I rush over and grab the most robust one I can find. A thin poker with a sharp-looking end.

I feel immediately more well-equipped with it firmly in my hands. I may be running around in my socks, but the makeshift weapon is weighty within my grip. Or maybe I am just so fatigued from being half-starved. My stomach continues to burn at the edge of my consciousness.

Nevertheless, I'll keep hold of it whilst I search for the gun, if there is one.

But then fear rises in me immediately when I hear movement behind me.

At first, I'm frozen in horror. Then I find the bravery to quickly turn all at once and face the figure that has emerged from the doorway.

When I do, several of my questions are answered all at once. For one, I've located the shotgun. It is being aimed right at my face.

Secondly, a two-year-long doubt that has burned a hole right through my insides is now put to an end.

The person on the other end of the barrel is so familiar, her face might as well be etched onto the inside of my skull.

It's Leah.

CHAPTER FIFTY-THREE

Now

'Leah?'

There is no softening of features immediately. It takes a few blinks for the woman standing across the room to show even a spark of recognition.

Her bleary gaze moves over me before coming back to rest on my face. 'Claire?'

'Yes, it's me.' I drop the brass poker on the sofa and rush over to my friend.

She doesn't put down the shotgun but allows me to push it aside enough so I can pull her into a hug.

I'm only able to embrace her from the side, due to her reluctance to let go of her weapon. Nevertheless, this is the hug that has been two years coming. At times I feared it would never happen.

'I can't believe you're here.' I pull back again so I can look into those familiar patterned irises. Leah's face is pale as though starved of the sun. Yet, the summer freckles she would sometimes have pop now more than ever on her nose and cheeks.

She isn't quite as thin as I had pictured recently though. Her cheeks are fuller than ever, in fact. Her fingers are puffy too beneath my grip as I squeeze her hand.

I blink away tears of joy, relief and disbelief. 'He told me you were dead. He said he had killed you and thrown your body in the sea.'

Leah says nothing. She just blinks at me.

'Have you been living in here since he took you from the other building?'

She nods.

'It must have been horrible on your own.'

'He locks me in when he goes away so I can't go over and talk to Katrina.'

Like the other captive, Leah's voice is flat. It breaks my heart to fear how dull her tone is; it is so far removed from the vivacious, laughter-filled voice that has haunted my consciousness these past two years.

Like Katrina, Leah has a thick blanket wrapped around her shoulders to keep away the cold, except my friend's is knotted at the side to keep her hands free. And unlike Katrina, Leah's blanket makes her look bigger than I know she is. I dread to think how thin she is underneath it all.

She watches me blankly, as though I am a television program she is only half-interested in. The rest of her mind seems elsewhere. This isn't the reunion I have fantasised about.

I prise the shotgun reluctantly from Leah's grip and rest it against the back of the small sofa nearby. Then I grip both of her hands in mine. 'Are you OK?'

'I don't know. Why do you care?' She shrugs. Her vague reactions trouble me. There is something really wrong here.

'Leah, it's me. It's Claire.'

'I know who you are,' she retorts quickly.

'What's the matter? I've been so worried about you. I thought you were … gone. I didn't think I would ever see you again!'

I reach out and stroke her cheek with my hand. It isn't as icy cold as I expect. The crackling fire, low as it is, gives out a surprising amount of heat.

'I'm surprised you have even spared me a thought. I heard you were busy with your new husband.'

'Husband? What are you talking about?'

'James. Ed told me you got married less than six months after I got here. You gave up on me pretty fast. It sounded like you decided I wasn't coming back and thought you should stumble into the first bloke you could find and have his baby.'

'His what? Of course not! None of that is true. I see James at work, that's all. Everyone has been so worried about you. Helen and Tony too. We have all been desperate for any news!'

Leah stares at me. Her mouth opens slightly. 'My mum is dead. So is Uncle Tony.'

'No, they're not. They are both fine. Worried, but fine.' I bite my lip when I consider explaining Helen's accident, but decide against it. Leah seems confused enough.

Unfortunately, she notices this. 'You're lying.'

'No! Of course not. Your mum is fine. She is soldering on - you know her. She won't rest until she finds out what happened to you. And Tony is taking care of her. She moved in with him a little while ago.'

'Mum wouldn't do that. She hated living with Tony when they were kids. She likes her own space.'

I nod hurriedly. 'Yes, I know. But your mum, well, she had a little accident. She got hit by a car - but she is OK. She bounced back pretty quickly after she left the hospital. She can walk again now, she just has a little limp, otherwise, you wouldn't notice. You know she is tough as nails. Like you.'

Leah doesn't react much to this. It seems to be taking too long for her to follow what I've said.

I glance over my shoulder towards the

window. 'Look, we need to get out of here. Thompson could come back any moment.'

'He won't. He goes off to the shack on the other side of the island after a hunt.'

'Shack? I don't know where that is. We still have to hurry. Come on.'

I pull her by the hands and pick up the shotgun again. But Leah digs her heels in with surprising strength.

I look at her in surprise. She just watches my eyes carefully with her intensely coloured ones. 'Are you saying, you and James aren't married?'

'Yes, I'm not definitely married. James and I are just coworkers.'

'So you don't see him outside of work?'

'No.'

'What about your baby?'

'I don't have one. Not even close. You know me.'

She studies my face for a trace of deceit. 'Are you telling the truth?'

'Yes, *definitely*. There is no baby and the closest I get to seeing James is at lunch at work sometimes, or in the car park on the way in or out of the park.

The last time I really spoke to James springs to my mind now. 'The last real conversation I had with him was in the summer. He told me you had a talk with him. He said you were the one who said I wasn't into him and that is why he ended things with me.'

Leah blinks as though she can't quite believe what she is hearing. Then she stares down at the rotten old floorboards. Even an estate agent would have a hard time passing them off as merely rustic. 'Yes, I remember saying that. I wanted you to break up with him. That seems like so long ago.'

'Well, it sort of was. I've moved on since then. He is in the past. No more James for me, OK?'

I give Leah's puffy hands a reassuring squeeze. 'Look, I don't know why Edward Thompson has lied to you. Katrina said he likes to mess with our minds. It is one of his sick games, that's all.'

'He does that sometimes. It is hard to tell fiction from what is real. But Ed had a difficult childhood here.'

Leah casts her gaze over to the nearby shelf. There are faded photographs in little old frames. The nearest one is of a man and a woman in a rugged landscape. Between them is a little boy with a brooding demeanour. The thick eyebrows and familiar dark green eyes can't be mistaken. They form a key part of the face I've come to hate with a passion I've never felt before.

'Is that him in the photo?'

Leah nods. 'I don't know why he keeps the photos. He hated growing up here. Plus it's another thing I have to dust. I know I don't have to. But it keeps me busy. Ed goes away for ages and there isn't anything else to do.'

My friend's use of a nickname for our captor troubles me. 'Why do you keep calling him that?'

She shrugs. 'He told me to. It's what his wife calls him as well.'

I glance over Leah's form for signs of injury. I conclude she seems to be standing fine. 'Are you hurt? Does he take you out and hunt you like with Katrina? He said he has eased off her a little bit before I got here.'

Leah closes her eyes and grimaces. 'He doesn't chase me anymore. I stopped cooperating, so he took me away from the other farmhouse. He tied me up upstairs and found another purpose I can serve. I've been locked up in here for ages.'

I swallow. 'I'm so sorry, hun. But you aren't tied up now. The door is unlocked. I walked in here, no problem. You could have gone out and got away when he hunts Katrina.'

'There is nowhere to go.' The flat tone of Leah's voice is more pronounced than ever.

'There's a boat.'

'I know. But it is just another trick of Ed's. He is twisted. He has been his whole life. His mother died right in front of him when he was seven. She fell off the boat going over to the mainland. She was a strong swimmer, apparently, but the water was too deep and choppy that day. It gets like that a lot here. His father couldn't find her soon enough and she drowned.'

'That's horrible. It's hard to have sympathy for the man that boy became. He has caused so much hurt to so many people.'

'Now he is sort of reenacting it over and over again with these women. That's why I have to call him Ed when we … when we're together. It was his mum's nickname for him.'

'Katrina is out there now. We need to hurry and help her.'

'She'll be fine. He won't kill her.'

I look at my friend in surprise. 'What about Crystal? She was killed.'

Leah looks down at the floor again suddenly. 'Katrina knows how to play along better than Crystal. She has been here the longest.'

Leah seems to have the same less-than-urgent attitude as Katrina. Both of them have been conditioned to believe they can't really escape.

I use my firm grip on Leah's hand to try and pull her towards the front door, but she won't budge.

'Leah, come on. We need to go. Where is the boat? It was on the jetty before and now I can't find it.'

'Ed moved it.'

'To where?'

'I don't know. It doesn't matter.'

'Why not?'

'He has the keys on him all the time, in his coat pocket.'

'No, I saw them through the window of the boat.'

She shakes her head quickly. 'Those are just a decoy. He got the keys from something old and broken and hung them up in the window so people can see them. He even added a key float to make them look like boat keys. Ed's really quite smart, you know, in a way. He wants his women to think they can just escape. He gets a real kick out of that. I've realised why after all this time. It's something to do with watching his dad trying to save his mother. I think they both thought they were going to rescue her. She just narrowly missed getting out of it alive.'

I take a moment to marvel at Leah's total lack of urgency. She is talking as she did the day we went out on a mother's day tea with Helen at our local garden centre.

'OK. So that puts a slight dampener on the plan to sail away. What about phones?'

'There's no signal out here. Don't you think I've thought about all this?' Leah's face suddenly contracts with an unexpected wave of misery.

I pull her into a one-handed hug. My other is reluctant to release my grip on the rifle as I know our captor could be closer than we think. 'Yes, I know. I'm sorry. We just have to get you out of here, that's all.'

Leah suddenly gets caught between crying and laughing now. 'Are you the rescue party? Come on, Claire. You are just as trapped as me and Katrina out here.'

She pulls back from my grip and sinks down onto the high-backed armchair nearby. She closes her eyes briefly, as though exhausted.

I crouch down beside her. 'We are armed now. That creep has to hand the keys for the boat over to us if the alternative is being shot.'

'We are both stuck. Just admit it. There isn't anything worse than realising all hope has gone, so you might as well do it now. Don't let it hit you in the middle of the night when you aren't expecting it.'

I stand up again and take hold of Leah's hand, giving her a tug towards the door. 'We aren't trapped. We can just walk out the door. We just need to hurry!'

'OK, maybe you aren't quite as trapped as me yet, hun. But I'm sure you still will be. If you won't play along and be hunted, then Ed will find other uses for you. The only reason Katrina has gotten out of it is that she kept miscarrying.'

'What are you talking about?'

Leah stands up again and unknots the thick throw around her shoulders.

My eyes are immediately drawn down to her middle. A large rotund bump is clearly visible.

'So you see, I won't be running off with you,

Claire. Sorry. You've had a wasted visit.'

CHAPTER FIFTY-FOUR

Now

I'll admit, my mouth falls open at Leah's revelation. It takes me a good ten seconds to recover.

'That's OK,' I say. 'It's OK, Leah.'

'No, it's not. You know it too if you have to keep saying it like that. I know this is a disaster. If you had got here eight-and-a-half months earlier, then maybe things would have been different.'

'Don't be silly. You can still walk, can't you?'

'Walk where? There is nowhere to go. He controls the only way off this wretched little island. We can't get away.'

'But we have a weapon. It is loaded, isn't it?'

Leah blinks at the gun in my hands. 'I don't

know. I've no idea how to use that really. When I got hold of it and tried to shoot Ed it didn't work. But Crystal was shot with that gun afterwards. It was one of his games. I just didn't realise until it was too late. He wants you to think you can get away, even when really there is no hope. I tried. I really did try.'

'We *can* leave. I'm not planning on spending the rest of my life here. Neither should you.'

'I used to be like you ... Claire.' Leah blinks up at me suddenly, as though recognising me properly for the first time. She seems too confused. I don't want to imagine what she has gone through for her to even forget temporarily our life together.

I look down at the gun. It looks completely alien to me. Cold and hard and heavy. But after a few moments of fumbling, I get the thing open. My heart sinks to find two empty barrels.

'It's OK,' I say again.

'No, it's not. Ed will know it isn't loaded. It won't do us any good.'

I drop the rifle on the sofa and switch it for the brass poker instead. It is marginally heavier and much sharper. It feels much more dangerous in my hands than the gun.

'I can probably take him on with this. Especially if I catch him by surprise.' I look back up at Leah. 'It's the dog that is the real problem.'

'Yeah. That's what Crystal didn't think of. She just went at Ed without thinking one day.

The dog protected him. Her arm was so badly hurt. It took ages for her to stop bleeding. I kept pressure on it for hours down in that cellar. We fell asleep like that.'

Leah looks dreamily at the peeling wall for a second, as though replaying the past in her mind.

I brush her hand with my thumb. 'We can learn from Crystal's mistake.'

'She is dead. It was my fault. I shouldn't have tried to escape.' Leah's face screws up again and tears leak out the corners of her eyes.

'It's OK.'

'Every time you say that I don't believe you.'

'We can let her family know what happened to her. They will get the closure they have been searching for all this time.'

'She didn't have any family. She lived on the streets ever since she ran away from her addict dad when she was fifteen. She reminded me of you a little bit.'

'Thanks to you, I had the chance to be part of a real family. I'll never forget what you've done for me, Leah. You and Helen and Tony. You are all my real family as far as I'm concerned. They want you home just as much as I do.'

'Are they really still alive?'

'Yes.' I nod adamantly as Leah's face creases up again. She hides her face behind her thick fingers.

'It's OK.' I wish I could think of something

more reassuring to say, but I can't. It just keeps coming out of my mouth. 'Your fingers are so swollen. Your face is too. We need to get you to a hospital.'

Leah touches her fingers to her full cheek. 'It's the pregnancy. I haven't felt so good for a while. It's making me confused. I couldn't remember mum's name last week. Yesterday, I put my hand on the stove to brush some crumbs off and I forgot I'd only just switched it off and burned myself.'

Leah brushes her thumb over a tight pink mark on her left hand. 'I don't know what's happening to me, Claire. I'm so scared.'

'We will find out when we get you out of here. Come on. You are going home today. You can tell your mum she is going to be a grandmother. She will be delighted. So will Mia. She will love having a little friend.'

'Mia?' Leah repeats in confusion.

'The little girl who lives next door to your mum. Helen babysits her quite often now. Remember when we picked her up from school a few times?'

Leah stares at the wall again. 'Fuck. That's where I first saw Ed. He was there when we picked up Mia from her nursery class.'

'I thought it might be. Anyway, Mia is six now. You'll be amazed when you see her. She is so grown up.'

Leah's brow creases with a frown. She opens

her mouth to say something but stops and freezes.

It is immediately obvious what is troubling her. Outside, the distant barking isn't so far away now. It is getting closer by the second.

CHAPTER FIFTY-FIVE

Now

We both stare in horror at the front door. Any minute now it will open and we will be faced with "Ed".

I turn to Leah quickly. 'How are you with the dog? Does it obey you?'

'A little bit. I keep out of the way mostly when it is here. It doesn't go for me any more.'

'Maybe you can get it into a back room?' I grab hold of the doorway and peer through to the kitchen. There is another door to what looks like a food storage area. 'Get the dog into the pantry and shut the door. Do you think you can do that?'

'I don't know.' Leah's eyes are wide and fearful like Katrina's as she stares towards the door. I pull her to her feet, but she seems in a daze still.

'Leah! Please listen, just get the dog out of the way. I'm going to hide upstairs.'

She turns to me and grabs hold of my injured wrist. 'Don't leave me, Claire!'

'I'm not going to. I promise, hun. Just do what I said. I will be back in a second. Our only chance is if we take him by surprise.'

I nod encouragingly, but Leah just stares at me as I turn and tread hurriedly up the small staircase. The metal rod digs painfully into my arm as I trip up the last step.

I turn and crouch myself against the landing just in time. From here, I can just about see downstairs without being seen.

Leah puts a hand over her bump as the front door bangs open.

'What are you doing?' Thompson demands as he strides in, without shutting the door behind him.

I see the back of his scraggy grey head as it turns from the sofa where the abandoned shotgun was thrown then back to Leah's retreating form.

'I thought I heard a noise,' Leah says as she disappears into the small kitchen.

'Is she here?'

'Who?'

'Your old friend! I can't find her anywhere else. I thought I locked her in. But she is gone.'

Frustratingly, the dog lingers stiff and still

in the living room as it watches the pair through the doorway. The black nose twitches from side to side.

He knows I'm here, I think.

I watch in horror, not daring to move or even breathe.

Come on, I pray silently. *Come on*. Go into the kitchen.

There are noises in the kitchen and I think I hear plastic being torn off something.

Leah's voice is high-pitched now and it alarms me for a second until I realise what she is doing.

'*Duke?!*' she calls. 'Come on boy. Lunch!'

'What are you giving him that for you stupid bitch?' Thompson demands suddenly. 'That's the good bacon!'

But the plan works.

The dog relaxes his shoulders immediately before he trots straight ahead into the kitchen.

Not being able to see if he has gone all the way through to the little room at the back, I realise I have to take a risk now.

Thompson will know something is wrong by Leah's behaviour and I only have the element of surprise on my side.

I tread quietly down the small staircase in my wet socks and towards the kitchen doorway, still hardly daring to breathe.

I round the corner just in time to see a snapshot of Leah shutting the pantry door with a snap.

Ed stares at her. I can't see his expression from the back, just his gormless body language. He looks like an aggressive ape with his arms out at the side in an unspoken question.

He is about to say something else when my brass poker comes down on the back of his head with all the strength I can muster.

The first blow forces him to stumble onto his knees. The second causes blood to spatter across the vintage checkerboard tiles of the floor. I raise the poker again, but wonder if it is necessary as I stare at the unmoving form in front of me. A red puddle has formed where the cheek is pressed against the floor.

'Is he dead?' Leah stares down at the crumpled figure, her eyes are wider than ever. I realise there is blood spattered on the white knuckles holding her throw.

'I don't know.'

Leah is frozen in horror as she stares down at the figure on the floor.

I step gingerly forward and crouch as I press my finger into Thompson's stubbly neck. 'There is a pulse. But it is pretty weak.'

'What should we do?'

I'm already rummaging through the pockets of Ed's dark green coat. Just as Leah said before, my fingers close around a large bunch of keys.

I stand up and grip her hand tightly in mine.

'Now we get out of here.'

CHAPTER FIFTY-SIX

Now

'I don't believe you. He can't be stopped.' Katrina looks between Leah and I stubbornly. She crouches in her duvet in the front room of the other farmhouse. Her voice is determined, even a little sulky. 'You're lying.'

'No, we're not. I hit him so hard, he can never hurt you again. Look.' I gesture to the blood on my hands. To be fair, not all of it is Thompson's, some of it is from my ankle bite which Katrina seems determined is the explanation. I've thrown open the front door and light floods in as much as it ever does in this place, illuminating the dusty corners and the crumbling walls.

Even in the gloom, I can see the red colour staining my hands. Katrina surely has to believe us, but she refuses to move. She sits shaking her head stubbornly, drawing her old duvet around herself.

Leah seems to have drawn the same conclusion on this issue as I have. 'She won't budge, you know. Ed had her trained pretty well. She thinks we are part of his game now, acting on his orders. I wouldn't believe he is gone if I hadn't seen it myself. She still thinks she has to do what he says.'

Katrina makes a noise as she looks down at Leah's full belly, visible now beneath her hastily wrapped throw. 'Huh! Looks like I'm not the only one who has done as she was told! She looks a bit more well-fed than me, that's for sure. It's all right for some, isn't it!'

'Don't be ridiculous,' I say. 'Leah didn't want to be over there at all. None of us deserves this. Neither did Crystal.'

Katrina nods her stubborn head towards Leah. 'Has she told you what happened to Crystal on the day she died?'

Leah looks distressed all of a sudden, but I shake my head. 'Look, I don't know what you are talking about. Come on, Katrina. Just get up.'

I move forward and try and force the other woman to her feet. It sort of works, but now she leans back against the wall in a last-ditch attempt to stay in the familiarity of her prison.

Another flash of red catches my eye. I look down and realise that fresh blood has erupted from Katrina's calf. A new dog bite.

She sees where I am looking. 'That miserable mutt got me on the hunt. I've got you to thank for that. He would have left me alone today if you had just played along. So thanks for that, Claire.'

'I'm sorry. But Edward Thompson is finished now. He is too injured to hurt you again. Let's just get out of here before he dies.'

'Ha! Get your story straight. I thought you said you killed him.'

I sigh and look at Leah for support. But my friend just stares blankly at the other woman, glazed over and lost in thought.

'Hey,' I say to her as I glance down doubtfully at her belly. 'Do you think you can get one of Katrina's arms and I'll get the other? We might have to frogmarch her to the boat.'

Leah nods. She is dreamy and vague again and says nothing.

She and I both put a hand on Katrina. I put mine behind her back and steer her towards the door. Katrina's own pulse is visible beating beneath the thin edge of the duvet she clings to. She shrinks slightly at the light, despite only having been back in the farmhouse for less than an hour.

As we pass the other farmhouse a loud barking pierces the air, I feel Katrina jump in fright beneath my arm. She stares in fear up at the nearest window as Juke's booming bark erupts from behind the single glazing.

Despite our mutual negative experiences with Ed's pet, Leah and I left out food and water out. We also left the pantry door ajar enough for him to escape right before we slipped out the front door.

It seems it worked. He stares ferociously through the glass as he watches us leave. Our offerings should keep him going until we reach the mainland for help. I don't like to think of what will happen to him after that, but that is for the authorities to decide.

I can picture forensics teams crawling all over this island soon. Only then will the full extent of Edward Thompson's crimes come to light. I wonder how many people he has captured and harmed over the years. Helen said he associated with a certain type of woman in town. I wonder how many of them have been hurt, even if they were never captured. Not to mention Thompson's little girl and wife.

At least he can't hurt them now. His injuries were causing too much blood loss; I doubt the emergency services will be able to get here in time to save him.

Leah doesn't flinch at Juke's snarling and simply stares at the overgrown grass the three of us tread over. I'm still in my socks. The grass soaks them through again within seconds. I've almost forgotten what it is like to have feet that aren't permanently cold and numb.

At the brow of the hill, I look all around. This spot provides a good overall view of the island, aside from the jetty. The boat is luckily immediately obvious from my first glance around. It is positioned near the rocks on the other side of the island. I suppose Thompson put it on show there on purpose as a lure; a trap, with decoy keys.

He would have enjoyed me spotting the thing and then being crushed with terror when the key didn't fit into the ignition.

I jog down the hill and rejoin the others. They didn't need to ascend the steepest slope. The three of us set off again. Katrina and Leah struggle even on the flatter areas. It will be a while before they can regain their full strength.

I glance at Leah. 'This place reminds me of Cathy and Heathcliff's moors.'

'Oh.' Leah seems even paler outside than she did in the farmhouse.

I look at her in concern. 'Are you all right? Do you need to stop for a minute?'

'No. Let's just keep going to the boat.'

The vessel finally looms properly into view. The thing looks so tiny compared to the grey sea around it. It bobs with the waves. Was the sea this choppy earlier? I don't say it out loud, but I just hope there is enough fuel to make it to the mainland.

The three of us climb over the dark rocks, most of which are slimy and green. Somehow it seems easier for me and Katrina to grip without shoes in our socks and bare feet.

Leah seems to have managed to keep hold of the trainers she was abducted in. Thankfully, they are not at the bottom of the water around us as Thompson had told me. The dark red neck of my friend's Costa t-shirt is just about visible beneath the throw she still keeps wrapped around herself. She is still dressed in her work clothes, Katrina too I suppose in her revealing red dress. But both women are so much different than the respective nights they were snatched off the streets.

I think of my relief when I remember how that body in the quarry turned out not to be Leah. Now that I see my friend on the other side of Katrina's matted hair, I'm angry with myself for ever thinking she could really be gone. All the while Leah was here on this island, having goodness knows what happen to her.

At the same time, she too was under the impression her mother and uncle were dead and I had moved on. Playing happy families with James, no less. Thompson has so much more to answer for than physical abuse.

As we reach the boat, I shift position into the lead. I spot the rope mooring the boat and pull it closer. The waves want to win our game of tug of war. I'm exhausted. My body isn't used to missing so many meals in a row. My dehydration headache returns, pounding in my head. I make a grab for a rusty railing as it nears my outstretched fingers.

Got it. Rain spatters in my eyes now. I blink it away. Just drizzle, but it makes everything harder than it has to be.

'Here, Katrina.' I turn to the woman standing behind me as I straighten up, but her face has changed. She stares past me towards the boat with a look of horror.

Then she screams.

CHAPTER FIFTY-SEVEN

Now

I turn and stare around me in a rush of adrenaline. Then I spot what Katrina and Leah have their vision fixed upon.

Edward Thompson's bloody form emerges from the back of the boat. He uses the rusty old handrail to push himself up into an almost-standing position.

I let go of the boat in surprise and it drifts out of my grip, moving with the rhythm of the waves.

My thoughts get stuck in a loop of panic. *He can't be here. He was too badly injured. No way could he have got up from that. Didn't I hit him hard enough?*

I hadn't checked his injuries too closely.

Why didn't I take the bloodied brass poker with me? Or the shotgun even, empty or not. It still would have come in handy at this moment. Anything would be better than nothing.

I've never felt so small. I'm unarmed and backed up by one emaciated shell and an ailing pregnant woman, neither of whom truly believe freedom can be theirs again.

Then I realise that Ed has the very weapon I've been thinking of. He faces it towards us now. I stare right into the dark barrel as his bloodstained finger moves to the trigger.

'Get back, all three of you.' His voice is weak, however, especially above the sound of the waves and the wind. 'Get back into the farmhouse. Now.'

Katrina shrinks behind me.

I step forward. 'We won't do any such thing! That gun isn't loaded and you know it! I checked it earlier. So come off it and let us leave!'

Ed adjusts the position of the firearm. His shot hits the water beside me with a loud bang and a very obvious splash. It proves his point.

He aims the weapon back at me. His bloody squint is locked firmly on my chest, despite the fact he seems to be trembling quite badly. 'Move back to the farmhouse - now!'

I shake my head. I've brought these two women this far. Right to the brink of escape. I'm determined not to allow them to be locked up again. He can't shoot us all at once, I reason silently.

I turn my head to communicate this, but as I do so, I catch sight of Leah's arm swinging through the air. I'm suddenly reminded of skimming stones with her across BorrowPit lake one time when we were absconding from our self-defence classes. She has launched a rock at Thompson.

Her sudden attack hits him on the temple. He looks dazed for a moment, his mouth opens stupidly.

Then, to my surprise, I see Katrina reach down and follow suit. Hers is a piece of thin slate. Her aim is terrible. She completely misses, in fact, but the sight of her springing into action triggers me too.

I dash forwards and scramble into the boat. It is almost too easy to slide the rifle out of Thompson's hands. His grip is almost non-existent. He is weaker than he pretends. As I find my footing on the peeling white floor of the boat, I realise that this last stand of his was more desperate than I realised. His blood makes me slip. I grab the rusting handrail for support.

Before I know what is happening, Katrina's hands reach out of nowhere. She tugs on Thompson's weak form with her claw-like fingers. She snatches him by the coat and attempts to drag him towards the back of the vessel.

'Help me!' she cries desperately.

Hurriedly, I place the shotgun next to me on the torn old captain's seat and turn back. But then I realise she must have been talking to Leah who has now clambered into the boat by herself too.

The two women roll, kick and shove their captor towards the back of the vessel.

Thompson makes noises of dissent all the while. I open my mouth to protest, but his bloodied figure is already upon the side and then slipping beneath the waves.

I put a supportive arm out to Leah who is panting hard now. 'He was the only one who knew how many women he took and who they were.'

Katrina shakes her head. 'Nah. His wife will have some idea, I bet. She can't have lived with him for so long and been completely oblivious. I mean how stupid would you have to be not to notice what your husband is up to? I know a lot too. He's left loads of evidence behind in this place. The stupid shit.'

Leah sobs deeply all of a sudden. Or is she panting? She seems much more distressed all at once.

I put a second arm around her and pull her close to me. 'It's OK.'

'You always say that when it isn't.'

It is now that I realise my best friend's panting is rhythmic. Her whimpers are too. I look down and realise there is a dark patch on her leggings that I know has nothing to do with the sea.

'Leah? Are you - ?'

'Yes. I'm in labour, Claire. I have been for the last twenty minutes.'

CHAPTER FIFTY-EIGHT

Now

'OK. It's -'

'Please don't say it is OK!' Leah closes her eyes and crouches in the corner of the boat. 'I was never going to make it off this island.'

'Don't be silly.' I rub her back reassuringly then pull Thompson's bunch of keys out of my coat pocket.

Leah takes a deep laboured breath. 'It's the little one with the black handle!'

Panic sets in as I step over to the little cockpit and try to find a place to insert the key. When I do find the small and rusted ignition, nothing happens. 'Oh, come on. Please!'

The engine roars to life on the third nerve-

351

wracking attempt.

But that doesn't calm me much. I look down at the rusting old controls in front of me. It takes me a moment to get some kind of bearing. I know nothing about sailing.

'Try the right lever.' Katrina's voice is close. She grabs the rusted old lever and the boat lurches. We drift quickly into a nearby rock. The impact seems strong on the tiny vessel. I fear it may have gouged a hole in the hull. Then I push the lever the other way and take hold of the steering with my bloody and still shaking hands.

Cold rain is drizzled over my face. I blink it away. Then I realise what is wrong.

'We are still tethered to the rocks!' Katrina shouts at the same time.

'Hold the wheel for a second! Just keep it turned like this.'

I turn around to see how I can detach the rope from the boat, but my mouth opens in surprise as I do. Leah is clambering back onto the rocks.

'I'll cast us off!' I shout to her, reaching across and grabbing her arm to pull her back. 'Get back in the boat!'

Leah shakes her head. 'I can't!'

'You can't what?'

'I'm not going back, Claire. I've done something terrible.'

'It's OK! It's a good thing Ed Thompson is gone now. You won't have to face him in court or anything like that. Besides, Katrina was involved too. It was self-defence. I was a witness. I'll tell everyone what happened. I'll even tell them I did it if you want. But don't worry about that now.'

Leah takes another sharp breath. 'No - I'm not talking about him. I'm talking about Crystal.'

'What about her? Can't this wait? Let's just get out of here first. We need to get you to a hospital. Please.'

Despite her weakened state, my friend manages to pull her arm back from my grip. I almost lose my balance and grab onto the edge of the boat in time.

'I'm not going, Claire.'

Leah whimpers in pain as she crouches down for the mooring of the boat. Her full fingers work on the knot tied around a rusty hoop driven into the rock.

'Leah!' I have the sudden sense that I am about to lose my friend again. No way can I let that happen.

So I tug on the rope to pull the little vessel back towards the rocks. I swing my leg out onto the large rock Leah is working on.

Katrina calls out behind me. 'What's going on?!'

I ignore her and crouch down where Leah has slumped. I put my arms around her as she winces through another contraction.

'Come on,' I tell her. 'We have to leave now. I know you've been here for so long. But we have to go. It's over now, hun. We have to get your baby out safely.'

'I can't be a mother! Not after what I've done.'

'I don't understand. Let's talk about it later.' I slide my arms beneath her shoulders and attempt to heave her to her feet. She is heavier than I expected. Worse than that, she isn't cooperating.

I turn over my shoulder to Katrina. 'Help me!'

Katrina almost slips between the rocks and the boat as she slides her thin figure over the side of the vessel. She swears as salty sea water splashes the fresh wound on her ankle. We couldn't find anything clean enough to put on her injury. All my hope and focus are pinned on getting to the mainland. Everything is up in the air until then.

Katrina takes hold of one of Leah's arms. 'Come on, you silly cow. Up with you.'

With surprising strength, Katrina's tug combined with mine gets Leah to her feet.

Leah still resists as we march her back towards the boat. 'I can't go back. What will Mum say?'

'She will be pleased to see you. Helen has missed you so much. So has little Mia. She has asked after you too.'

Leah bursts into tears now. She digs her heels in as Katrina and I attempt to steer her into the boat. 'I don't want Mia to know either. How can I bring that into her innocent world? It's all so horrible.'

'I know.' I smooth her hair down. The finer strands are getting wet in the drizzle from the sky or sea. I can't tell the difference any more. 'But we have to go home now.'

'I don't want to go to prison!' She whimpers through another contraction.

Katrina sighs impatiently. 'You won't! Just tell everyone it was him. He can't argue now, can he? I won't say anything either.'

I look between the two women. 'What are you talking about?'

Katrina rolls her eyes impatiently and nods her head sideways at Leah. Her teeth are noticeably yellow even on this dull day. 'She was the one who shot Crystal.'

CHAPTER FIFTY-NINE

Now

Rain splashes harder down upon the three of us now. I barely notice my shivering anymore though. 'What?'

'It's true.' Leah recovers from her contraction enough to speak again. Tears roll down her face, which I'm sure aren't entirely from the pain. 'I killed her. It was my fault.'

'I don't understand.' My mind reels. I think back to the skeleton I shared my confines with on the other side of the island. Am I to believe the remains I suspected were Leah's for a time was actually caused by my friend?

I nod as I try to process this new fact. 'But it must have been an accident. Or Thompson made you do it.'

Katrina shrugs. 'It was both! It doesn't matter now, does it? I won't tell if you won't. I'll say it was that shit at the bottom of the sea. I want to get out of here now. I've had enough of this place.'

She attempts to drag Leah, but my friend has a slight weight advantage on her side.

She frustratingly remains planted on her rock, inches from the boat. 'I can't just pretend! I know what I have done. I see her face every day and the gun in my hands!'

'OK. It's OK.' I cringe at my use of the phrase again. 'So what happened?'

Katrina shuffles impatiently. 'That creep wanted to punish Crystal for attacking him. He handed Leah the gun and told her to shoot her. She refused at first, then pulled the trigger.'

'Why?'

Leah wraps her arms around herself. 'I thought it wasn't loaded. I'd tried to use the gun earlier when I got hold of it. But Ed must have left the gun lying around on purpose. I didn't realise it was part of the game at that point. I tried to shoot him and he just laughed at me as I kept pulling the trigger. He must have set the whole thing up. He made me believe the thing wasn't loaded. I was adamant it wasn't, as I'd seen it for myself.'

Leah pants through another contraction. 'So later, when he handed me the gun I believed it was still empty. I'd pulled the trigger earlier and it didn't work. So when he told me to shoot Crystal I just wanted it to look like I was playing along so he would leave us alone. But pulling the trigger the second time meant Crystal actually got shot. He must have loaded it between me trying to shoot him and picking up the gun again later. Either way, I did it. I shot her. It was *my* fault. I should have just refused to do it. I should have let him hurt me instead. I'd rebelled against him before, so why didn't I just do it at that moment?'

'No. You did nothing wrong. You didn't know.'

'I should have known it was a trick. Now a woman is dead because of me. I can still see her lying there in that cellar. The door was open so it was light enough. I can still see the look of shock on her face before she died. How can I go back home after that? Crystal will never get to go home because of me. So this place is my home now. I'm not going anywhere. I'm sorry, Claire.'

It takes a few moments for Leah's revelation to sink in. 'That's horrible. But it wasn't your fault. You need to understand that.'

'No. I can't get over what I did.'

Katrina groans. 'I've had enough of this place!'

She stares at Leah. 'Don't you want to get out of here? You've got people who want you. You should be grateful! I've got no one. Nobody cares I've been stuck here for six years of my life! I haven't even been reported missing. It is all right for you.'

Leah shakes her head. 'I don't want my mum to know what I've done. It will eat at her, as it has me. She doesn't need to go through all that. I've been wanting to escape all this time when I thought she was dead and wouldn't find out everything that has happened to me and what I've done. She can just keep thinking I went missing. It will be better for her if she doesn't know the truth.'

I reach out and squeeze Leah's cold hand. 'No, it won't. Helen has been distraught. The hardest thing has been not knowing what happened to you all this time. Trust me, I know. It's been hell. We haven't known whether to mourn you or not. I never wanted to give up hope. I sort of did and it was awful, the darkest time of my life. Helen needs to know you are OK. She will just adore a grandchild too. You can't deny her that.'

The stubborn clench of Leah's chin softens a little. 'It's *his* baby though. What will it turn out to be?'

I shake my head. 'Thompson has a little girl already. Her name is holly. Mia has made friends with her at school. She is lovely really. A little disturbed maybe - but only because she has spent her whole life under her father's roof. He is gone now. So this baby won't know its father at all. His or her main influences will be us and Helen.

Holly will have a little sister or brother. It might be what turns her life around and brings out her softer side.'

'I don't want to have a baby on my own though.'

'You won't be alone. You have me and Helen and Tony. Hey - *Great* Uncle Tony.'

Leah laughs suddenly and it immediately turns into a sob. Then a contraction.

She whimpers in pain again.

I look at Katrina pointedly. She and I use the opportunity to grab hold of our friend and pull her towards the boat.

We settle her securely in a back corner beneath the seats and I cast the rope off and return to the controls.

It isn't so hard to figure them out. Lucky really, as I know time isn't on my side. How long will it before we have a baby on our hands?

CHAPTER SIXTY

Now

It's a choppy ride. The vessel is churned around like a toy boat in a bathtub. Leah's cries become louder as we grow nearer to the mainland. No longer can they be carried away by the wind.

Katrina huddles close to her in the back of the boat. She keeps her duvet over the pair of them and has her arm around Leah. She has one of her bare feet on each side of the vessel's seats to keep the two of them grounded and stable. I keep both hands on the steering and lean my weight to one side to stop myself from toppling over. I remember how I slid around blindly in what must have been this boat on the journey over. No wonder I had the intuitive feeling I was about to slide to my peril that day.

The fuel gauge reads low during the whole journey. I keep praying silently that we can make it to land before the thing drops to zero. What if we run out of juice before we make it?

Seagulls screech above the wind as the mainland becomes bigger. Through the rain, I see details becoming clearer as we approach. Craggy dark rocks and cliffs loom into view. The island we have just left behind must once have been connected to this piece of land. It has the same look about it, from the wild weedy grass to the type of stone used for the huts and buildings before us. A pale beach looms into view.

The needle of the fuel dial is in the same position when we finally approach the mainland close-up, so I assume it must be faulty. Nevertheless, it has added another layer of stress to my already tense state.

I've no idea where Thompson would have sailed this vessel to when he came back and forth in it. Perhaps he used to journey to a specific harbour somewhere, but I can't find it in a hurry. He must have known a good place because he made the trip so frequently. I haven't a clue where that could be though.

Whether or not the fuel gauge is faulty, I can't afford to take the risk of sailing about aimlessly and maybe running out. It's a miracle I've brought the three of us this far with my non-existent knowledge of boats. I vaguely noticed a name painted on the side in faded old paint. I assume Thompson's father dubbed the vessel, *Sunny Daze* himself. I wonder if it was a joke, or if he really had better hopes for the environment around here. But it doesn't matter now.

My sketchy sailing skills mean I manoeuvre the boat into a rocky section of a beach.

The little boat judders violently. The vibrations course through my hands and up my forearms as I fight to hang on to the steering wheel. There is a scraping sound audible even above the wind that suggests this will be the last ever voyage of *Sunny Daze*.

The three of us are dangerously cold and damp. My only priority is getting Leah to a hospital as quickly as I can. The fact that it isn't just her own life on the line weighs heavily on my mind.

The three of us scramble off the boat and onto more rocks. They are sharp and slimy beneath my socks and undoubtedly, Katrina's bare feet too.

Progress is slow making it onto the grassy slope and up the hill. The terrain feels so familiar after being on the island. But there are buildings nearby. I separate from the other two and race up ahead to the nearest one - a farmhouse. It looks much so more modern and inviting that the ones we left behind.

A young couple with a hyperactive cockapoo answers the door. It turns out his place is an Airbnb rental, not a working farm. The woman calls an ambulance immediately as the man welcomes the three of us into the lounge and away from the cold. A log burner bathes us in warmth as soon as we step into the room. This whole place is so dignified in contrast to what we have just left behind. It might as well be another planet.

It would be nice to breathe deeply and think the nightmare is over now. But Leah has a hurdle to climb first. I'm so empathetic to her, as I always have been, I feel like it is me who is about to give birth.

My best friend looks in a bad way as I turn to face her. She looks as though she wants to disappear into the brown leather sofa Katrina and I steered her onto. Her face is pale and clammy with damp strands of dark hair clinging to her forehead.

She has finally relinquished her throw in the warmth of the cottage. I'm alarmed to see how skinny Leah looks, aside from her bump and her obvious swelling. The contrast between the two features looks odd, and unnatural.

I grab the soft teddy throw slung elegantly over the side of the armchair and tuck it around her loosely. I have no idea what to do. I feel so helpless.

Somehow Leah's frail condition seems more obvious in the chic and refined conditions of the cosy cottage around her.

She looks too delicate for the task she has to go through next.

I just hope she makes it.

CHAPTER SIXTY-ONE

Three Months Later

Helen coos softly over the baby in her arms. 'You're beautiful, aren't you? Yes, you are. You look so much like your mother, don't you?'

Baby Krista has grown so much in such a short space of time, it seems. Or maybe these past few months have just been a blur of night feeds, adjusting to having Leah back and keeping the press at bay.

Helen tilts her head as she looks down at her granddaughter. 'I'm still trying to decide who else this little one looks like. Obviously, she has her mummy's eyes. You know, call me crazy, but I'm sure she has the same shaped face as you, Claire.'

Leah is reclining on her mother's sofa. She catches my eye and pulls an amused face whilst her mother is still occupied with the baby.

I grin back. I assume this is Helen's coping mechanism. It's obvious Krista might take some influences from her father. Leah and I are prepared for that. Helen, however, seems determined to dismiss all of Edward Thompson's influence from the precious bundle in her arms and find other explanations.

Helen is back in her own home now. She walks with a limp after the accident with the car. She ditched her walking stick at the first available opportunity and is grateful to have her independence back. Although Edward Thompson never admitted he was the one who had been behind the wheel, the police have chalked it up to him.

At least Helen can live without fear of further attack now. She is delighted to have a surprise baby in her arms to fawn over. Krista's bright blue eyes share a similar sparkly pattern to her mother's. They stare up at her grandmother adoringly.

Her big sister, Holly, was at first disappointed that the baby didn't share the same dark green eyes as her, but she got over it quickly. She throws herself into full sibling duties when she visits once a month.

When Holly visits Helen's house, she mostly spends her time reading books to her baby sister. Currently, Holly and Mia are engrossed in reading, Danny The Champion of The World, which happens to be their favourite present from Holly's seventh birthday. Holly has now decided that it is therefore Krista's favourite book too. The pair of girls take turns reading to the baby.

Helen has taken well to being a grandmother, but that's no surprise. I would have liked to have seen Helen's face when I told her the news. But she was back home in England when I called her from the hospital in Anglesey to tell her. She had a triple shock that day.

Even though I wasn't gone for more than a few days, Helen noticed my absence. She had sent Tony over with a pasta bake to drop off, and the pair became alarmed when they couldn't get hold of me. Helen then called my boss at the park and managed to ascertain I hadn't shown up for work for days. That was when they realised something was wrong.

Thankfully, they didn't have long to wait for answers. Not like they had with Leah, anyway.

Helen tells me she had to virtually mop herself up off the floor when I told her the news about Leah. And the perhaps even happier news that Helen was now a grandmother. She loves her new role. The four of us have hardly had any time apart since we have been back. Great Uncle Tony has spent a lot of time over here too. He can't stop expressing his disbelief at his niece's return, mentioning it every time we see him. He pulls us both into a tight hug, most uncharacteristic of him. 'I can't believe you're back, love.'

We have both wondered if Tony will ever get over the shock.

The birth wasn't as quick as I had feared in the end. Thankfully we had enough time to get Leah to a hospital. It was well into the night before little Krista emerged.

The doctors told Leah she was lucky that I found her when I did. She had developed preeclampsia. At least what was causing Leah's swelling and confusion was temporary and not something permanent.

We were told at the hospital that if it was left any longer then the mother and baby may not have had the happy outcome they had. The sudden stress and activity my arrival caused are what triggered the labour. And it may have actually been beneficial in this case.

Despite being several weeks early, baby Krista was in good health. We were allowed to take her home after five days of care during which time Leah had time to recover too.

My friend has gained some weight now. She would look almost like her old self if she had clawed it all back in the same places as before. I guess her experiences and motherhood have changed her. But it's OK. I love her no matter what. I always have done.

It turned out her veganism went to pot on the island when she was forced to rely on whatever Edward Thompson gave her. But she is back to making her own choices again. In fact, Leah is revelling in the freedom of it and I've been delighted to make her favourite dishes during her path to recovery.

The press got hold of Thompson's story. It has been hard to avoid the headlines. Luckily, Leah and I have been so busy with the baby we haven't had much time to scroll through endless news feeds on our phones.

The last thing Leah needs is to relive her experiences so soon and read the user-submitted words that make up the bottom half of the internet. Most of the comments are sympathetic and convey positive messages for the surviving victims. But then you always got at least one that isn't so nice on each article or social media post, like when trolls speculated I was to blame for my best friend's disappearance. We don't need that in our lives right now.

Leah and I have been assigned a therapist to talk to. But I know we both find the most useful thing is to talk to each other about what happened. Leah finds she can only really open up at times she feels most comfortable. It could be whispered during a night feed. I'll warm the bottle and Leah will soothe the baby until the nourishment arrives. Then the new mother will pour her heart out to me as Krista feeds. Or it could be when we take the baby out for a walk in her stroller.

Leah confesses something new just a week or two later as we fed the swans in the Castle Grounds. I find little snippets come from her when I least expect them. The healing process will take a long time. Our therapist says it could take a lifetime to fully accept what has happened. I'm prepared for that.

As we approach the river, Leah explains how she would sometimes get through tough nights alone in the farmhouse by pretending Crystal was still alive and locked in there with her.

'I don't know how I could have faced the guilt in that quiet building on my own,' she says as she tears off another piece of leftover cabbage from Helen's latest roast.

'When you showed up, Claire, reality sort of slowly sank over me. I realised Crystal was really gone. It really hit home when we went over to free Katrina and she was alone too. I bet it was even harder for her to be in the dark all that time. It was so tough in that first year, but at least I had her and Crystal for some company. I can't imagine doing it for six years, alone for most of it too.'

'Was she always so … ' I cast around for the right word, but Leah beats me to it.

'Tough?' She laughs. 'Yes, she was like that when I got there. She had been locked up for a few years already by then, but I think it might just be her natural personality. She will need to be thick-skinned if she is going to stay working at the sandwich shop with mum. My mother has always complained about how strict June is.'

'Did Helen find premises for her own cafe yet?'

'Yes. Actually, that's what she was talking about on the phone earlier. She is going to sign the lease with a landlord later. But she hasn't told June yet, so don't pass it on. Mum says Katrina is ready to get started on the project and help her set everything up. Apparently, Katrina is tired of working for June already.'

I smile. 'She has only been employed there for a month. Do you think she will last working in Helen's new cafe?'

Leah shrugs. 'I think she will. Katrina probably doesn't want to live with Mum and Tony forever. She is having a hard time adjusting to real life again, but she knows she has to get herself on her feet eventually. As do I.'

I shake my head. 'Don't worry about going back to work now. We have my income and Tony has gifted us the house. We are rent and mortgage free now. I can cover the bills. You know that.'

'I feel like a sponge. You're exhausting yourself working and then taking care of Krista when you get home as well.'

'I don't mind. Looking after a baby is hard

work. Honestly, I feel like I'm having a break going to work and leaving you with her. Besides, I love our little one.'

I lean down into the pushchair and engage Krista in the baby voice that it turns out I was capable of all along without realising. 'Yes, I do! Don't I?'

When I straighten back up, I catch Leah watching me with something unfamiliar in her eyes. I look at her enquiringly, but she looks away across the park.

Since we have been back, we seem to have fallen into a routine. We have come to an unspoken agreement with regard to our living arrangements. It has all just felt so natural. But Krista is growing bigger now and we are more than used to having her in our lives.

So will that agreement come to an end soon?

CHAPTER SIXTY-TWO

We walk past the floral terraces in the Castle grounds as we have done so many times recently. It tires baby Krista out. She can sleep in her pram whilst Leah and I talk.

As we near the children's park, we talk about how it will be surprisingly quick before little Krista will be clambering up the climbing frame we pass on the way. My best friend tells me how much she has missed her favourite haunt beside the nature reserve.

I tuck the blanket carefully around a now sleeping baby Krista. Spring has finally rolled around and even though the sun warms my and Leah's faces, Krista is shaded in her pram.

I look across at her mother who strolls beside me, hands in her coat pockets. 'Are you still not ready to go back there?'

Leah shakes her head. 'I don't feel ready yet. What if I freak out and imagine Thompson and Juke are going to be there when I turn around?'

'I'll be there with you. We could feed the swans over there like we used to. I did that quite a bit when you were away. It was a way to feel close to you, even when you weren't there.'

Leah smiles and slides a hand over mine on the foam stroller handle. 'Thank you for never giving up on me. It means so much. I was devastated when Thompson told me you'd got married without me.'

'Without you?' I laugh playfully at her choice of words.

She lifts her head in mock diva style. 'Well, I'd want at least the position of maid of honour.'

'Would you now?' I laugh but I'm aware Leah still hasn't let go of my hand.

She shrugs and looks down at the ground like she does when she is embarrassed. 'To be honest, Claire, I think it would hurt to see you marry someone else, even if I was there.'

I stay quiet, not knowing what to say. Does Leah mean what I think she does?

She chances a slight glance at me with those bright blue eyes I believed at times I would never see again. 'I had a lot of time to think when I was on that island. It made me realise certain things.'

'Oh?'

'You know, the thing I missed the most was

you. I was distraught thinking Mum and Uncle Tony were both dead, but imagining you with James just drove me crazy. I thought you had given up on me and moved on. You and James had a sort of spark when I saw you together. You seemed happier with him than with anyone else. It made me jealous.'

'That's why you told him things weren't working out. You wanted to break us up?'

Leah sighs. 'It sounds bad when you say it like that, doesn't it? I'm so sorry, Claire. I promise I never meant it that way. I just thought you moved on too fast after how you said you felt about me.'

'It was kind of a rebound thing with James. But I thought we gelled pretty well compared to other guys I'd been with.'

'You did. That's what got me. I wasn't expecting you to admit your feelings for me as you did that night. It caught me unexpectedly and I probably didn't react the way you hoped. But because of that, I feel like we didn't explore the possibility of what we could have had together. It was my biggest regret.'

We walk in silence for a few moments more before I break it. 'That's why you made up Adam - that guy you said you were dating. You wanted to test the water?'

Leah nods.

I grin. 'You know the police actually investigated Adam as a lead when you disappeared. I told them everything I knew about him.'

Leah laughs now with a cringe. 'Oh no. It's probably just as well I never made up his last name. Some poor bloke would have been in for a shock when the police knocked at his door.'

We both laugh as we imagine this possibility. Things had seemed so dark at the time, I can't believe I find any part of the situation amusing.

We fall quiet again before I ask the question that has been burning inside me for so long. 'So how do you feel about us now?'

Leah brings us to a standstill. 'I thought my life was over when I was locked in that farmhouse. I thought it was the end and I'd never get the chance to even see you again. But now I realise you haven't been having a nice life without me, it changes things. I want to give us a chance.'

'You do?' I'm trying to keep my reaction subtle, even though my heart is doing a little leap inside.

'Yes. I decided a while ago that there was a reason neither of us could ever find someone we really liked. At the end of the day, we were happiest when we went home to each other, weren't we? We know each other inside out. And now, with everything that's happened, you know the most about it all. I've told you things about my experience I would never admit to anyone else, even in therapy.' She pauses. 'I love you, Claire.'

My heart swells with emotion at Leah's words. I've spent years thinking about this moment and now it has actually happened. 'I love you too.'

Leah's whole demeanour seems to relax at my confirmation. She steps towards me and closes the gap between us.

Instinctively, I close my eyes as she presses her mouth to mine.

The house felt so empty when Leah was away. It wasn't my home any longer. But this is. Home isn't a place, it's this feeling right here.

Krista interrupts the tender moment with a wail.

Leah and I pull back from one another with a smile.

'Her highness has noticed her carriage has stopped.' I lean down to tend to Krista. 'Oh. Actually, I think there might be another problem. Time for a nappy change, I think.'

I consult my mental map of changing facilities. 'We can take her to the toilets near the cafe.'

We turn around and retrace our steps towards the eating establishment. This part of the journey feels so much different now. When we headed along this path half an hour ago we were something else. Now we take the journey hand in hand as much as Krista's buggy will allow. I couldn't be happier. Even my very tread feels lighter with each step I take.

Leah and I can't stop smiling at each other.

Outside the toilets, Leah reaches down and unstraps Krista.

'Don't you want me to change her?'

My partner shakes her head. 'It's OK. I'll do it. You do so much.' She nods towards the open cafe door. 'Why don't you order us a slice of cake each? I'm starving.'

'OK. See you in a minute.'

Leah disappears inside the door with the baby in her arms and the changing bag slung over her shoulder.

I look across the castle grounds for a moment. The sun has really come out now. Patches of bright blue sky are visible and it makes the sprawling grass seem greener. For the first time in a long time, I know everything is going to be OK.

I'm about to turn and step towards the cafe when my phone buzzes in my pocket. I wonder if Leah has forgotten something and needs me to take it into the changing room for her.

When I see my phone notification, however, I am surprised to see Carole's name on the screen.

My heart sinks as I open her Facebook message. I thought I had seen the last of her when she realised I wasn't going to give her any money.

Hiya, Claire. Long time, no see - again! I've seen your name on the news a lot lately. I'm so glad you found your friend. I told you and Helen not to give up hope, didn't I? I was right. I'm sorry to hear what you went through at the hands of that monster. You aren't used to the bad side of life. You got whisked away to a better one at such a young age. So when bad things happen in your perfect world, it probably seems like being on another planet!

The thing is, I've seen the other side. I live in it 24/7. I know it's my fault. I've got no one else to blame but myself. I didn't deserve to have a beautiful daughter like you. Not that I expected to have you in the first place. I don't have to tell you how I've earned money on the side all these years, even when I didn't have an official job. You've probably heard all sorts from your new friend Katrina. Reading between the lines in all the online news stories, I'm guessing she can tell you what it is like.

I'm really sorry we didn't get to be friends now that you're grown up. I thought maybe we were going to have a second chance, but never mind. I get why you don't want me around. I'm nothing but trouble. But I wasn't lying when I told you there were things I wanted to say to you. I never told you about your father, did I? As you have probably guessed, he was a paying client. No surprise, eh? Your dad was a regular back then. He used to visit me often, even after you were born. I never told him who you were though. He probably just assumed you were the product of another customer and thought nothing more of it.

That's if he even noticed you. He was always so busy with me when he came over to the flat. Your dad had very specific interests, you see. He paid well for them. I suppose he was one of my favourites for that reason, in a weird sort of way. Is that romantic? Probably not when you are living the dream with your new girlfriend, I bet. Did you get it together with Leah in the end, or is she still not interested? You looked quite close in one of the newspaper photos I saw online.

Anyway, I was telling you about your father. You probably don't want to hear it, but he liked to be rough. He always liked games that involved me having to fight him. He always requested that I should try and get away from him. He turned violent often. I always used to hope you couldn't hear from your bedroom. You would have been too young to remember any of that though.

I would be lying if I said I wasn't scared for my life a few times when he was over at my flat. But his money meant I would never say no. I was in desperate need of it back then. I can't say I'm not any more, but that is a different story. I just want to be clear that this isn't me asking you for money now, Claire. I don't deserve your help. I know that.

Your father, or "Ed", as he always liked to be called, always kept coming up with these scenarios *for us to play out. He liked me to pretend to be a woman drowning and calling his name over and over. That was his favourite fantasy. I guess I will never know why now that he is gone for good. It just said on the news that Edward Thompson had a "troubled childhood". I'm guessing he had specific issues with his mother. All these nutters seem to, don't they? At least you turned out normal, despite me being less than perfect. I suppose social services rescued you in time, eh? Plus, you have Helen who seems just wonderful. I heard she had an accident. I hope she has recovered well and whoever did it gets what is coming to them.*

Was it you who killed Ed, Claire? The news stories don't make it clear. If you knew he was your father when you were on that island of his, would you have tried to save him? I guess not. He did terrible things to you and your friends. You don't seem that bothered about me and I'm only half as bad as he was. I know that it is my own fault you don't want to keep in touch. I even admire you for that. You have a backbone. That is something I've never had. So many times I've wished I could be a better person, especially when I've been up to my eyeballs in filth, weirdos and debt.

My biggest regret was not being a good enough mother to you, sweetheart. But my addiction came first. I guess it still does. You were right not to let me into your life as an adult. I wouldn't want to mess it up. If you had handed me the money I asked you for, I would only have come back asking for more when I had blown it.

I wasn't lying when I said I was proud of you, Claire. I'll always love you in my own way, even if you don't feel the same. You are the only good thing I've ever done. Love, Mum xx

I stare at the message in horror for a good few minutes. My head is trying to process the details. I'm desperately trying to apply logic to Carole's suggestion that Edward Thompson was my father. I don't want it to be true. But something in the back of my mind nags me.

Carole has come up with things that haven't been released to the press. Only Leah knew Thompson's nickname. She started referring to him either impersonally or by his last name as I did by the time she had to make a statement to the police. I also know the police haven't released the full details about his mother.

Neither has Thompson's wife. All along, she has denied all knowledge of her husband's private interests and the island too. She had no idea he even owned such a place. She mentioned she was selling the land when she was here last dropping Holly off for a visit. Whether she truly knew more or not remains a mystery.

Part of me thinks she must have had an inkling though, especially if what Carole is saying is true. When Helen broke into the Thompson house that day, she found Mrs Thompson seemed to have taken refuge in her daughter's bedroom. No surprise, if her husband wanted to play out on repeat what was going on in his disturbed mind.

There is one way to tell for sure if Carole is telling the truth. I could take a DNA test. But the samples would surely be taken from little baby Krista, or Holly.

I couldn't get the thing done without other people finding out. Do I want anyone to know what Carole has said? It could turn out to be completely false. Hasn't our family been dealt enough lately?

And Holly's too. She and her mother want the town to forget the legacy of Edward Thompson just as much as we do. If what Carole is saying is true then Holly is my half-sister. As is Krista, the baby I'm raising. Both Leah and I are related to her.

Helen has suggested several times that little Krista even resembles me. It's true, Krista does have a similarly shaped face. I've noticed myself since it has been pointed out. It's the same broad one Edward Thompson had. It seems so familiar after spending a lifetime seeing it in the mirror, as do his dark green eyes. Holly seems to have inherited those traits too. The gene responsible must be strong. I wonder if Thompson's mother passed that down to him.

I hadn't paid that much attention to those faded old photos in his farmhouse living room. Had those been my grandparents in that photo where they flanked their little boy?

Then a thought strikes me. Had Thompson had any idea he could have been my father? Was that knowledge going to become the ultimate part of one of his twisted games? The pièce de résistance. Perhaps it was something he would have worked up to revealing had he been given the opportunity. But as it happened, he never got it.

The sound of a hand drier echoing out of the nearby toilets brings me back to the here and now. The sunny day is still here for me. As is Leah any moment.

Everything was going so perfectly. Can I let a message from Carole disrupt our new path?

It occurs to me that Carole and I are the only ones that know about this now.

Leah emerges from the toilet building. She beams at me as she approaches with baby Krista in her arms.

I quickly hit delete on the message from Carole. It's gone. She is in the past. It's time I took the advice I've been hearing and started looking to the future.

It's so much easier now that Leah is here. And baby Krista too.

Leah makes a wonderful mother. So do I, as it happens. How things are now is perfect. It is hard to imagine how such a horrible situation could have turned into something so wonderful.

Now my life is so full and has the promise

of new beginnings. I know that no matter what might come our way, my partner and I will face it together.

That's all that matters.

THANKS FOR READING

Did you enjoy The Victim? If so, please consider taking the time to write a quick review on Amazon or Goodreads. It really does help other readers find the book! :)

Also, if you would like to get news & be the first to know when my next book gets released, then visit my official website and enter your email address. It is only used to make sure you are the first to know this kind of news!

www.RuthHarrow.com

MORE BOOKS BY RUTH HARROW

In Her Footsteps
You're All Mine
In Her Wake
Dear Sister
Just One Lie
The Silent Wife
The Victim

Printed in Great Britain
by Amazon

42077645R00229